HER HUNTER

Her Hunter

E. M. ROSELYNN

CONTENTS

To Michael, Emily and Luna
We did it b

CONTENT WARNINGS

- Mention of suicide/suicidal ideation/self-harm/character death by suicide (in the past)
- Emotional abuse
- Physical abuse
- Torture/mutilation
- Alcohol abuse
- Trauma/PTSD
- Graphic descriptions of rape (including torture, gore, and body mutilation)
- Graphic violence and death
- Unplanned pregnancy/pregnancy caused by rape

Your mental health matters.

ACKNOWLEDGMENTS

There are so many folks who made this book possible.

First off, my partner, my husband, my love. A novel would never have been in the cards without your constant support, love, and encouragement. And of course, helping me with "research."

Emily, here it is. Our babies in real life. This literally never would have happened without you. Without spending literal years coming up with stories together. Not only that, your friendship and support through this and every other journey. Love you, b.

Krissy. Without you and your friendship I don't think this ever would have been completed. Not only have you helped keep this project going by listening to me for literally hours at a time, (up to at least ten straight . . .) but you've honestly kept *me* going. Thank you. I love you.

Viv, girl, you read the drafts of this that never should see the light of day. Thank you for suffering alongside me, helping me work through the rough patches, and loving our boy Mutt like he deserves.

Caitlin, yet another patient soul who listened to my rambling and loved me the whole time. Thank you, babe.

Brett, Alex, Bo, and Alex, y'all listened and dealt with my shit while I rambled on about vampires. Thank you.

The support group of friends and family, my incredible editor, y'all truly made this possible and helped my dream become something real. Holy fuck. Thank you.

Part 1

A Vampire And Her Hunter

~ 1 ~

CHAPTER 1

E^LLE
    She was screaming.

The darkness was consuming. She couldn't escape. She couldn't breathe. It was in her bones, in her blood, in her throat, her eyes, her lungs. She was dying. She was dying, and *he* was dragging her to hell.

She could feel his hands. Everywhere. Everywhere at once. They were tearing her flesh, ripping her apart. She could feel his teeth. His claws. The knives. He had taken everything: her body, her mind, and her soul.

She was screaming into the darkness and no one could hear her. No one could save her. No one was going to save her. She was going to die there. She was going to die. Pregnant and alone in the purest blackness. In complete and utter darkness. Her child was going to die. She was going to die. And it was all because of *him*.

Months before
She was seated in front of a mirror lined with everlight in clear glass balls. The room was small, smaller than others she'd had before, but at least they had given her a space to dress. It was both more and less than she'd had in other theaters, but certainly more than she'd expected, and it was enough. She reminded herself regularly. It was enough. Torzen was *enough*.

3

Having danced in a variety of shitholes, she'd learned what actually mattered, what was actually important, and dancing at the Silent Stag was surely not the worst. She had somewhere quiet to hide away before she was the center of everyone's attention on stage, somewhere to be alone before she was consumed by the eyes of the crowd. She was nightly entertainment at the Stag, danced every night except Sunday, and she brought in more money than any performer they'd hired before.

There wasn't much to the room, her mirror and vanity, hooks on the wall where her dresses hung before and after her performance. The vanity held her makeup and jewelry—though she wore little jewelry when she danced. A few long-dead roses sat on top. *I really need to throw those away.*

She sighed and leaned toward the mirror, raising her top lip to check her teeth. *They're still filed. Relax. They're not going to change back. They've been filed for years.* They looked perfectly human, completely disguised. She had plenty of precautions in place, plenty of wards and spells, and practical measures like her teeth to hide what she was. Even now, after eighty years in hiding, those precautions still didn't change how anxious she was before a performance. Even with everything in place, if anyone found out what she was—what she'd done—she'd be killed, and every night she was all the entire room looked at.

She sat back from the mirror and began to pull her hair back into two sets of braids on either side of her head, which outlined her face and blended into her long brown, nearly black curls. Once her hair was up, she lined her emerald eyes, pulling the dark black to sharp tips just off the outer corners. Green. Her eyes were still green. She didn't know what color her eyes actually were, what shade of red . . . The green was a spell her parents had placed on her so many years ago. Then, after their death, the couple who took her in continued her parents' work, raising her as a human, helping her learn to hide her nature. They were the ones who'd filed her fangs.

Another sigh left her lips as she continued to stare at herself. She hadn't looked like a vampire in so many years. She wondered what it would be like. Her disguise had held for so very long, it wasn't going to vanish overnight. It certainly wasn't going to vanish before this performance. She was going to be fine like she always had been. Like she always was. But regardless of her reassurance, her constant reminders to herself that she would be fine, she couldn't shake the anxiety swelling in her chest.

She stood and turned to her dresses. A pair of them hung on the wall behind her, one a pale pink beside the other, her favorite. She traded her street clothes for her dress and the shorts and top that hid underneath. Everyone always *loved* the reveal. The silky fabric of her dress fell over the curves of her hips. The pale-yellow material with pink trimming made her feel like a spring flower when she wore it, and it had become one of her most loved dresses to wear while dancing. She twirled just a moment before the mirror, watching the fabric swirl around her legs, and smiled softly to herself.

"Elle, get out here!" The familiar male voice screaming outside her door pulled her from her thoughts.

She took one last heavy breath, savored one small moment, before she was forced back into the world.

*****

The group waiting for her was drunk, as they always were, and she could smell it on them immediately as she stepped onto the stage. The everlight was blinding, enough that she could never see the audience's faces when she danced. In most ways that made it easier. She could get lost in her performance without the distraction of their eyes running over her. She'd learned to keep her distance from the patrons. After Alder . . . after Alder she'd learned that well enough.

They cheered her stage name. *Jezebelle.* It had been chosen for her by the man she worked for. Stephan seemed to have convinced himself it was some clever play on her true name, but more than likely, he'd chosen it because it was close enough to her actual name that the dumb bastard would be able to remember it when he announced her every night. She paid it all little mind. Jezebelle was a character, only a character. An opportunity to enjoy being a different person for a moment, enjoy the fantasy of being someone else, someone free. Because she'd always been someone else, Jezebelle was just as much a cage, just as much a mask as Elle was.

Sometimes she hated how Jezebelle twisted the art she had once deemed beautiful. Dance had been an expression once. It still was an expression of sorts, but it was different. Maybe the name was fitting. Maybe her character was just a tease, a siren, and she was only there to tempt men into emptying their pockets for a beauty they could never attain. They'd go home and begrudgingly fuck their wives, wives who were surely beautiful women. Women who deserved better. Elle missed what dance had been, before it became a tool to part men from their money. Before it became only survival.

The band tucked into the corner of the room began their soft serenade. The crowd hushed, and every eye turned to her. Every man and woman fell silent, entranced by her movements. The flow of her dress and the gentle motion of the fabric following the lead of her body captivated them. The silence was filled with small gasps, moans even, as she slid the dress from her shoulders and it fell to the floor. *The reveal.*

Free from the fabric, she grabbed hold of the silks hanging from the ceiling, and she danced. She shut them out of her mind, the humans that watched, the sounds, everything other than her body and the dance. There was only the steady rhythm of her heartbeat, and she followed it. It pulsed through her limbs, resonated in every drop of sweat that ran down her neck. It was beautiful, painful, and gentle.

The audience didn't even know how much she withheld. Should she bear her soul to them, dance as she used to . . . Should they truly see her, they'd die in their seats. She wrapped herself in silk, wrapped and twisted her way to the ceiling. And then came the gasp. She loved that gasp. That gasp as she let herself fall, spiraling in the silk as she let herself drop inches from the stage, nearly to her death. Then she caught herself, and they erupted in applause. Even those who'd seen her over and over seemed shocked each time. Fair enough. If she slipped up even a moment, she could be dead on that stage. It made her feel alive.

Then it was over. Her performance was complete. The music quieted, and she slipped back behind the stage, avoiding the humans searching for her. She hated that part. Maybe it was because her art had become someone's fetish, maybe it was the ghost of Alder tormenting her, but she hated it. She ran from them. Adoring fans. Hungry men. All of them.

But it kept her and June in their room. Sometimes, it kept the doors to June's apothecary open. She'd been lying to June about their rent. It'd been increased twice in the last season, but she would do what she had to to keep the roof above their heads. Even when June told her to leave the Stag, stop dealing with Stephan, and find something else . . . She couldn't, and she didn't tell June just how important keeping her job was. She didn't want to burden her any further. All of this could only pay back a fraction of what June had done for her. June had saved her life and continued to. Every day, she was *literally alive* because of June. Paying for their room was so small compared to that. June carried enough.

June. Her roommate. Her best friend. *June.*

Her bare feet met the cool floor as she hurried to her dressing room. She'd left her performance dress on the stage, but someone would bring it back to her. The air was cold against her body, which was nearly fully exposed. Her hands ached as they did after every dance, her palms torn fresh each night. A surprising downside to being a vampire. She healed quickly, so calluses could never form on her hands, and every night they blistered and bled on the way from the stage. Healed, of course, by the time she got home, but annoying nonetheless.

She returned to the dressing room, changing out of her performance attire and back into the simple dress she wore most days. She slid a cloak over her shoulders and slipped back into her boots. Her makeup was slightly undone as sweat pulled it from her face, but she'd clean up when she got home. She wanted to gather her pay and get back to June.

Quickly, she found Stephan. A short man, overweight and constantly sweating. His hairline was far behind where it had lain in his younger years. His eyes were dark, nearly as dark as the heart in his chest. His meaty hands wrapped around the coin he owned her. It was damp as he dropped it into her hand.

She counted the coins as they fell into her palm and didn't think before her thoughts left her lips. "This is less than last time." She knew as she spoke, that was a mistake. *Shit.*

"Excuse me?" Stephan's eyebrow rose as though he hadn't heard her or did not register what she'd said. "Listen to me, you little monster." His gaze ran over her. "Out of the kindness of my heart, I continue to hide you here, give you work, pay you more than your kind is worth." His tone was laced with rage. "How *dare* you question what I pay you?"

Stephan knew what she was. He'd revealed that to her long ago, though she didn't know how he'd come to know. She feared asking him, feared that pushing her luck any further would only get her killed.

It didn't matter how he knew, in the end. What mattered was *that* he knew. He knew what she was and what she had done. Him not immediately turning her in was a mercy she hadn't understood for some time. He didn't turn her in because she made him a fuck ton of money. She wasn't sure if she made him more money dancing than he would get if he turned her in, but she dared not mention that part either.

Maybe he got off on the control. He knew she was a vampire, and he knew she was a vampire *wanted for murder*. He held the ultimate power over her. He knew he could turn her in at any moment, and she would be put to death. She couldn't argue with him. He owned her. If she wanted to stay alive, if she wanted to stay with June, she would have to take what he gave her. Even his fists.

She hated that June was mixed up in all of this. June was harboring a fugitive vampire. Elle was being hunted, and every human who knew only complicated the whole thing. If she chose to argue with Stephan then, or at all, this life she had begun to love could all go away. It would risk June's safety if she argued, and she could never put June in more danger than she already did.

"Yes." Elle took a step back. "Of course." *Fuck.* Sometimes she wondered if this was punishment from the moon. Atonement for what she did to Alder. Atonement for being a monster walking among men. She slid her pay into the pocket of her cloak. "Forgive me, Stepha—"

He slapped her.

She winced, squeezing her eyes shut and stumbling only slightly, as his hand collided with her face. She took a shaky breath. This wasn't the first time. It wouldn't be the last.

*****

"Stephan, please." She stumbled backward from him.

His hand was raised, ready to strike. "Fucking cunt." He slapped her again. "Vampire bitch."

Her hand was pressed against her now-stinging cheek. "Please."

Again, he struck her. His fist was closed that time, his knuckles colliding with her jaw and sending her to the floor. "Stop begging, little bitch. You're mine, and you do as I fucking ask. Do you understand?"

*****

"Get out, *vampire*," he hissed.

A chill ran down her spine as she left his office. She glanced around as she ran through the door, checking the hall for anyone who might have heard him utter what she was. No one was in sight. *Thank the moon.* She slid her hood over her head and slipped into the darkness of the evening.

*****

It was already long past midnight. The moon lit the street, and the stars were ready to lead her home as she stepped out of the side door of the Stag. She pulled her cloak tighter over her shoulders as the brisk evening hit her face. It nearly sucked the breath from her. The cold of the air bit her lungs. She loved it. That bite. That energy. It woke her up and drew her out of her own thoughts when they began to spiral.

She loved the stars and the moon. She loved the night. Even though humans were afraid of the night because it held monsters, terrors, *vampires*, she found it so beautiful. The way the stars shone brightly, dancing in swirls around the moon. The moon's soft glow that seemed to gently caress her children as they danced by her. Ben had told her that the moon was the mother of the night sky, her children the stars. The sun was her lover, though they were cursed to be apart. All children's tales that had comforted her once.

Lio had once told her all the vampire folktales and legends she knew. She let herself wonder for only a moment if he was alright.

The mother moon was a legend among vampires. She'd birthed the first of their kind and given them dominion over the darkness. Vampires viewed the moon as a goddess, a deity. They revered her and considered her the mother of their entire kind, though all of her temples had been destroyed in the war hundreds of years ago.

But Elle did not love the night because of her blood. She did not love the night because she was a vampire and the moon watched over her. Elle loved the night because it made her *feel*.

As she walked toward her home, she smiled softly at a few bar patrons who recognized her, townspeople she'd come to know from their frequent attendance of her performances. She kept her interactions short and polite, she just wanted to get home, but she didn't dare anger the people who kept her in a job. She'd grown practiced in the polite but swift exchange. A couple gushed over her a moment then let her continue on her way.

The moon guided her home as her mind was elsewhere. She had to figure out what to do with less pay. She had to tell June.

*****

Their home wasn't more than a room in a small building a few yards from the house where the people they rented it from lived. The girls were saving for their own home, and they were getting close to having enough . . . but with rent being raised multiple times, Elle wondered if the owners were trying to drive them out without having to actually kick them out.

She closed the door behind herself as she stepped into the room and let her cloak slip off her shoulders. She was exhausted, but she knew her nerves were going to keep her up late.

The room was simple. Two beds with a dresser between them on one wall. Elle had clothes hung over the bottom of her bed, her things piled neatly at the end atop a chest where she stored what little she had. There wasn't much left. She had significantly fewer possessions since she'd last run.

The end of June's bed was adorned with a variety of weapons, her gear and clothes thrown into a heap below it.

Lining almost any free wall space were shelves of medical supplies, herbs, and books detailing a variety of magics. All of it June's work that didn't live at the apothecary. What she was studying on her own time, and the things she studied that she didn't need her patrons asking questions about. In one corner was a small stone stove that just barely kept the room livable for June.

June rolled over on her bed. Her dark eyes opened sleepily, and she rubbed them as she sat up. Her long brown hair fell around her shoulders. The shirt she slept in was sleeveless, barely much fabric at all actually, revealing the dark runes tattooed into her shoulders, down her arms, and all the way to her fingertips which were tattooed entirely black. June was a human mage and the person Elle had come to consider a sister. It had been years since they'd met in the woods, and they relied heavily on each other.

"You're back." Her voice was still thick with sleep, and her half-opened eyes vanished behind a gentle smile.

Elle only nodded.

June blinked the sleep away, her smile dropping entirely. "What's wrong, Elle?"

Elle fell back into a seated position on her bed. "Stephan . . . docked my pay." She began untying the braids in her hair, strands falling free as she did. "And when I argued, he reminded me that he knows what I am." She paused, her fingers trembling as she struggled to continue to free her hair. Her eyes lifted to meet June's across the room. "Gods, I can't run again, June." Panic settled deep in her stomach. She wasn't sure if she'd survive it if she had to run again.

The blankets fell from June's legs as she swung them off the bed. She sat beside Elle, scooting toward the wall and crossing her legs underneath herself as she got behind her. She tried to hide her anger, but they could read each other well enough that Elle saw through the attempt.

"He didn't pay you enough as it was, Ellie. Why the fuck would he dock it?" June began to take out the braids, ushering Elle's hands from her head to fall into her lap.

"I don't know. Because the bastard can."

June ran her fingers through the strands of Elle's hair. The sound of her taking a deep breath through her nose and letting it out from between her teeth nearly echoed in the room. "I'll talk to him tomorrow. That's absolutely unreasonable."

"I can't afford that." Elle shook her head. That panic sank deeper. "*We* can't afford that."

June scooted off Elle's bed, rubbing her eyes. "You can't afford to have him dock your fucking pay." She grabbed a tie for her hair and began to put it up, every movement stiff with the anger building in her.

"It's better than my last job." *The one where I killed a guy.* Her voice rattled as she said, "What could I do, anyway? I can't— June, I *can't* jeopardize this." She gestured to their room and then between them.

June poured some mead into a glass before handing it to Elle. "You can come with me if you want, but you're not changing my mind. Tomorrow, I'm talking to that bastard." She took a swig directly from the bottle. "The men in this city are fucking pigs, Elle."

Elle nodded slowly, staring down at her glass for a moment. She took a sip then raised her eyes back to June's. "Fuck men, *fuck men*, and fucking men." She forced a small smile onto her lips, holding the mead out toward June again.

June smiled softly, tapping the bottle against Elle's glass.

Elle knew she'd unleash her anger the next day.

"Now you've got it."

June always had
a look about her of
cold stone, like
granite, unsettling
and anything
but warm...
Permanent
tattoo
She wears one
star earring as a set.
I don't dare ask her
about the fact that
Bliss has one that
he wears as well...
Star symbol
of the moon?
Except of course
when she looked
at Elle.

~ 2 ~

CHAPTER 2

E^{LLE}
Elle turned as she heard June roll over. The sun peeked in through the small window, just catching the crack between the two sides of the curtain covering it. Her hair was tied up into a ponytail, and she brushed the loose strands that fell into her face behind her ears. She'd been humming softly as she made June breakfast like she usually did since she almost always woke first. June's magic took such a toll on her body, she could sleep for days if Elle let her. Elle, however, found herself sleepy for only a few hours most nights. A mage and a vampire had incredibly different sleep needs, and it worked well for them.

June smiled at her initially, but Elle saw the moment when concern took hold and June noticed how badly Elle's hands trembled. She sat up and swung her legs off the bed. "Elle, you need to eat."

Elle shook her head. "I'm alright."

"It's been what . . . a week? You're pushing it too far, Elle. And I fucking let you too." She rubbed her forehead and sighed. "I should really be pushier about this."

"I said I'm fine." Elle turned from her, her attention back to June's breakfast. She was trying and failing to hide her hunger from June. The truth was, she was starving. Exhausted and weak. She was absolutely pushing it too far.

She could practically hear June roll her eyes. "We're *bonded*. I'm fully aware of how fine you are, Ellie. I won't eat unless you do."

15

She sounded a little smug. She knew Elle's weakness: *her*. With a wave of a finger, she summoned a shadow.

Elle glanced at the entity now with them in the room. "You're the laziest person I've ever known." She rolled her eyes, a small smile just barely slipping onto her lips.

June laughed softly. This was one of her most used spells, shadows. They were figures, simple and without a soul, that she could summon and direct. She used them to retrieve things, move things, do all sorts of simple tasks that she could pawn off. The shadow reached into her bag, removed a knife, and brought it to June. June nodded at it then waved her hand, and it vanished. She reached over and grabbed a cup from beside her bed, then eyeballed it quickly to make sure it was clean . . . enough. She placed it back on the table and ran the blade over her arm. "Stop doing this, Elle," she commanded as the blood from her new wound ran into the cup. After a few moments, it was about a quarter of the way full, so she whispered another spell and ran her now-glowing fingers over the cut to seal it closed, leaving not even a mark in their wake. Holding the vessel toward Elle, she said, "I wouldn't have agreed to this if I wasn't willing to bleed."

Elle took the cup and nodded. "I know . . . That doesn't change the fact that I feel bad about it." She sipped. Nearly immediately, her shaking ceased and her vision grew clearer. She had pushed it way too far, again. She did often. She would push it as far as June would allow. She hated seeing June bleed for her. She dreaded it. It made her feel like the monster she was. Her filed teeth meant that she had to watch as June cut herself to feed her. She couldn't bite June without leaving jagged and horrible wounds . . . like she once had. But that morning, the blood tasted sweet. Its warmth soothed her, and she tried to let the worry wash away. June's blood was willingly given. That was what mattered. She hadn't taken it. She would never take it. Never again.

The room was quiet as June ate, Elle sipping delicately at the blood. It all for a moment seemed like a normal morning for the girls.

Until June set down the bowl her breakfast had been in and stood, breaking the silence and peace of their morning. "Now," she huffed. "This bastard who's docking your pay . . ." She ran her hands through her hair, guiding the strands into a ponytail. "Stephan, right?" Once her hair was in order, she dressed in simple pants and a white shirt, leaving the buttons undone deep between her breasts. Then she strapped a leather harness across her back, shoulders, and chest where she sheathed a small dagger. Her boots went up to her knees, and she laced them before she strapped a few small bags with some of the herbs and other trinkets to her belt.

As a mage, she kept some of her most used components on her always, just in case. That was how her magic worked. She used components, specific words, with her own energy in exchange for some sort of effect. A human required an innate ability to transfer their energy into magic, and from there, *most* magic could be learned, taught, or trained. June's mentor had taught her to use shadows, and he had taught her healing magic. Mages tended to master only a few types of magic and put their time and energy into perfecting their craft rather than expanding it. June had always been determined to learn *all of it*, even the dark magic her mentor had been killed for.

But she was good at healing. She was incredible at healing. Elle teased her, telling her it was because she was such a kind and caring soul, and June would huff and say it was because it was the easiest to make money with. Both could be true. Most recently, June had learned transport magic. Magic to move people and items, from one location she knew to another. This magic drained her for days, but she'd learned it as a safety measure for Elle. As much as she'd saved Elle's life, and Elle felt this need to repay her . . . Elle knew June loved her. She knew June felt that Elle had saved her life just as much and that June would do anything to keep her safe. Elle hadn't replied yet. She didn't want to confront Stephan. But she knew June well enough to know she wouldn't let this go.

Elle fiddled with her hands, her fingers anxiously moving over each other. "You shouldn't confront him, June. It's just not a good idea." Her voice exposed the nerves that consumed her. "Please. I'll figure out another job I can do during the day to make up the money." Elle knew June considered her . . . hers. That June would want to protect her.

June cupped Elle's cheek and shook her head. "No, Elle. Come on. We can reason with this bastard and get your pay back to what it's supposed to be. You're worth more than this, okay? Don't let him treat you otherwise."

"June—"

"Even if he knows what you are"—June hushed her, running her thumb over Elle's cheek—"you're still worth more than this. Listen, I'll use magic if he gets out of hand and glue his mouth shut forever." June's eyes softened when she looked over Elle. Her regularly cold expressions melted entirely around her. "You've suffered enough."

Elle felt her heart swell slightly for this powerful mage who had never hesitated to protect her. This strong woman before her who was all Elle wasn't: determined, unwavering, and tenacious.

"Use your magic and expose yourself?" Elle asked, raising her voice a little. June was far more powerful than anyone knew. If Stephan found out . . . "So he has power over you too?" Elle shook her head aggressively.

"I'm better than that, Ellie." June smiled then grabbed a jacket from the pile of clothes at the end of her bed and tossed Elle's cloak to her. "Come on, let's go." She slid another dagger into its sheath on her harness and a third into her boot. "Now come on. I still need to open the shop today, so let's get this over with, yeah?"

Elle swallowed a knot in her throat as she watched June slip yet another knife into her boot.

*****

Elle and June walked through the streets of Torzen, the city that now hid them both. A pair of runaways who'd managed to find each other in the vastness of the world. Patrons of the tavern smiled at Elle and a few waved. A woman ran over to June to ask her about a salve she'd purchased a few days before. June told her to come by the apothecary later, and she'd get her another. The girls had become comfortable here. June was relied on by the city, Elle beloved. They felt safe here. This had become home after they'd found each other. After June had found Elle in the woods. Now this place welcomed them. *Or at least it welcomes what we've given them to see.* Both kept their secrets, and the people of this city seemed to love the image they portrayed. Elle was famous for her dances, loved by everyone she met. June was a powerful healer and made herself invaluable as such. She was respected despite her cold demeanor.

They approached the tavern, and Elle grew increasingly nervous. Confronting Stephan felt like a terrible idea, but she couldn't sway June. She was thankful June didn't know *everything* Stephan had done. That her bruises were always healed by the time she made it back to the house and June didn't know the extent of his abuse. She didn't want to risk what they'd built, she didn't want to risk the safety they'd found here, even if that meant a few bruises from a piece of shit man. She healed so quickly, bruises meant little to her.

She owed June everything. She'd saved Elle's life in the woods that day, pulled her from the ground as she'd lain there begging for death. It was so different, then and now. Then Elle had not been able to imagine feeling joy like this again, and now, as they walked together toward the Stag, the fear that this joy would be taken was overwhelming.

The main room of the tavern was large. A bar against one wall was lined with many imported spirits from the coastal cities. Clumps of wooden tables and seats were arranged in the center of the room, their tops covered with deep red tablecloths. But the true heart of the tavern was the lifted stage against the wall opposite the bar. The floor gleamed with polish, and small glass balls of everlight illuminated the front of the stage. Long, heavy green curtains were daintily tied back by thick gold ropes on either side. A door tucked behind one of the curtains led off the stage.

A man stood by a table adjusting the tablecloth, straightening it and smoothing out the wrinkles in the fabric. He shifted the everlight in the center of the table, and Elle waved when he glanced over.

"Lynn, is Stephan in the back?" She tried to keep her anxious tone at bay.

Lynn nodded, straightening his back. "Yeah, sorry fuck just rolled in." He smiled and nodded at June then returned his gaze to Elle. Lynn was around June's age, maybe a few years her elder. He had long red hair that he kept braided back, and bright green eyes nearly as vibrant as Elle's over heavily freckled cheeks. "You're here early, Jez."

"Elle."

"I just need to speak with him." She glanced at June, then set off for the door to the side of the stage.

As they started toward the back, Lynn raised his voice to say, "He's in a gods-awful mood, Jez."

"Elle," June corrected him again with a bit more force in her tone.

"It's *fine*, June." Elle pulled her by the arm toward the door.

"Your guard dog seems to be in a bad mood too." Lynn grabbed a cloak from the counter and turned to leave. "I'm headed to grab flowers for tonight. I'll see you later, Elle. And you, mage."

*****

Backstage, they passed the room where Elle prepared for her performances, a few other rooms with supplies, and then, at the end of the hall, was Stephan's office. Elle was so very familiar with that room.

She knocked on the door. "Stephan? It's Elle."

June pushed past her and barged in.

Stephan was seated at his desk. He looked up when June came crashing into his office, his annoyance clear in his eyes. "Elle." His eyebrows furrowed when he looked at June. "I remember you. You're her roommate, right?" He looked hungover. His skin was ashen, and he winced, his hand moving to his forehead, when he stood too quickly. "What exactly do you two fucking want? And so fucking early in the gods-damn morning, for fuck's sake."

June was quickly in front of Elle, protection in her stance and her hand resting on Elle's hip. "Her pay. Her full pay."

He stepped around the desk and shook his head. "I paid her her full amount last night."

"You shorted her. You know damn well you did, and I wouldn't be surprised if it's happened before," June hissed. Any control over her temper was quickly vanishing.

"*Really, Elle?*" He glanced at her. "You send her in to fight for you?" He stepped closer to June. "I have no need to pay a vampire any more than I did, and if you want her to stay alive and well, I'd advise you to let it go."

June pushed her shoulders back, her hand poised and ready to reach for her knife. "Being a vampire isn't illegal."

"But being a murderer is, and being a murderer *and* a vampire is a death sentence." He looked at Elle. "Leave, and take your bitch with you."

Her hands grew damp. Her neck went cold as beads of sweat ran down from her hair to her collar. "June, we should leave."

"Fuck you." June stepped toward Stephan. "Pay her the full amount, or I'll—"

He slapped her.

June's hand darted for her knife, but Stephan surprised them both.

He moved faster than Elle would've thought he could ever be able to. He was a well-connected man, deep into the underground, and he must have spent plenty of his life fighting to get into his comfortable position. Stephan was clearly practiced. His hand wrapped around June's neck, and the other had drawn a knife of his own. June's knife clattered to the ground in the struggle.

"And you, I could get quite a pretty payday for your little head, too, huh? You worked for that twisted black magic fuck from Holdtag."

June pressed back into the wall, trying to make any room between her throat and the knife he now had pressed against it. The blade just barely dug into the flesh of her neck. "Fu—fuck off." Her hands began to glow.

No. No. No no no no no. If June used her powers . . . If she used her powers, it was all fucking over. They wouldn't be safe anymore. But that look in Stephan's eyes . . . He was going to kill her. Elle had seen that look before. She'd seen that look in Alder's eyes. Stephan was going to kill June. He already knew who she was. He could expose her. He could get them both killed, even if he didn't do it by his own hands. *Shit shit shit shit shit.* It was overwhelming, the panic crashing into her mind. The fear was going to bring her to her knees. She needed to protect June. She needed to keep her safe. In the moment she hesitated, June screamed.

No.

No.

No.

NO!

June grasped at her throat. Blood poured from the slice across her neck. Her hands glowed as she desperately tried to heal the wound.

Stephan stepped back, June's blood dripping from his blade, and his eyes turned to Elle.

A flash of light burst from her.

Stephan fell backward, his knife dropping from his hands and clattering on the wooden floor.

Elle ran toward him as he stumbled. For a moment, June's eyes caught hers, and her expression was familiar, a combination of fear and concern. It was a look Elle had seen before. The look she'd seen when they'd first met. When Elle had been nearly feral.

Elle plunged her hand into Stephan's chest. Her nails seemed to have grown but were consumed in the residual glow of that same light that had burst from her. Her other hand clamped over his mouth to muffle any sounds before they escaped. As she tore his heart from where it beat within him, she clamped her teeth down on the side of his neck. Vampiric urges and needs took full control. Her dulled teeth tore his skin apart, and she left a messy wound where she fed as he died.

He dropped to the ground.

June sat on the floor, her back against the wall, her hands still holding tightly to her neck. Gurgles left her throat as she tried desperately to heal, her eyes locked on the vampire now the only one left standing.

Elle turned to her. She could feel her nature. Herself. Vampiric power coursing through her veins as it hadn't in years. It felt like the spells keeping her hidden wavered. Hot blood poured from her mouth. Her eyes met June's, then looked down to see that in her hand . . . in her hand was the heart of the man dead on the floor behind her.

June didn't speak, she didn't move, she only stared at Elle.

Elle began to tremble, swayed a moment, and then collapsed.

$\sim$ 3 $\sim$

CHAPTER 3

E lle

"...Elle...Elle..."

She felt June's breath on her face.

"You *have* to wake up, Ellie."

Elle's eyes fluttered open. "June . . . ? June?!" Her head was pounding, and she winced as the light flooded in between her lids. "You're— You—"

"I managed to close it up." June's voice was quiet. "You have to get up, Elle."

"June . . ." She sat up slowly and leaned against June's chest. They were on the floor in Stephan's office. She looked over, then pushed away from June when her eyes landed on the body. Stephan's body. "Oh my gods. *Oh my gods!* He's dead. June, he's dead. June, I killed him!"

June pulled Elle back against herself. "Yes."

"I KILLED HIM!" Elle began to shake violently in June's grasp.

"You . . ." June grabbed Elle's face, both her hands holding tightly to Elle's cheeks. "You protected me, and he fucking deserved it. He tried to kill me."

Elle's chest heaved as she fought to hold back a sob. "I just . . . I just got so scared, and I needed to protect you. Then there was light, and I-I killed him." She ripped her face out of June's hold to look at his body again. "What do we do, June? What do we do!?"

June began to stand, pushing herself up off the floor and onto her shaking legs. We have to hide him, and we have to clean this room. And us. Come on, Elle. We need to fucking focus." She reached down to Elle to help her up.

June must be so tired. She'd lost so much blood. Elle had almost seen her life entirely fade from her eyes, only barely held back.

Elle held as tightly to June's hand as she could, adrenaline the only thing granting her the ability to stand at the moment. "What do we do?" There was blood *everywhere*. It was even on the ceiling . . . They were covered. His blood was drying against her face, streams now hardening and flaking off from where they'd run from her mouth. She'd lost control entirely. Panic began to build again. The man on the ground before them was not small. There was more blood than she understood around them. How, by the moon, were they going to hide him? Her stomach twisted into knots. She'd killed *another* man.

June started pacing, her boots leaving prints in the puddles of blood. "First, we get rid of him." She ran her hand through her hair, brushing back the strands that had fallen from her ponytail. "Fuck. Fuck. Listen, we can get a keg, okay? I can hack him up if we need to, but the blood . . . Fuck. Fuck, there's so much blood. But we can stuff the bastard in a barrel. He fucking deserves less. Fuck. But we could—"

Elle's eyes darted to his body, then quickly back to June. The sight of him made her stomach turn. His blood in her belly threatened to make its way back up. "Just transport him with your spell."

June's hand dropped from her head. "Yeah . . . yeah, that makes sense." She looked around them. "Still doesn't help with the blood." Her neck arched as she looked at the ceiling. "I'm not unfamiliar with cleaning up blood. There's cleaning supplies around here, right? In one of the rooms we passed? I'll use . . . I can use the shadows, summon a few to get the blood cleaned quickly. Water. I'll need water. I can make water. Elle, do you have any gems, like any, in your dressing room? I need them for the spells. I'll buy you more, I promise." Already shadows began appearing around June as she summoned them.

Elle could remember June speaking of her mentor vaguely, about cleaning up after his work. She wondered how much of that cleaning meant *cleaning*. "It's fine, June." Elle shook her head. The gems she had were what she'd been able to take of the gifts from Alder. She'd taken them to sell, if need be, but maybe using them now, not staring at them anymore, might relieve some of the weight of his ghost. "I do. I do. I'll be right back." She looked down at her boots. Blood entirely coated them. She moved out of the puddle on the floor and her boots, stepping carefully to keep her feet on the clean portions of the floor. She didn't want to make more tracks for them to have to clean. They were already working on a short timeline before Lynn might return. Another employee could come in early. *Literally anyone could show up.* "Be careful, June. Please." June couldn't have much energy left. How much had she used to keep all of her blood from spilling? The image of June with her hands wrapped around her throat, blood seeping through her fingers, flashed before Elle's eyes, and she fought that vomit down again.

*****

June started to clean the office as Elle rushed out the door and to her dressing room. Thank the moon Lynn had left and the farm where he purchased flowers was a decent walk away. Elle had made that trek herself before. He'd be gone for hours. And if he stopped to see the girl he was in pursuit of, she'd have enough time. They could pull this off. They could.

Elle caught sight of herself in her mirror for only a moment. She didn't have a second to waste, but gods, it frightened her to see her own reflection. Her face was covered in blood. His blood. She'd tasted it. She'd fed on him as she ripped his heart from his chest. *Fuck. FUCK.* Her hands shook as she grabbed a towel to wipe off with. She cleaned up as best she could and stuffed the blood-stained cloth into a bag, then changed out of her clothes and into spares she kept in her dressing room. Her bloody dress went into the same bag as the cloth she'd wiped her face with.

She could hide this. They could hide this.

She rifled through the drawer in her vanity for the few gems she'd stashed there. A ring, an earring, another ring. Hopefully, these would be enough for what June needed. It was all she'd dared to keep there. She'd separated what she'd made out with, hidden them in various locations should she need to run from anywhere. She was always ready to run. She had to be.

You lost control again, you fucking monster. The thought twisted through her mind and around her heart, threatening to squeeze until it stopped. *Fucking. Monster.*

Once she was clean enough to get home without being caught, she grabbed the bag of bloody evidence and went to help June. She didn't have time to spiral yet. If nothing else, she had to keep her shit together to keep June safe. Once June was safe, she could let the tidal wave of emotion crash.

*****

She walked back into Stephan's office. The shadows were already hard at work cleaning while June knelt over the body. She looked up at Elle as she entered. "The coin I gave you." She held out her hand expectantly. "I'll get you another."

Elle nodded and fished the coin from where she'd tucked it in her brassiere. The spell June had practiced. The transport spell. She'd focused the magic into a coin that she'd instructed Elle to have on her at all times.

The spell worked one of two ways. June could send someone to a location she knew. Depending on her energy level, the distance to that location changed, and she had to be intimately familiar with the location, able to fully see it in her mind. Or, should Elle be in immediate danger, the coin could bring her directly to

June, wherever she was. Using the spell in that manner, however, required both parties of the transport to be alive.

June shoved the coin into the hole in the man's chest, the hole Elle had placed there. She closed her eyes and breathed in deeply through her nose. "I'm sending him as far as I can. As far as fucking possible." June's tone was harsh, nearly a growl. "If I could— If I fucking could, I'd send him into space, directly into hell itself . . ." She breathed again. "But I can't, I fucking can't."

The body vanished.

"I've sent him as far as I can. It's all I can do. We have so much to clean."

Elle stared at the space where he'd lain. He was gone. Thank the moon, he was gone.

Now just the blood.

*****

They cleaned the room as well as they could. The shadows worked quickly to clean the surfaces of any of Stephan's remains. June stripped her clothes and shoved them into Elle's bag, then borrowed one of Elle's dresses. It was far too short for her, but it would do well enough to get them home without too much suspicion. Elle knew there were rumors that she and the mage were lovers, and coming back in each other's clothes would only reinforce those rumors. Couldn't be helped though.

Then they left. Quickly.

They walked as calmly as they could as they trekked back through the streets of Torzen, a bag over Elle's shoulder they would have to burn as soon as they arrived home. June leaned heavily on Elle's arm as they walked. Her eyes were already drooping closed with just how much energy she'd used. They took the shortest route, avoiding June's shop which likely had frustrated patrons out front waiting for her to open her doors as she was supposed to. "Just get home," Elle whispered gently as they walked.

Elle saw a flash of red hair, but she was fairly sure she'd ducked her and June into an alley quick enough that Lynn didn't spot them as he returned to the Stag. *Just. Get. Home.*

*****

Elle paced in their apartment, her hands on the sides of her head and her fingers twisted in her hair. "Fuck. *Fuck.* Fuck me, June!"

"Elle." June's voice was weak. "There's no way to trace it to you. There's no way they're going to figure out who did it. They're going to have to find him first, and no one knows you're a vampire. The only person who did is dead. It was clearly a vampire attack. There's no way it could have been a human."

Elle's stomach twisted into knots as June continued. *No way it could have been a human because I tore him apart. Humans can't do what monsters do.*

"And everyone believes you're a human, Ellie. If anything, they'll go after the vampires in that creepy-ass castle." June lay her head back, her eyes half-open at this point. The amount of energy she'd used . . . She'd nearly passed out the moment they'd stepped through the door. Elle had managed to get her to bed, but only just. June's eyes appeared heavy, only half-lidded as she looked at Elle.

"And I worked for him." Elle continued her pacing. "They're going to look into his staff, and the moment I'm asked a question, I'm going to break." Her hand rested on her chest. She felt like her heart may explode. She tried desperately to breathe deeply, but it was like her lungs were filling with water. "I have no idea how I'm going to dance tonight. I don't know how I'm going to keep it together." The last time—The last time she'd killed a man, she'd had to run. She'd run into the woods, and she'd begged death to take her away. How was she supposed to handle it all a second time?

"I'll go to bar"—June took a deep breath—"after I take a nap, and I'll tell Lynn you're unwell. Stephan not showing up for work isn't that abnormal. They won't realize he's missing for a while." Her voice was quiet. Fatigue had settled in deep.

"It will only be more suspicious if I don't show tonight. I have to dance." Elle grabbed the bottle of mead they'd sipped off the night before and took a healthy swig. It burned her throat. She wanted it to burn away the taste of him in her mouth, burn away any trace of it. "Gods damn it."

With apparently great effort, June looked over at Elle. "Stop pacing." She turned her head back and closed her eyes. "I'll come along tonight. It's been a long while since I've had the pleasure of seeing you dance anyway. Focus on me. Just make it through tonight." She sighed when the pacing continued and struggled up into a seated position again. "The bastard deserved what happened." She slowly and shakily shoved her legs off the bed and rubbed her forehead. "Do you want something, Ellie, for the nerves?" She moved toward a shelf of herbs without waiting for an answer, her steps unsure and her hands trembling.

Tears began to roll down Elle's cheeks, and her hands covered her face. "He hit me."

June froze, her hand hovering over the jar she was reaching for. She did not turn to face Elle. "How often?" Her tone shifted; it grew cold but sounded more alert. The anger must have been waking her up.

"Very."

June grabbed the jar. "Then he deserved far fucking worse." She grabbed a few more and a small bowl and then began to mix something.

"I *killed* him, June."

"I would have if you hadn't, Ellie."

*****

June slept hard in the few hours before Elle had to go to work. Her gentle snores filled the silence of the room.

Elle only heard the ringing in her ears.

She began reciting the moves to her dance, each step, each motion. Over and over. Focusing on ensuring that night's performance would be perfect. It had to be perfect.

They would know. They would know if she wasn't perfect.

She debated letting June rest, not waking her when she left for work. But she could already hear June's scolding, and she chose to rely on June for this. She was right, if Elle didn't have her to focus on, she would not make it through this performance. She stood, tying back her hair, then gently nudged June's shoulder. "It's time to go."

June's eyes opened and she nodded. "Of course. Let's—let's get moving." She pushed herself up, blinked a few times, and rubbed her eyes a moment. "Let's get you to work, yeah?"

*****

As they approached the Stag, her stomach turned yet again. The image of his heart, the sight of his blood, his body, the taste and the smell of it. It all crashed into her. It had tasted so fucking good at first but now was bitter in the back of her throat. What she did to him rushed into the front of her mind. She shook it away as best she could and forced a smile to Lynn with all the effort she had. She kissed June's cheek as she let go of her arm to go to her dressing room and prepare for her performance.

June smiled so softly. "Good luck tonight, Ellie."

After a quick bob of her head in reply, Elle darted to the backroom, just barely hearing June saying to Lynn behind her, "Alright, I need something to drink, red."

*****

Over and over and over she recited the steps, the movements. She'd always felt her dances, followed her heartbeat, but that night, she needed to focus on every step. Every deliberate movement. She could not fuck it up. Not that night. *Not tonight.*

As she pulled up her hair, applied her makeup, changed into her clothes, she repeated the steps over and over and over under her breath. She focused on how it felt as her feet made contact with the floor. She walked onto the stage. The blinding everlight was familiar. It was warm.

His blood was warm.

No. No no no. Focus, Elle. Focus. Three steps until the dress falls.

One.

Two.

Three.

They gasped as the dress slid from her shoulders. The air was cold against her skin, nearly fully exposed now. Thank the moon. It jolted her back into focus. Focus. She had to focus.

She had to focus.

She felt the pull of the silks on her body. She felt that familiar pain and tension. Sweat ran down the back of her neck. She couldn't see June in the crowd, but she knew she was there. June was watching her. So was everyone else. Everyone was watching her. Everyone knew. Everyone knew what she'd done. What she was. They were going to figure it out, and she would be killed. *June* would be killed.

Just like she'd killed Stephan.

His blood on her tongue, his heart in her hand. She felt eyes on her. She felt a hand wrap around her throat. *Alder.* She could feel him grab her neck and squeeze. She couldn't breathe. *No no no.*

But it couldn't be Alder. Alder was dead. He wasn't there. She was in the air . . . No. She was falling.

She'd lost her focus.

She'd lost her grip.

She was falling.

People screamed as she collided with the stage.

~ 4 ~

CHAPTER 4

E^{LLE}

She opened her eyes. The mattress beneath her was familiar. It was hers. She was in her bed. She turned her head and saw
June sitting in a chair pulled up beside her bed, her head tilted
back and her arms crossed over her chest. Her feet were propped
up on Elle's bed. She was snoring softly. "June . . ."

June shot up, her feet sliding to the floor and her eyes immediately meeting Elle's. "Oh thank fuck, you're awake."

Elle took in a breath. Her ribs hurt. They had been broken. Her
head ached from crashing to the stage floor. "How long—"

"Only a day, Ellie." June leaned forward and cupped Elle's cheek,
her eyes searching Elle's face like she would find new wounds.

"You didn't—"

"No. No, just your vampire magic." Her lips curved into just a
touch of a smile. "But if anyone asks, I've been healing you since I
carried you out of there, yeah?"

Elle winced. "I hit the stage . . ."

"You dropped straight fucking down." There was a hint of fear
in her tone, like watching Elle fall was something she would not
shake for a long time. "Your hand fucking slipped, and you hit the
ground. You were . . . broken."

"They're going to—"

"No. No, they're not." She shook her head. "Lynn came by. He
dropped off your pay. He just wants you to take a few days to re-

35

cover, okay?" She sniffed, her face twisted a bit. "I'm just sorry I let you dance . . ."

"June—"

"I should've stopped you. You were in your head." She grabbed Elle's hand, pulling it to her face. "Thank the gods you're okay."

Elle could tell by the way the light peeked into their room it was morning. "You should go."

"Morel can wait one more day."

"I'm fine, June. I swear." Elle squeezed June's hand wrapped around hers. "Go. If I'm not dancing, we need the money."

June huffed, "Ellie."

"Go. I'm okay."

June squeezed her hand once more. "Fine. Fine. Don't open the door for anyone, and just rest, my dear, okay?"

"Of course."

She lingered beside Elle. "We maintain as much normalcy as possible still. We have to. I'll be home soon." Her shoulders were tense as she spoke. Elle felt June's eyes run over her as if she were searching for blood, for broken bones . . . signs of what she must have seen. June's tone shook slightly. "I'll not lose you." She leaned forward and kissed Elle's forehead before she departed.

Elle was left alone in her thoughts that day, lying in her bed as her body continued to heal. Her mind raced, swam through wave after wave of fear. She could not slow her thoughts. She could not calm the anxiety that rattled through her bones. She'd killed *another* man.

~ 5 ~

CHAPTER 5

ORZEN

A body was found in a ditch four days after he had gone missing. The community hadn't felt a stir like this in years. The man—Stephan—had run a local tavern and theater, the Silent Stag. He had worked for a powerful landowner by running the day-to-day of the tavern. The man was known in the community, but not beloved. He was known to be cruel. Employees had left his place of business reporting foul treatment, but the Stag brought in enough income that the man Stephan worked for had little care for his methods. Whatever he did worked quite well for them both.

The few other employees of the tavern, a bartender, a dancer, and a few barmaids, none of whom had much pleasant to say, all reported to Stephan.

His heart had been removed, torn from his chest. Sharp claws had been dug into his face. Jagged teeth marks were in his neck. He'd been killed by something vicious. Something intending to tear him apart.

That Stephan had enemies shocked no one. There were plenty who would've been happier to see him dead than alive, except he wasn't killed by a man. This death was not by human hands. The beast that ripped out his heart and apparently consumed his blood could not have been human. Immediately, the community concluded it had been a vampiric attack. A creature human enough to walk directly into the Stag, a creature fueled by a drive for human blood, a creature that could rip out a heart with such ferocity.

The guard who found him described the aura around the body as chilling—overwhelmed with death.

The word in Torzen quickly became *vampires*. The people's fear of an ancient creature was renewed when one seemingly walked among them and had killed one of their own.

Hundreds of years before, vampires and humans had been locked in a conflict that had waged on for years. Men defended their homes against monsters that fed on their blood, monsters that seemed crazed for it. Vampires trying to survive, hunt, eat, feed. Once they'd tasted the blood of a human, they could no longer survive without it crossing their lips. The vampires' numbers weighed so little against the humans', but their strength seemed almost equally matched. Their power granted them only enough of an edge to equal the humans' strength granted by sheer numbers. Eventually, after their casualties had grown far beyond what either side of the war could have imagined, a treaty was drafted. The human kings and vampire lords signed an agreement. The war had ravaged both peoples, both sought only for an end. The law deeply favored men, humans, but the war needed to end. It just needed to end. Vampires were to live in their own communities. Cities could allow them, but they were required to be registered. The murder of men remained entirely illegal and outlawed, and so vampires were forced to find blood by ethical means.

Some tried animal blood, finding it could only take the edge off for so long. Most vampires tucked into their castles, or what was left of them, their keeps and large fortresses that had survived. They kept to themselves, forced to feed within the human rules. For some vampires, this was easy. Men and women would gladly give themselves to creatures they viewed as nearly gods. Old-blooded vampires with plenty of coin could make arrangements, for a price. Could pay humans enough to consume their blood.

Some vampires and humans formed bonds, mutual agreements exchanging power for blood. But some, some were unable to feed under the new rule—lesser vampires, poorer vampires—and if they were to survive, they were forced to murder, to hunt human blood if they wanted any hope of life.

This was how the hunters came to be.

Hunters. Human men transformed into something else entirely. They were trained, tortured, designed to find and kill the vampires who refused the rules of the treaty. Dark magic twisted in their veins and turned their blood black. The color of their human eyes remained until their power was summoned, then their eyes grew dark as the night. The same dark shade as their blood. The transformation hunters endured gave them power far beyond human limitations. Their senses were honed. They could see and smell vampires like dogs bred to track prey. They were faster, stronger. Some hunters acquired powers when mutated into the creatures they became. Some controlled water, some gained physical strength far beyond a human man, and their most powerful controlled flame. Their order was ancient, their rituals had not changed for hundreds of years and were considered quite barbaric. Yet the brotherhood remained, taking young human men and creating more of their kind to hunt and kill. Even vampires joined their ranks, though they were not transformed into beasts like the human men, and this led to superiority of the turned hunters over the vampires who'd joined to help eliminate the conflict their brethren caused. A vampire only held the power they were born with, and a vampire who did not consume blood, less than any other. Hunters held strength far beyond them, and so the power was imbalanced.

Their numbers dwindled as the years marched on. The need for hunters lessened, and the grandeur of being a hunter faded. The number of vampires rebelling ticked away. Vampires were entirely cast out of the hunter brotherhood, the group becoming more and more hostile toward their vampire members.

The initial rebellions against the human laws were stamped out, and the hunters' relevance slipped. Men no longer dreamed of the day their sons became hunters. Hunters scoured the land for initiates, buying young men, taking the homeless and broken, and creating beasts of them.

Years turned the violence slowly into unease, distrust. The war was over. The hunters had removed what was left of vampire rebellion, and the two kinds lived in a strained peace. Men kept to their cities, vampires their castles. Vampires in human cities were registered. Vampires were far more lax with humans within their walls. Hunters were hired when a vampire was found to have killed a human and sent to eliminate the, usually individual, threat, then they retreated to the crumbling ruins of their keep.

Torzen's vampire registry held one name, a half-breed.

Elle had not lived the life of a vampire in the human world, or a vampire in a vampiric domain. She'd been disguised as a human her entire life. She wasn't sure entirely why her parents had chosen to hide her, why they had gone to seemingly great lengths to keep her existence secret, but she'd spent her entire life hiding her nature. The couple who raised her, though as in the dark as her, carried on her parents' work, placing blind trust in the vampires who'd died at the hands of hunters. She'd grown to assume it was to protect her from the discrimination of human society, to keep her from living the life of a vampire in a world owned by men. She did not remember them, her parents, but she desired to trust their judgment. Not that any of that mattered anymore. She had to hide now. After what she'd done.

The couple who raised Elle had filed her teeth once her adult fangs came in, giving them the appearance of human canines. The experience had been nothing short of horrible, but she'd known it was the last visible trait she held of her blood. Her eyes, the red that quickly identified her as vampire, had been turned green by a spell her parents had placed on her. She'd been raised without blood. Until much later in life, she had never tasted what her ancestors had killed for.

A vampire could live without blood if they'd never known it. At around six, a vampire child would yearn for it. Their body would adjust fully to desire the liquid. If, however, a parent kept it from them, a process that could take weeks to years of torment, they would not crave it again, and they would not die without it.

Unless they tasted it of their own accord.

Then. Then it became entirely consuming. Worse than a vampire who'd had blood from their childhood. Without blood, they were weaker, *nearly* human by a vampire's standards. Unable to heal as quickly as other vampires without the full extent of their strength or their power. Most vampires would never choose to live without blood. Though Elle had known nothing else for years. But after what happened with Alder, she was, as most were, controlled by bloodlust. After she'd torn into his neck and tasted the honey that dripped from the wounds, she needed blood like oxygen.

Elle still *appeared* human, but she needed blood. Then she met a mage who agreed to bond with her. An exchange of vampiric power for a supply of blood. Elle could continue to live in the shadows, her hunger satiated.

The vampiric bonds were one of the most powerful tools vampires had to continue to survive without hiding, though Elle had argued relentlessly with June about it. There were three kinds of bonds: mutual, cursed, and soul. A mutual bond was a bond of consent between a vampire and another creature, often a human. The vampire could share their power, their strength, spirit, energy with the human. The human only need give their in exchange to the vampire in exchange. Often these bonds would connect the two emotionally, leaving each able to sense danger, pain, and hunger from the other. Should one member of the party no longer consent to the arrangement, the bond would snap.

Cursed bonds were barely a bond at all. Cursed bonds could drain a vampire's power quickly, and only the strongest of old bloods were able to hold cursed bonds for any amount of time over another creature. These were ties that bound the cursed creature to the vampire who cursed them, granting that vampire power over their very organs in some cases.

The third kind of bond was a soul bond, and these were not something a vampire could control. They required intervention from the moon herself, and she only rarely bound two vampire souls. Should these souls accept their bond, each bleeding for the other, the pair would become like one. They would share each other's power, each other's strengths and weaknesses. Their very lifespans would become intertwined. Should one of them die the other would quickly lose themself, falling into ruin, driven entirely mad, often ending their own life because half of their soul had died. Some bonds had been known to kill nearly instantly should one half fall, leaving the living partner unable to exist further.

All three types of bonds were sealed with a physical mark. These marks, their contents, would vary. In a cursed or mutual bond, the mark could be chosen. A vampire cursing another may use their house seal, a mark of ownership, or in Elle and June's case, their mutual bond was sealed with a simple spot. They dared not draw attention to their bond, as both hid their nature, but they each knew that the little mole on her wrist had a sister.

*****

Elle shook her head. "You've done enough. You don't have to. You really don't."

June held both of Elle's arms. "I want to do this, Elle." She laughed softly, squeezing Elle's arms just a little. "I've studied them, the bonds between vampires. They can be beneficial to both parties—well, this kind can. I'd get stronger, Ellie. I could make more powerful spells, and you would be able to resist your bloodlust because you wouldn't hunger anymore. You'd be free from it."

"I'd feed on you, June." *The thought sent a shiver down Elle's spine. Feeding on a human, even a willing one, petrified her.*

"Less often. And you'd feel better. You'd be safe. You could stop hiding. You're going to die if you don't, or you'll—"

Elle froze, knowing what June was going to say. "I'll attack someone again."

"Elle."

Her head drooped. "You're right. It's fine. You're right." *She could feel herself slipping back into that madness. She couldn't hang on much longer. June was right. Of course she was.*

June's smile grew. "It's a good idea. I promise. It will be good for both of us." *She shifted her hair to the side as she spoke, her movements unselfconscious. She clearly didn't intend to reveal it, but Elle's eyes immediately darted to the large scar on her neck. The scar Elle had put there. A scar deep enough that even June could not heal it.*

Elle withdrew as a wave of guilt washed over her. "Are you really sure?"

She rolled her eyes. "For the last goddamn time, Elle, yes."

~ 6 ~

CHAPTER 6

"A hunter?" Elle's voice shook. "They've hired a *hunter*?"

"So I was told." A hint of fear flashed over June's face, a rare occurrence. "Bliss overheard."

Bliss was seated in the corner of the room. A half vampire, he was the only vampire registered in Torzen. He was also a friend of Elle's and June's lover. June adamantly refused to admit she harbored feelings for the male, but that hadn't stopped either of them from enjoying each other's company. *Or being madly in love with each other.* He was thin but toned, only an inch taller than June. June kept his black hair managed for him, shaved on one side of his head and braided along the other. His face and ears were covered in metal piercings, his arms heavily tattooed, some that June had done herself. His black eyes had red flecks dancing in them. But what really made the male memorable was his single fang, prominently protruding from his mouth. Half vampires had the luck of the draw with the traits they got, and the single fang was certainly unique. Bliss dressed simply in tattered clothes that were only hanging together because Elle regularly mended them for him.

He spoke with a voice that was known for its song, should he get drunk enough. "Heard the guards discussing it." His legs were crossed beneath him as he sat on the floor, rocking side to side as he spoke. "Apparently, Duke Dumbshit isn't a big fan of a vampire killing folks in *his* city." Bliss was full of rumors and gossip.

Regularly drunk and wandering the city, he overheard many *many* things. He helped June around the apothecary, ran errands for the Stag, took any odd job to get him enough coin for his next drink or enough bread to keep him until June or Elle fed him.

The girls hadn't initially told Bliss about the murder, the one *they'd* committed, but it hadn't mattered. He'd come by after he heard about Elle's fall, and immediately, he'd smelled Stephan's blood on them. June had held her knife to his throat and threatened him to keep his mouth shut, but they both knew he had no reason to turn either of them in. He didn't wish them to be caught. Ellie was like his sister, and he was in love with the ice queen of a mage. However, he did seem to quite enjoy her knife against his throat. Elle recognized the look in his eyes, and she wondered if knives would come into play in his and June's next *encounter*.

Not all half vampires were lucky enough to gain a vampiric power, but Bliss, cursed with his face, had been given that one mercy. He'd been born with a sense of smell that rivaled even the king's hounds. He'd smelled Elle's vampiric blood through every spell placed on her the moment he'd met her. He casually brought it up with June, and she'd threatened his life then too. But he had proven trustworthy and over the years had grown to be part of their strange little family. Not once had he betrayed their trust and not once would he, Elle had no doubt.

Elle was pacing again. "So I *have* to leave." Saying it felt like a rock dropping into the pit of her stomach.

"No. Elle. A hunter has passed through the city before, and they didn't sense you then." June handed Bliss the food she'd been preparing for him. She fed her little stray when he stumbled into their home. Another sign her coldness was only a front with him.

"They weren't looking for me then. They weren't looking for *you* then. This hunter is here for me. For us."

"He won't know that." June's tone was calm again, as she always was around her anxious friend.

Bliss looked at Elle, bread now hanging from his mouth. "It'll be okay, Ellie." He smiled. "Just lie low until the bastard passes through."

"He's going to go directly to the Stag. He's going to question me." She sighed heavily as she rubbed her temples. "Shit."

~ 7 ~

CHAPTER 7

Kirk

The hunter stared at the city before him. His hair fell around his neck in loose waves, a few braids keeping it away from his face as gentle winds tossed the strands. Handmade metal beads threaded throughout clattered together. A deep scar ran over his right eye. It was white and aged. He'd carried it for a long while. Gold streaks danced and swirled in his soft blue eyes, like golden ink dropped in water. He ran a hand through his hair and urged his horse forward. "Almost there, Love."

Torzen. A city he had yet to have the pleasure of visiting in his years hunting. Large stone walls surrounded the city, and the guards kept posts at the gates. A thick forest rested to the west, and just beyond that a castle. A castle he had heard of before.

The Red Castle was from legend, housing ancient vampires and the home of the oldest vampire bloodline left after the war. Relatively young as far as vampires go, but unheard of by the standards of men. They had kept to themselves for centuries, the vampires who lived there, staying far out of the affairs of men. The only humans who interacted with those who lived in that castle never exited its walls. However, by all accounts, most willing walked in.

The lord of the castle, of the House of Blood, was named Dae. He was worshiped by some, and those enamored enough with the male would throw themselves on the stone steps that led to his castle. Steps that old hunter stories said had once run red with rivers of blood. The ancient lord was supposedly the most power-ful vampire left and, by some standards, strikingly handsome. The combination alone was dangerous enough for human souls, so easily lured behind his walls. All that said, Dae had done nothing to bring down the wrath of the hunters, as far as they knew. He either kept his nose clean or hid it well enough. And until proven otherwise, he had nothing to do with Kirk's arrival in the city. But Kirk wasn't stupid enough to disregard a neighboring vampire keep when a vampire attack in Torzen hadn't occurred in decades.

A few small farms dotted the fields around the walls, echoing with the sounds of cattle, sheep, dogs, and poultry. The leaves on the trees fell lazily from their branches, their colors bright yellows and browns. Fall had settled deeply around the city. These people's sleepy lives seemed so peaceful. It brought him some warmth. This was what his work provided. They lived within half a day of ancient vampires, but they knew peace. For so long, that peace had been undisturbed, and he felt proud to have been even a distant part of that. As a hunter, he protected this. His duty upheld laws that for hundreds of years had kept humans safe. But he was here because someone had threatened that peace. A body had shown up, murdered by a vampire. He was here to find that vampire and kill them. That was his job. Return the peace that had been taken from the residents of the city.

He rode up to the gates and spoke with the guards that stopped him. He showed them the carved metal disk that held the symbol of the hunters, imbued with magic that identified him as a true hunter. The emblem of his brotherhood: a skull with a vampire's fangs, a sword driven through the top of its head and the tip jutting out below the jaw, surrounded by flowers and thorny vines. A message straddling the border of elegant and foolish with its simplicity.

They opened the gates and he rode in, taking in the sights and smells of a bustling city. He dismounted his horse and led her through the streets to an inn the guards had pointed him toward. He would get her settled and get himself situated with somewhere to rest. Then he would begin his hunt.

*****

A sign rattled as the wind shook its chains. He approached the inn, the Sunflower. The sign was carved with sunflowers surrounding its name, it seemed inviting and warm. Almost out of place in a busy city, but a welcome retreat.

He tied Love off out front, then slid his bag off her back and over his shoulder. "I'll be back shortly, Love."

The furnishings inside were plain, modest. The main room just past the entryway held a few chairs and tables, the walls nearly empty. A fireplace on one side of the room, though currently without flames in its core, would offer a great amount of warmth and light when ignited in the evenings. Everlight glowed in the center of the room. A portrait of a man hung above the fireplace. His expression was nearly as warm as the inn, and for only a moment, Kirk wondered who he was.

The head of a stag was mounted to one wall, everlight hung from its antlers. On the opposite wall, another.

A woman smiled and approached. She had to be in her mid fifties with bright red curls streaked with silver hanging down past her shoulders. Her kindhearted nature was potent enough to shine through her eyes paired with the kind of smile that could put anyone at ease. She tightened an apron as she trotted up to him. "Welcome! Welcome!"

Kirk smiled politely at her. "A room if you have one, ma'am."

She nodded, ushering him in farther, her smile still on her lips. "Of course. Of course. Straight to business!" She walked toward a counter in the corner, motioning him to follow. A vase of flowers brightened the counter, and she stepped around them to grab a paper to write. "You're the vampire hunter, yes? You look like one. I've never seen one, but I've heard of them. You look like what

I'd think. That's why you're here right? The murder?" She shook her head and rested a hand on her hip. "It's really quite a scare. We have a normal amount of crime here for a city as big as this, but so rarely does someone turn up dead—and then it's a vampire! We haven't had an issue with a vampire in a hundred years, those beasts stay up in their castle and leave us alone down here. And we leave them alone up there. How it should be, in my opinion. They just stay the hell out of our business, and we can leave them alone. But now one's walking through our streets! Can you believe it? A vampire willing to kill a man in the middle of the morning. Heard the poor bastard was torn apart. Vampire must've been crazed or something." She shuddered. "Scary stuff. But that's why Duke Kinsley hired you, yeah? Get this all sorted out?"

"Of course, ma'am."

"Fria." Somehow that broad smile grew, and she tapped her chest. Her kind eyes sparkled. "Name is Fria, sweetie."

"Kirk." He tilted his head.

"Lovely to meet you, Hunter Kirk." Fria motioned that he follow her as she started down the hall. "This way to your room, yeah? There's a stable where your horse can get some rest." She opened the wooden door when they reached it. "Should be all you need. Our very best for our city hero."

"I appreciate that, ma'am."

She laughed. "Just Fria, sweetheart."

*****

After he settled himself into his room and Love into the pasture, he set out to find the tavern. The Silent Stag. The man who'd been killed had managed the establishment, an apparently quite busy tavern with, according to Fria, a locally infamous dancer who graced their stage most nights. He strolled down the street, his sword swinging at his hip still slightly obscured by his cloak. Fria had given him directions to the Stag, and he wound through the city toward it. He'd arrived in Torzen late morning, and by the time he was walking through the streets, it was early afternoon. The air was cool and bit at his nose and ears. It smelled like it may rain, snow even, whispers of winter's threat looming in the wind.

A sign swung in that same breeze. The Stag. There it was.

He tapped his knuckles against the door as he pushed it open and stepped through. "Hello?" he called into the room.

A man looked up from behind the counter. Bright green eyes met Kirk's. The man's red hair was tied in a ponytail, and freckles danced across his cheeks and nose, even dotting his ears. He smiled at Kirk and began to walk around the counter to approach the hunter. "Welcome in, good sir!"

Kirk glanced around the room, taking in as much as he could before he returned his gaze to the redhead. "I'm looking for Gen."

The man nodded. "I can go get him for ya, but I must ask who exactly you are."

Kirk slipped his hunter's mark from his pocket and held it out. "I'm the hunter."

"Ah! Yes!" He nodded. One of his hands ran through some loose strands of his hair. "My name is Lynn." He tilted his head slightly. "Do let me know if there's anything I can do to help or questions you have. I worked here with Stephan . . ." His eyes lowered and his voice shifted as he got lost in the emotions of it for only a moment. "Let me go grab Gen from the back, yeah?" He picked up his tone again, shifting his shoulders back. "He settled in here to keep the place rolling after everything happened."

"After I speak with Gen, I have a few questions I'd like to ask you too, Lynn." Kirk's tone was firm but not cruel. His eyes followed Lynn as he walked through a door to the back halls of the tavern, leaving Kirk alone in the room. It was only a few moments before Lynn returned with another man in tow. A man a few inches shorter than Kirk but with shoulders nearly as broad. His hair was shaved clean to his head. Dark brown eyes with a glint in them met Kirk's.

"Gen?" Kirk asked as he stepped toward the new figure.

The man who'd followed Lynn extended a hand. His handshake was firm, sure of itself. "So you're the hunter."

Kirk shook Gen's hand, his own grip matching Gen's. "Yes, sir, I am."

"You got here quickly." Gen released Kirk's hand and slid both of his into his pockets. "Good, good. This has been such ugly business, and it's done quite a number to our profit. People are scared of vampires again and barely leaving their gods-damn houses." His hands quickly exited the pockets he had just shoved them into and he gestured around the room, his movements exaggerated.

A man is dead, and he seems far more concerned about the lost profits. Not impressed by his priorities. "Tell me what you can, please, and I'd like to be taken to where the body was found."

"Of course." Gen walked toward the wall where the spirits were stored. "A drink and then we can talk all you want."

*****

Kirk sat back in the chair. The tavern was still empty. The patrons of the day had not yet begun their trek to enjoy a night of liquor and entertainment, most still hadn't completed their day's work. He sipped at the cup of mead Gen had poured him, a far heftier pour than need be. "So he worked for you? Here?"

Gen nodded as he took a hearty swig of his own drink. "He did. He ran this place for me. Technically I own it, but he invested enough we were almost partners, you could say. But day-to-day was all Stephan. When he passed, it all fell into my hands, and I'm back to managing it myself."

"And his murder?"

"He was found on the edge of the city. His heart had been torn from his body, and a vampire had ripped the side of his neck to shreds. They said it looked like the monster tried to cover its tracks but didn't do well enough." His eyes kept moving around the room, never settling too long before something else took his attention. "The last person who saw him was the dancer who works here. She came in to speak with him that morning, and no one saw him afterward."

"And she had nothing to do with his death?"

Gen laughed, loud enough it echoed against the ceiling. "Gods, no. Pathetic little thing is tiny, delicate, and very, very human. No way she could do the damage the beast did to him. But if you need to ask her questions, she comes into work shortly. Her, Lynn, and two other barmaids are the entire staff here." He rubbed the corner of his eye. "Tomorrow a guard will take you to where he was found. I'm not sure how you complete your hunts, but I pray you find the bastard and handle it. I've chipped in a hefty bonus to whatever the duke has offered to pay you, as a thanks for handling this little issue for the city. And for my business in particular."

"I appreciate that, sir. I'll have it handled as soon as possible."

~ 8 ~

CHAPTER 8

Kirk

Lynn knew little of what had happened. He told Kirk he'd seen Stephan wander into the tavern, hungover and in a piss-poor mood. Then the dancer had to come in early to speak with him. Lynn said after he greeted the dancer, he'd left to run a few errands for the tavern, pick up a few things. He hadn't seen Stephan since. He mentioned that Stephan having enemies, Stephan being wished dead, would not shock him, but a vampire attack seemed so unrelated to any affairs. The office had appeared undisturbed when he'd gone looking for Stephan, and initially, he'd assumed Stephan had simply left again. Lynn seemed anxious, but it wasn't the anxiety of deceit. Kirk got the impression he was simply nervous about the threat of a monster—the threat of a vampire—and the presence of a hunter.

Lynn showed him to Stephan's office. After opening the door and gesturing Kirk in, Lynn made his excuses, leaving Kirk alone. He began studying the room while he waited for the other tavern staff to arrive so he could question them. He looked through Stephan's things, through his desk, his shelves. Stephan's knife was laid on the desk alongside a few books with the finances of the tavern written in them. Nothing seemed out of place. He could smell Gen, Lynn, and other people in the room, but that was almost entirely unhelpful, any of the staff's scents would have been in the room with Stephan's, anyone who had come and gone before or after the murder.

He turned to exit the room when he looked at the back of the door. Lynn had closed it behind himself, and it appeared just barely off color . . . just barely. He approached and leaned close, examining the wood carefully. The color was darker than the wood of the walls, of the doorframe, but it did not seem burned, rather almost stained? He noted it. What he would do with the information, he wasn't sure yet. The room seemed recently cleaned, which likely was Gen setting up his new office, but there was little dust or dirt anywhere.

On his way through the halls toward the main room, he walked past a closed door. Lynn had mentioned it was the dancer's private dressing room. He stopped and opened the door slowly before stepping into the room. It was small, less than half the size of Stephan's office. On one wall was a mirror mounted above a vanity, a small stool seated before it. There were hooks on the opposite wall where two dresses hung, one a pale yellow and the other a delicate pink, both quite lovely, but he noted they wouldn't leave much to their viewer's imagination. A few other items rested on top of the vanity. Makeup, hairpins, a hair brush. A few wilted roses lay on the side of the vanity, likely gifts from patrons or maybe a lover. But were they from a lover, would they not have been in a more loved position? These seemed . . . tossed.

"Oh! I— Ah!" A feminine voice shook behind him, evidently with surprise.

He turned and faced her.

Bright green eyes looked up into his. Full pink lips and cheeks just touched with red. Dark curls fell over tiny shoulders, and delicate features held a look of shock at the sight of a strange man in what he quickly assessed was *her* dressing room. The dancer.

He felt his chest tighten suddenly, and a chill rushed up his spine. It became difficult to swallow, and his stomach felt like a bottomless pit. He shook his head, unsure what had just come over him. He *ached*. He tried to shove the feelings aside. He must've been tired . . . or something. "Forgive me, ma'am."

She was shaking.

"My name is Kirk." His blurry vision cleared. "I'm the vampire hunter hired to find the beast who killed your boss." He lowered his head, bending deep, nearly into a bow. "You're Elle, the dancer, yes?" When she just barely nodded her head, he continued, "You were the last person to see him alive, if I'm correct?" His eyes took in every inch of her. Gods, she was exceptional. His heart picked up speed, his cock began to rebel against him, his hands were sweating. *Why are my fucking hands sweating? Gods be damned.*

"Yes, sir." She nodded. She kept her eyes fully averted from his.

He towered over her. She was so small, delicate, lovely . . . Should he hold her, he could consume her. *I want to hold her desperately. What am I even doing?*

"Sir is not necessary, love." He shook his head, trying to keep his composure. "What happened that morning?"

"I came here to speak with him, collect my pay from my performance the night before." She motioned that she needed to step into the room, her hand flicking toward her vanity. "Let me get ready while I answer your questions, good sir."

He shifted out of her way as best he could. He took up much of the space in the room. He was an imposing man.

She brushed against his chest as she pushed past him and seated herself before the vanity.

He prayed she had not felt the stiffness in his pants as she grazed him. She smelled like flowers. Honeysuckle. "Of course."

She leaned toward the mirror, reaching to apply dark, black lines around those green eyes. "What else do you want to know?" Her shaking seemed to have calmed slightly, and she applied the lines with the precision that comes with having applied that same makeup many nights before.

"Did anything happen during your conversation with him? Anything after?" He shifted on his feet behind her, watching her hands as they began to run through her hair to pull it into braids. His hands ached to wrap around that waist which stretched as she reached.

"Not really, no. He gave me my pay, and I left. I didn't see where he went after that. I—" She paused only a moment, something wavered. "I've already spoken to the guards about this. Everyone who's come to ask, I've answered everything." She sighed, her fingers seamlessly twisting the strands of her hair into braids. "Do they really believe it's a vampire?" She looked at him through the mirror, her eyes meeting his watching her with such intensity. "We haven't had a vampire in Torzen in so long . . ."

"It was certainly a vampire." He couldn't control himself as his gaze roved over her body. "This is your first performance back after an accident, I hear. The night he was last seen?"

She paused. She fully froze in her movements like the memory of her accident held her in a tight grip. "Y-yes." She stuttered. "I was in my head, with Stephan missing, and I lost my grip." She swallowed hard, seemingly forcing her hands to continue their work. "A mage worked a long time to help me heal as I have." She closed her eyes, her expression suggesting the memories of that pain washed over her. "So tonight is my first night back."

"I appreciate your answers, dearie." Kirk stepped backward just a bit toward the door. "I will see you again, I'm sure. I may need more information." He tilted his head, his hand motioning goodbye. "It's been a pleasure, love." He couldn't shake the ache as he left her room. Whatever it was about her that made his body revolt against itself . . . He needed a drink. Or a nap. Or both.

*****

Gen grabbed Kirk's arm as he exited the back hallways into the main bar. "Stay for the dance," Gen commanded. "All your drinks are on the house!"

"I really should get going-"

Gen's grip tightened. "I insist, dear hunter."

Kirk sighed heavily. He did not wish to anger his employer, appearing to decline their hospitality. "Of course." He forced a smile. "How could I say no to free mead?" He ran his hand through the loose strands of his hair.

*****

It was not long before the room was buzzing with patrons. Members of the city coming in, chatting loudly, laughing and drinking, excitedly waiting for the performance. Kirk found himself somewhere to stand with his back pressed against the wall. A mug of mead was balanced in his hand. He had already made it through another by then, his eyes quietly taking in the people in the room.

He was left well enough alone. A woman or two made a pass at him, a few gazes from men in the room shot to him, running him over, sizing him up. But not only was he unknown, he was visibly threatening enough that folks rarely desired to talk to him let alone start something.

A small band in the corner was preparing to play. Aerial silks hung from the ceiling. The everlights grew a bit brighter.

The room hushed when the lights signaled it. She was going to dance.

Her delicate figure stepped out onto the stage. That pale yellow dress he'd seen in her dressing room fell over her body. Her legs and arms were entirely exposed, free for mobility as she began to dance. Like he'd thought, the dress left little of her to the imagination. High slits to keep her legs free revealed toned hips. The back of the dress entirely open all the way down to just above her ass. She moved around the stage, her limbs gracefully following the rhythm of the music. Her feet seemed to barely touch the floor before they were moving again, each step deliberate and delicate. The yellow dress was short-lived. The fabric would have gotten in the way as she moved toward the silks. The dress slid easily from her body as she continued, every movement appearing effortless. His cock ached against his pants. Underneath that dress was a tight top and even tighter shorts, the bottom of her round ass just barely exposed. The top plunged deep between her breasts with strands of fabric crisscrossing between them. Her hair was pulled up, those nearly black curls tucked into a variety of braids he'd seen her begin to weave during their earlier meeting. He barely realized he held his breath. His heart felt like it was being crushed. His eyes were entirely fixated on her as she performed. Knots formed in his gut. His palms grew sweaty again.

He was entranced as she climbed, fell, spun, twisted, and twirled with the silks wrapped around her body. He was damn near jealous of the fabric.

Then her dance ended.

He felt as though he'd watched her for hours, yet only seconds at the same time. He shook his head as reality grabbed him and dragged him back. He took another sip of mead, the burn down his throat waking him up. It was as though he'd witnessed a deity, a goddess who graced the realm of men, if only for a moment—a moment deliberately designed to drive him mad. To burn so deeply in his chest it became hard to breathe. This little dancer had to be a mage. She had to have cast some spell over the room . . . The rest of the room felt as he did, right? Like they were consumed, like their bodies *ached* for her. Like their chests would burst if not near her? After she vanished, it was like his lungs could collapse. He was possessed by her, owned by her very existence. He did not wish it to end. He only felt driven to be nearer to her.

*****

Kirk returned to the Sunflower that night, strolling through the darkened streets until he saw that wooden sign, the carved flowers barely visible in the dark. The everlights were dim, but one of a hunter's gifts was vision at night, to hunt their prey that preferred darkness. He could see each step clearly. Sometimes he wished, however, that they were blessed with no need to rest . . . he'd even settle for needing less rest. Vampires were creatures of the night, humans creatures of the day. A hunter needed to be able to be both, and he was *tired*.

When he reached his room, he slid his cloak off. It fell onto the floor, and he rubbed his forehead. He glanced at the bath in the attached room and waved his hand. A fire began to warm the water as he continued to settle back into the room. His brothers envied his gift of fire, a gift rare among hunters. A gift that rocketed him toward hunter leadership, that meant he had power far beyond that of his brothers. Practically, it made camping simple, meant he had warm baths, and vampires . . . vampires burned.

He unbuckled his belt and laid his sword against the tub. He always kept his sword within reach. A beautiful blade, carved with their symbol in her hilt, he cared for the sword so she was always prepared to relieve a vampire of their head. In the handle, a small piece of carved wood was encased in metal and resin. A symbol of his past. A reminder of what he had done. Who he had become. And why he continued every step down his path.

Kirk slid out of the rest of his gear, his boots, his leather pants, his shirt. He stepped into the bath. The muscles of his back, his thighs, screamed against the water, eager for the heat to soothe the aching. Being trained and toned did not release him from aches. And that dancer. That dancer made his body feel like it had when he was no more than a young man.

The water always made his scars ache. His arms rested on either side of the bath, his head leaned back over the edge. He closed his eyes and let his chest sink into the water. It felt so heavy, his chest . . . his heart. The water gently moved against him, and he could not keep her from his mind.

She was so small. Like his hands could wrap around her and simply crush her. Like she could vanish within his grasp. His cock stiffened as he continued to think of her. It ached for her as the rest of his body, his mind, his soul did. He did not resist the fire in his veins as he wrapped his hand around the base of his cock.

He stroked himself as he thought of her, as he pictured her in his hands. He wanted so desperately to touch her. She danced through his memories behind his closed eyes, every movement of her body etched into his mind. The way the lights caressed her. The way the sweat running down her chest between those perfect tits reflected the everlight like stars. The way she moved, like she was entirely one with something unseen to everyone in the room but her. The way she'd smelled when she'd brushed past him in her dressing room. The delicate touch of her skin just barely making contact with his.

Something about her . . . This was unlike anything he'd felt before. It had awoken something deep in his being, something primal that he did not understand. He *needed* her. She must have cast a spell over him. She had to have.

His grip on his own length shifted as he felt an orgasm building in his core, and he moaned softly as he thought of her.

She didn't wear much makeup as makeup off
stage at the stage, just her delicate features unhindered
by frill and fuss. Her skin like snow and eyes like evergreens
A set of
earrings she
wore, said
they were
from Jian
Hair Black
as Ravens
A flower abandoned
on stage after her
first met, or rather the
first time I saw her in daylight

~ 9 ~

CHAPTER 9

KIRK
He was out of the inn at first light. His hair was pulled back and his leathers strapped into place. Even his release in the bath and the subsequent few in bed after hadn't shaken his desperate desire for that dancer. Something in him was changed. It was beyond a simple hope that he would see her that day.

The autumn air was crisp and attempted to shake him from within his own head as he trekked back toward the Stag. Gen had arranged for the guard who'd found Stephan's body to take him to where it had been found.

The young guard was waiting for him just outside the tavern doors, his spear gripped tightly in his hands. "Good morning, hunter, sir."

Kirk nodded in greeting. "Good morning."

"This way, sir."

*****

The guard led him from the Stag toward the edge of the city. Kirk learned his name was Helion. He was barely past twenty, and finding a body that'd been ravaged by a vampire was the most interesting and exciting thing that had ever happened in his short existence. The kid's armor barely fit him, hanging loosely on his slight frame.

"Are there vampires living in the city?" Kirk asked. He mapped the path from the Stag to where the body was found as they walked. Whether alive or dead, Stephan would have made some version of that journey. However, because of the time between or some other reason, there wasn't a single sign that Stephan had been through the way Helion led Kirk. "They require a vampire registry in Torzen, yes?" Not that a murderous vampire would necessarily be registered, but it was somewhere to start.

"They do, sir. There is only a half-breed that I'm aware of, sir." Helion glanced at him as he continued to walk beside the hunter. "His name is Bliss. The son of a human prostitute and some vampire sire."

"And do you know where I might be able to find him?"

"At this time of morning, he's likely stumbled his way to the apothecary. He regularly sleeps with the owner. He's a bit of a drunk, and I'm not sure he has a home of his own. I've personally had to shoo him away plenty of times."

"I'll seek him out next. Thank you."

The place where Stephan had been found was tucked back on the edge of the city, a ditch just outside of and alongside the stone walls. Kirk had seen no obvious signs of him being moved, even as he had observed their entire path from the Stag. Nor did it appear to be where he'd been murdered. Kirk was quite sure of that. This was only where a body had been dumped. Now there was nothing here. The body had been removed, and any blood had returned to the earth, been washed away by autumn rains, or been taken by animals before Kirk had arrived.

One of the issues with solving murders after too long was that clues eroded away. Kirk knelt where the young man pointed. He could smell the death there. His eyes darkened. There were no remnant signs of a struggle, nothing to indicate there had been an attack. He sighed and stood back up. "I'm going to speak with the half-breed."

*****

ELLE

Elle walked toward the apothecary with her arm looped through June's. Sleep had escaped her another night. *He* had been at the Stag. She knew he would've been eventually. As soon as Bliss had mentioned a hunter, she knew she would see him. But she hadn't expected to feel like her head was going to explode and her stomach was twisting into painful knots with *desire*. When she'd found him in her dressing room, a chill rushed up her spine. He was so tall with broad shoulders, a large chest, and muscles that his shirt barely contained.

His face was scarred, nearly every inch of skin not covered by leather littered with scars or tattoos. His eyes were so bright—the blue and gold held the vibrancy of an ocean filled with stars. For how much a man in his role must have seen . . . they were still so bright. Fear had radiated through her at first, that sword at his hip was meant to drive through *her* chest, but her eyes had drifted from that blade and he had been . . . aroused. That had only fueled her own twisted thoughts.

Gods, a man here to be her own death, and she desperately wondered what he looked like naked. What his hands would feel like gripped around her. What his teeth would feel like against her flesh. Fear twisted with longing, and she knew she needed to avoid him if she wanted to keep from grabbing him and begging him to fuck her until she saw stars. She needed to stay *far away from him.*

They approached the shop, Morel Apothecary. A small wooden building June had bought when she'd first come to the city nestled between a few others. She'd transformed it from a run-down disaster to what it was now. Her blood, sweat, and tears were nearly as a part of the building as the wood itself. She'd run from her past life to start a new one here, and she'd built everything she had with her own hands.

Her mentor, the man who had taught her magic, had gotten caught up, deep, in dark and evil magic. It ended in his death. It ended with June being cast out. June had had to run from what had been home, run from a community that had turned against her. She ran until she reached Torzen. Far enough away that she could start her life anew, start without rumors of her involvement. She'd built a life there for herself. She'd built a new life in a new city, and she'd started to become happy. She'd fallen for a half-bred vampire, she'd made connections to the townspeople as she'd offered them simple medicine. Then a bloody mess of a vampire had stumbled into her world.

A woman was already standing outside of the apothecary door, fiddling with her fingers anxiously. Her hands shifted to her skirt, then her eyes rose to meet the girls as they approached. "There you are!" she called to them. A few gray hairs fell into her face from beneath the hood pulled over her head.

June stepped past her and unlocked the magic lock only June and Elle could open. "Come inside, Leligh." She sighed, her eyes meeting Elle's for a moment before she disappeared through the doorway into the shop.

Bliss was already inside.

"How in the fuck did you—" June rolled her eyes. "Good morning, Bliss." Somehow this half-breed managed to get into everything of hers. *Everything.*

Elle wondered how she put up with him. And in that specific moment, just how he had gotten into Morel.

Leligh huffed, "June."

June forced her temper down, Elle could see her shove it deeper. "Give me just a second, Leligh. It's for the bump on your neck, yeah?" She rifled through jars that lined the shelves. A wooden table stood in the center of the room, spell books opened and tossed on top of it. June spent any time not supplying the city with spells learning new magic, learning *more* magic.

Bliss must have slept there last night. His eyes were sunken back, some of his hair falling out of the braids June had put into it the day before.

He smiled stupidly at Elle, waving from where he was seated on the floor in the corner.

She smiled gently, kneeling beside him and laying a hand on his arm. "You're never going to win her heart if you keep breaking in, Bliss," she whispered, laughing softly.

He shrugged. "I still get into her bed." Elle knew damn well that the man wanted into that mage's heart desperately. Her bed was not enough.

"You're disgusting." Elle rolled her eyes and stood back up, nudging his thigh with her foot. "C'mon. She's got work. I'll make you some breakfast, and it looks like this shirt needs another patch."

*****

KIRK

The apothecary. This was where Helion had said the half-breed would be. Likely. Kirk opened the wooden door and stepped through the frame, his boots heavy against the stone of the floor. "Hello?"

A woman glanced up from the books and papers spread out across the table before her.

Immediately, Kirk sensed power on her, in her. It radiated off her like a beacon as he took her in. She had it cloaked, which was a feat of power within itself. Her gaze was stone, cold and entirely calm as he entered.

"This is your shop?"

She took a step back from the table and crossed her arms over her chest. "It is my shop." Her chin was slightly raised, her eyes clearly assessing him as he stood before her.

Enough people had forced a cocky, though foolish, confidence before Kirk, in some desperate attempt to intimidate him, but she . . . she was not forcing anything. And judging by the power he could feel coming from her, she would be one hell of a fight. She appeared like a snake, ready to strike should he give her any reason to.

"My name is Kirk." He stepped farther into the shop, glancing around for a moment. "You already know what I am, I assume?"

Her posture did not shift. She stood firm, but not still, like a storm waiting to break. "I do. You're here to kill a vampire." She tilted her head to the side, her chin still raised. "What I *don't* understand is why you're here in *my* shop. Stephan's death was nowhere near here."

"I've been told there's a half-breed vampire around here. He goes by Bliss, and he regularly lurks around your shop." Kirk's gaze returned to her. "The wounds on the man were messy, his neck was torn apart, and I've heard reports that the half-breed, Bliss, has only one"—Kirk tapped his lip above his canine—"so if he were to attack a human, it would be quite a mess. Like Stephan." He could smell him, vampire scent mixed with human. The smell was almost more potent than one or the other. The combination was damn near sickening to some hunters. Kirk never considered it so appalling, just strong. "He's been here. Today." He watched her eyebrow rise only slightly. "Where is he now?"

"I don't know." She shook her head. "He left hours ago. Probably drinking already." Kirk noted something in her tone. He couldn't pick it out exactly, but there was just barely something about it . . . just barely.

"Very well then. He smells strongly enough. I'll track him easily. May I ask," he began as he turned to leave, "what a mage with power like yours is doing"—he gestured around the room—"here?"

"You may not. Now leave my shop."

"Yes, ma'am."

*****

A vampire with long white hair walked through the halls, his steps desperate and panicked. This isn't going to go well, he thought as he brushed some of his hair behind his ear.

He entered an office. Another male was seated at a desk with his legs crossed, a glass of wine resting between his fingers, and he was idly flipping a blade in his hand. He had dark hair and even darker eyes that pierced nearly through the first male as he entered. "What do you want, Silas?" he growled.

"A human was killed by a vampire, Dae." Silas forced his voice out. "In Torzen."

"The closest thing to a vampire in that city is the bastard." Dae's eyes lowered to the wine in the glass a moment, swirling it and watching it move. "And the little shit doesn't even drink blood." He sighed. "If someone from another house, or this house—"

"All of yours are accounted for, Dae." Silas shook his head. "No one left the castle."

"Investigate then." Dae sighed again, angrily, closing his eyes like the inconvenience ached deeply in his head. "I do not need some hungry low-blood complicating things and bringing humans up here. Eliminate it, yes?"

"Yes, sir."

~ 10 ~

CHAPTER 10

K^{IRK}
Finding the drunk was simple enough for Kirk. He followed the scent trail left behind by a half-bred vampire. The trail stumbled through the city, leading him to a small building near a larger house. He walked past the large house and up to the door of the smaller building. He heard voices from inside as he neared. One was an unfamiliar male's voice, the second he recognized immediately, and a chill ran down his back. It was *hers*.

Suddenly, it felt like electricity sparked through his bones, and he was achy all over. He tried to shove the feelings away, shake his head and shake away his reaction, but the weight in his head, his chest, was entirely overwhelming. *Fuck.* He really needed to talk to this woman about this spell and get it removed. It was making it hard to work . . . and it was going to be hard not to devour her the moment he laid his eyes on her again. *Surely, she's a mage, maybe even more powerful than the other if she can control a man like this.* His fist pounded heavily against the door, even his most gentle knock bellowing through the wood.

The voices hushed, and delicate steps approached the other side of the door.

It opened, and there she was. She looked up at him, those eyes raised to his, and she stepped back. She was in a simple dress, and her hair was only half pulled up. It cascaded over her shoulders in loose curls he desperately wanted to run his fingers through.

"Oh! Hunter Kirk. What are you doing here?" Her voice trembled.

He tilted his head to the side. *For fuck's sake, she's the most stunning woman I've ever seen.* "Forgive my intrusion, love, but I'm here to talk to the half vampire. I believe he's in your company. Could you send him out, please?" He caught sight of the room behind her. It appeared to be her home, and someone else's. He wondered why the male was in her home, he wondered if they were familiar, he wondered *how* familiar. He quickly found himself wondering if the half vampire was the other person who lived in the room . . . and he deeply hoped he wasn't. *Why would I care about that? Why would I care if she lives with a male? If she's with another . . . It hurt. Why the fuck does it hurt?*

She looked over her shoulder and made eye contact with the male. She gestured toward Kirk and the doorway with her head. "Bliss. He's here for you."

Kirk took one step back, remembering his job, his work, that this vampire would likely bolt at the very sight of a hunter. "I just need to ask you a few questions." He kept his tone even, his eyes as soft as possible . . . which was much simpler when he glanced at the girl in the doorway.

Bliss walked toward the door, sliding past Elle and standing before the hunter. His hand brushed her arm as he walked by in what appeared to be a comforting touch. "Listen, hunter. Sir. I know I'm half vampire, but I don't—I don't drink blood. I never have. And if I did, I wouldn't touch that ugly bastard."

Kirk ran his eyes over the man before him. The male swayed slightly. If he was the drunk the guards had claimed he was, he was either still drunk or hungover, or somewhere in between. This was confirmed by his sunken eyes and the wafting scent of liquor coming from him. Kirk saw the dancer fidget nervously behind Bliss, and the hunter found himself more concerned with comforting her, making sure she knew that she had nothing to fear from him.

He knew he was a daunting man, but she did not need to be anxious. He wanted her— He shook his head, dragging his thoughts back from her to focus on his task. His work. His hunt. *Shit. This fucking spell she holds.*

But he would be gentle with her, if she wished. He would hold her as delicately as she commanded. He spoke finally. "Can anyone account for your whereabouts the morning Stephan was killed?"

Bliss shook his head and ran a hand nervously through his hair. "Of course not. I was asleep in the apothecary. June was opening late because she wanted to walk Elle to work . . ." He glanced back at Elle briefly. "Listen I don't know what happened to him, I fucking swear."

He was nervous, he was lying, or maybe he just knew how *fucked* he was based on the situation and how poorly that boded for him. Kirk, however, had not sensed this male's scent anywhere Stephan was said to have been, not a single trace anywhere. "Don't lie to me." Kirk's voice was stone. "You know something." His hand shifted just slightly to his sword. A little intimidation might help persuade the male to speak whatever it was he withheld.

Bliss's voice began to rattle, cracking slightly. "Please, man. I didn't fucking touch him." He stepped back once. "I swear to you, I didn't touch him. I didn't fucking kill him. I didn't."

The male was lying and dodging something. Kirk grumbled, frustrated with the entire situation. He didn't think he'd killed him, but he knew something. The *only* thing on Kirk's fucking mind was the girl behind Bliss. The dancer shifting and fidgeting behind him. How her hair moved, how she bit her lip nervously, how her eyes kept darting to him, looking at him with a combination of fear and . . . desire. He looked back at the male, his grip on his sword tightening slightly. "Then what *do* you know?"

Bliss's hands began to shake.

But Elle stepped forward. "The castle." Her voice broke through the tension and commanded Kirk's attention like he was a dog. "The castle," she repeated.

His eyes locked on hers. "What about it?" His frustration, his tension, melted when she addressed him, and he her.

"It had to be one of theirs . . ." She stepped once more toward them. "He's afraid that if he says anything, they'll kill him." Fluidly, with all the grace of a trained dancer, she moved in front of Bliss, one hand reaching behind herself to grasp his. "Bliss is one of their bastards. He's afraid of the repercussions should he send you into that castle and one of them needs to be eliminated by your hand, sir." She looked at him, her chin tipped up to meet his gaze, her chest puffed out.

She was afraid. Kirk could read every false show of confidence. She was afraid. *Of him.*

"You did not mention this when we spoke yesterday." He felt his tone melt with her. He felt like his *bones* melted around her.

"I only spoke with Bliss this morning, hunter. And even now, I am not certain. I cannot prove it, but Bliss and I both believe it."

He realized he'd long since released the hilt of his sword. The tension in his shoulders dropped entirely. "Then I'll go to that castle tomorrow. If I find nothing, I will return here." He looked at Bliss who stood behind the tiny female. "I will find you easily if I learn you ran."

"I have nowhere to go, and no reason to run . . . sir."

"Good." Kirk sighed. "Leave us." His eyes left the male and shifted to the girl before him. "I need to ask her a few more questions."

Bliss pulled at Elle's hand, but she only nodded in confirmation. He glared at Kirk over her shoulder, then released her hand and began to walk away. Kirk wasn't entirely sure where.

He watched for only a moment as the male left, then, like a magnet, his attention was back on Elle.

She straightened her shoulders. "What else can I help you with, hunter, sir?"

"The magic." He needed this addressed. Whatever this was needed to be addressed before it completely derailed the entirety of his hunt. Or his life.

"What magic?" Her brow furrowed and her head tilted slightly, confusion painted across her face.

"The spell." He moved a bit closer. "Whatever you've used on me so I cannot keep my composure around you." He shook his head. He was frustrated by just how undone he'd become. "Is it something you've done for your work? Some kind of spell so you consume their thoughts? Bring them back to the Stag to see you dance over and over to satiate . . . whatever this is."

"I . . . I don't know what you're talking about." There was genuine confusion in her tone at first, but then something in her face changed, like she'd had a realization. "I have no such spell over anyone, sir, and I have certainly not put a spell over you."

"Then *tell me* why I *ache* for you," he pleaded. He needed answers. For fuck's sake, he needed answers. It weighed on his heart, in his chest, an ache of desperation. "Why can't I fucking focus on anything other than *you*?"

Her eyes met his.

She felt it too. *She feels it too.* That draw. That painful and overpowering need, to nearly consume each other.

"Sir, I don't know."

He knew in an instant she wasn't lying. She had no idea what it was, just as he didn't.

It was unnatural and entirely natural at the same time. It was everything and nothing. The woman before him made his guts twist, his head swim, and he had no idea why. But *she felt it too.*

His hands began to shake. "Do not deceive me, please. Tell me what this is, dancer."

She stepped toward him.

He felt his throat constrict as she drew closer. Her smell, only a hint stronger, overwhelmed his senses. Seconds. Seconds before he would need her more than he could control.

"I've done nothing." The magnetic attraction between them only grew stronger as she took another step. "I swear this to you." She placed her hands on his chest.

FUCK. Fire and ice collided within his breast as she touched him. He bent slightly, moving even closer to her.

Then she kissed him.

She stood on her toes and just barely placed her lips against his.

And for a moment, his entire world fell silent.

He wrapped his hands around her waist and lifted her as he deepened the kiss. Far beyond the gentle touch of her lips, he crashed into her. He needed her. Fuck. Fuck, he needed her.

~ 11 ~

CHAPTER 11

ELLE

He kissed her. She kissed *him*. Fuck. Fuck. Fuck fuck fuck. It was like her body had rebelled against her and moved on its own. She completely lost control, and she kissed him. The man who was her certain destruction, her certain death. But fuck, he tasted like life itself.

His hands were wrapped around her waist, and he pulled her against him. His chest pressed against hers. His breath matched her own. Frantic. His lips crashed into hers, his mouth desperate to capture hers. He was warm, so warm against her frozen skin. He didn't stop. He kissed her deeper, harder. His tongue sought entry into her mouth, and she granted it without hesitation.

His tongue grazed her teeth, where her fangs were filed—her *fucking fangs*—and reality and panic ripped her away. She pushed away from him, her hands flat against his chest. "No. No no no. This is a bad idea." She shook her head, her hands moving to her hair. Anxiety battled the sea of emotion and heat in her chest. "Forgive me. Forgive me, please."

He seemed confused. Rightfully so. Whatever was between them, dragging them together as their lips had entwined, it had felt right. She'd felt *whole*, and she'd been the one to kiss him. Then she shoved him away in a panic. Of course, the poor bastard would be confused. His brow furrowed. "El—"

"No." Her chest moved with anxious breaths even as she desperately tried to calm them. "Kirk— Hunter— Fuck. Sir, I . . . I don't know why I did—"

Those massive hands wrapped around her, and he pulled her back against himself. One hand moved to the back of her head, and he kissed her again. His fingers tangled in her hair, and the hand now on her back pressed her deeper against him.

She didn't resist. She didn't want to. She wanted to be consumed by him. "Kirk—" Her voice was muffled as he kissed her again. And again. And again. She felt every inch of him against her body, yet he didn't feel close enough. Gods. She managed to squeak out words, force herself to pull her mouth away long enough to get a few past her lips. "I have—I have to go."

He lifted his face from hers. His hands, however, remained on her.

She looked at him. "After I perform tonight, come find me. Out back. We *need* to talk about this. We need— I, ah." She stumbled over the words nearly falling from her mouth, nearly falling over herself directly into him. "Just come find me. I have to go. I have to go to work."

"Yes. Of course." He nodded, but his grip didn't release, his hands seemingly refusing to lift now that he held her. "I'll be waiting . . ." He finally let her go and stepped back, his eyes firmly locked on her.

She could feel it. He must feel it. The confusion, fear, desire, all swirling around together.

Elle stepped back once, and it felt like she stepped away from her own body. Suddenly, she felt cold, alone. Her legs begged her to move back. Everything was drawn to him. This was deep magic. Whatever this was . . . she was entirely and completely fucked.

*****

That night she sat in front of the mirror. She could barely hold her hand steady enough to apply her eyeliner. June would know what kind of magic it was, whatever it was that caused her to *kiss* him, the man here to kill her. It took more strength than she understood to stop there . . . It had been nearly impossible to pull herself from him and leave. After her dance that night, after her dance when she saw him, she wasn't sure what was going to happen. But she knew . . . she knew so certainly, she would not be able to hold back a second time. She knew that as surely as she knew being anywhere near him was fucking suicide.

But.

She was excited to see him. She wanted those hands to hold her, those arms around her again. She wanted those lips pressed against hers.

She was going to fuck the vampire hunter hired to kill her.

*****

She slid her cloak over her shoulders and untied her hair as she walked toward the back door of the Stag. Her dance had been nearly a blur, which, after her last distracted dance, frightened her. She would need to clear her head before she touched the silk next time. She couldn't fall again . . .

She sensed it in her bones as she grew nearer to him. Like the taste of him from earlier had awoken something. Like she could sense him now that she'd gotten his scent. She barely noticed that her steps hurried as she grew closer. She opened the back door, and there he was, waiting as he'd said he would.

As she closed the door behind herself and stepped into the cool evening air, anxiety swirled with the butterflies in her stomach. What exactly had she thought she was going to do with him when saw him? What exactly was her plan there? She had no idea why they felt as they did around each other. All she knew was being close to him was a stupid mistake, and she was walking into it directly because gods it felt *good*.

She looked at him a moment. Neither spoke.

Elle still stood in front of the door, about to open her mouth to speak.

Then he pressed her against the door and kissed her. One hand held gently to her cheek, tilting her face up to meet his, and his other hand wrapped around her hip. For fuck's sake, his hand covered so much of her hip as he grasped it. His kisses felt desperate. She knew why. She'd felt like every moment apart was torment now that she'd had the smallest taste of him. It seemed he'd felt it too.

"Not out here, Kirk," she managed breathily between kisses. If he refused to move, her resolve wouldn't hold. She'd fuck him right here on the street if he wanted. His hands began to explore more of her. She desperately wanted it to continue. Maybe she didn't want to find somewhere private. Maybe she wouldn't be able to hold out that long.

He released her and stepped back. "The Sunflower. It's close."

*****

KIRK

They only just made it to his room.

The door had barely closed before he had her pressed against it. His hands tightly gripped her waist. He was nearly shaking as he tried to control himself. One of his hands released her waist and slammed into the door above her head. He wasn't going to be able to hold himself back. Not even a little. He had to have her. So fucking badly. "Fuck." The need for her was overwhelming. That tugging at his heart, at his soul, at his cock, that weight in his chest would crush him if he didn't consume her. It was going to tear him apart.

Her hands grabbed his face. "What the hell are you waiting for, hunter?" she whispered as she pulled his face all the way down to hers before pressing her lips against his as though he were the very air in her lungs.

That was it. He lost all control. The blood finished vacating his head for his cock, and he let his desire take over completely. He began kissing her, each kiss more desperate than the last. His tongue darted past her lips as her mouth opened for him. The breaths between them were heavy, both gasping between kisses as their mouths crashed into each other over and over again. The hand that had been above her head moved to her hair, and his fingers tangled it in, grasping at her. *Closer.* He needed her closer. His hips pressed against her, but his back was angled harshly at the difference between their heights. He stood at just over six foot five, and she had to be at *least* a foot shorter than him.

He grabbed her by the waist and lifted her with ease, holding her against the door. His chest heaved, pressing against hers with each heavy breath. His hips ground against her. *Closer.* He needed her fucking closer.

A small squeak escaped those perfect fucking lips as he shoved her against the door.

She threw her legs around him, and his hand moved to her thigh to support her. Her arms were wrapped around him, grasping at whatever was in reach, his hair, his shirt, anything. Her ass was soft as his dick pressed against the bottom of it, and gods, he wanted to feel the skin.

His kisses shifted from her mouth. His lips grazed her cheek, her ear. He bit down on her earlobe a moment, pressed a kiss just below it, then grazed his teeth over the sensitive skin. His mouth continued down her neck, lingering on every new stretch of skin. His lips and his tongue needed to savor every taste of her.

She moaned softly, tilting her head back and inviting him even farther into her neck. "Bed." Her voice was breathy against his ear. It dripped with desire *for him*. It made his chest burn.

He quickly obeyed her command, lifting her from the wall. Both hands held her thighs just under her ass so she remained pressed against him. He stumbled away from the door, still kissing her, still gasping for breath as his need for her overwhelmed him.

He fell backward onto the bed.

He lay there, his legs still hanging over the edge as she straddled his stomach. Both of them were panting.

She sat above him, smiling at him. Fuck, she was teasing him. Gods, how was she able to hold it together? How could she so easily taunt him? Panting and staring at him, her chest heaving . . . sweat already running down her neck . . . *fuck.*

With a little quirk of her lips, she slid her hips down and over the bulge in his leathers. She ground against his cock that so clearly yearned for her. She leaned forward, her hands resting on his chest. "Your pants are in the way," she whispered.

He whispered through his teeth, "Take them off then."

She slid backward off him, again those soft thighs taunting him. She stood at the edge of the bed and began unbuckling his belt.

Kirk watched her fingers intently. Those delicate little hands, how soft their touch would be . . . He wondered how she'd kept them so perfectly silken. A chill ran down his spine as his belt fell to the side, and her fingers slid under the waist of his pants. A small gasp of anticipation escaped. Those hands were *exactly* as soft as he'd just imagined.

As she pulled down his pants, she followed them, landing on her knees before him. His length was then fully free of its prison. "Sit up." Her voice was soft yet still a command. Her eyes locked onto him hungrily.

Before he could do any more than follow her instruction, he nearly lost his composure entirely as she leaned forward and ran her mouth over the tip of his cock.

One of her hands wrapped around it, and she fucking *toyed* with him.

Every single movement of her mouth, her tongue, would have brought him to his fucking knees if he'd been standing. He planted his feet on the floor to steady himself. One of his hands pressed firmly into the bed behind him to try to keep himself upright as she tormented him with pleasure. His other hand gripped her hair. She held tightly to his leg, her hand so small against the girth of his thighs. She was incredible, and she caught him off guard.

Her mouth worked such miracles that he surprised himself by being completely unable to resist. His grip on her hair tightened as he came down her throat. He moaned loudly, and his head rocked back. *Gods.* She had made quick work of him. He was nearly embarrassed by it, but he was far too enamored with her. "Oh my *gods,*Elle," he growled.

She glanced up, smirking as his chest heaved. Wicked little thing she was, she enjoyed watching him squirm under her touch. "Yes?" She sat back on her heels a bit after she licked the tip of his cock, cleaning up whatever was left.

Sensitive, he shivered from her delicate touch and jerked his head back once, a motion for her to rise. "Come here."

She stood, stepping between his legs and smiling down at him. Her hands wrapped around his head and held him there. "Yes?"

It was his turn to make her squirm.

He leaned up and kissed her, their tongues twisting fully together again. He pulled at her dress. He needed this cursed fabric out of the way. He needed to touch *everything.*

She reached over her head, her mouth still pressed against his, and she pulled at the tie in the back of her dress. It loosened, and the garment began to slide off her shoulders.

The moment he realized he could remove it, he had it off her and onto the floor at their feet. Now all that remained was a delicate pair of panties. Those couldn't come off soon enough. His hands moved from her waist to wrap around her ribs, just below her breasts. The soft skin of them just grazed the tops of his hands. He felt her breath beneath his grip, every one of those ribs against his palms, her silken skin against the callouses he'd built up.

He flipped her onto the bed.

She let out a squeal as she collided with the pillows.

Swiftly, he moved over her. His hands pressed into the bed on either side of her, and he took her in. For just a moment, he stared at her. "Fuck . . . you're beautiful."

Her body was fully displayed to him, the body that had consumed every waking thought since he'd first seen her. Somehow, she was more beautiful than he had imagined. He longed to run his mouth over every curve, every inch of her bare flesh, mark her as his, feel every part under his tongue, his fingers, his teeth.

Then she smiled at him. Her hands moved to the buttons of his shirt, but she only had a few undone before he pressed against her and began kissing her again. His kisses moved down her neck, to her shoulder, across her collarbone. He dragged his teeth down her chest, between those beautiful breasts . . . then he kissed them, silken beneath his lips. He took one in his hand and bit delicately at her nipple. Gods, he wanted to consume every ounce of her. Every piece of her. He wanted everything.

He sat back on his heels, one hand still holding himself over her, his other now dipping under the edge of her panties. "Now something's in *my* way," he teased, then slid off the side of the bed to kneel beside it. Grabbing her thighs, he pulled her to the edge of the mattress. He hooked his fingers under the waist and slipped her panties down her legs, a smile spreading across his lips at just how soaked she was between her thighs. She desired him just as much as he did her, and it made his cock throb again. His chest ached. He wanted to taste her.

He took ahold of her knees and spread her legs, scooting himself closer between them. He turned to her right leg and leaned down, pressing his lips against it, just beside her knee. His eyes darted up to her. She was still lying back on the bed, one hand tangled in her hair, the other grasping one of her breasts. She was panting with anticipation of his touch. He ran his tongue slowly up the inside of her leg, teasing, inching closer and closer to where she desperately wanted his mouth.

The gasp was *loud* when he finally reached his destination, and her legs wrapped over his shoulders. His tongue danced with deliberate strokes. As though he instinctively knew every ounce of her desire and how to give her everything, yet keep it all just out of reach.

One of his hands released her thigh and moved toward his mouth until his middle and ring finger slipped inside her. Her back arched. His free hand moved to her pelvis and pressed down, holding her firmly against the bed, against his tongue, against his fingers.

She squirmed under his grasp, her little raspy sounds of pleasure only assuring him of every movement.

He paused.

Her breaths paused with him, as though he'd sucked the breath from her. "*Fuck.*" He'd kept it just out of reach. "Please. Kirk, oh my gods. Kirk . . ."

He licked just beside where he knew she wanted him. "Please?"

"Please, Kirk. Please let me—"

He smiled, then his mouth returned. His tongue pressed against the nerves outside and his fingers inside until her back arched and she yelped. She came hard around his fingers, her legs clenched and her muscles tightened as the wave crashed over her.

"Such a good girl," he praised. As he stood, her legs slid off his shoulders. He licked his lips, then his fingers. "You taste so fucking good, Elle."

Grabbing her by the ribs again, he shoved her backward onto the bed and climbed between her legs. With her feet pressed down and her knees raised, she tilted her hips up toward him and looked at him intently, deep desire in her gaze, her eyes falling to his dick between her thighs. Her eyes were half-open, and he could see small shivers run through her body as she recovered from her last orgasm. "Fuck me, Kirk."

"Absolutely." He guided himself inside of her.

She gasped.

Fucking gods, she felt incredible.

Back and forth, pressed against each other, they continued to dive deeper into the other. She moaned softly into his ears, and he whispered in hers. His teeth grazed her neck, and her mouth slid down his. Their bodies moved together nearly as one. It was beyond their physical connection. In those moments, their souls combined.

She grasped at his back, and her nails dug into the skin, just barely scratching as his muscles tensed.

Intensity and speed picked up until they both toppled over their edge together. Elle called his name as her release rolled through her. He growled as his followed after.

They lay together for a while, sweating and panting still against each other. Her hands rested on his back, her fingers tracing the lines of his muscles. He kept kissing her, gently then, softer, each kiss delicate and deliberate. Their breaths were still synchronized, soft sounds leaving both of their mouths.

He rolled onto his side beside her, and his hand landed on her stomach, his fingers gently running up and down from her navel to her throat. "Elle . . ."

She smiled softly, turning her head to face him. "Yeah?"

"Gods, you're fucking beautiful."

Neither of them were likely to get much sleep that night.

~ 12 ~

CHAPTER 12

They needed to talk. They needed to talk about what the hell had happened between them. He had to know it too. They'd been entirely unable to keep their distance, nearly feral with how badly they needed each other. She had to talk to June about what kind of magic did that. Not that she hadn't enjoyed him. Oh gods, she had enjoyed him. She wanted to be as close to him as possible, but they both knew—she knew, certainly—this was far beyond any attraction she'd ever felt before. Both of them had had lovers before, she had been *in love* before, but this wasn't the same. She wondered if he had ever been in love before . . . *Not that that should matter.* What mattered was why she had fucked a vampire hunter, and why she desperately wanted to do so again.

Now she lay beside him, both on their sides facing the other. His hand was on her hip, and his thumb was slowly moving over it, a gentle caress. His eyes were closed, and he looked so calm, so at peace. She wished she could feel calm like that. She wanted to feel peace like that at his side. *But he's not the one who's going to get killed at the end of this.*

She took in every inch of his face. Gods, he was the most handsome man she'd ever seen. Every scar, every *flaw* in his face only made him more beautiful, more perfect. Her heart fluttered with butterflies unlike any she'd felt in such a long time. His hair, still a little sweaty from their lovemaking, fell over his face, a few strands falling into his eyes. The scars that ran over the flesh of his chest, exposed by the blanket only just barely over his waist, were deep. Each had to hold a painful story, and she found herself desperate to know *all of them.*

She wanted to know everything. Everything about him. Every secret he held. Her fingers moved gingerly over the raised skin of a scar over his breastbone. It was rough beneath her hand.

"A vampire tried to drive a knife into my heart." He smiled softly as his eyes opened at her touch. "Thank the gods he missed."

She thought a moment, still tracing the scar. "Do you hate them? Vampires?" Her eyes stayed on his chest, and she pressed her hand against him to hide its trembling.

"I . . . hate what they do." His chest rose and fell with a heavy breath, his brow furrowed in thought. "And there are times I . . . pity them."

Pity. That stung.

His hand moved to her chin and lifted her gaze to meet his. "Let's not talk of monsters."

Monsters.

"You truly have not put a spell over me?" he whispered, leaning forward and kissing her nose. "No powerful magic?" he asked gently, his eyes not leaving her.

He had no idea that a *monster* lay beside him.

Elle shook her head. "I understand this as little as you do."

"But you feel it. As I do. Whatever it is."

"I do." Her voice was small. She tried to mask the fear in her tone. "But I don't know what we do with it. With this."

He ran his thumb over her cheek. "Then tell me about you."

She pulled back, only slightly, just enough his hand fell from her face. "I don't want to get close to you if you're going to leave this place, Kirk, or if this is only some cursed desire." *Or if you have to kill me.*

"Please."

She couldn't look away from him. " . . . fine."

*****

The following morning, she awoke still beside him. She looked at him for a moment. His breathing was gentle, and he snored just a bit. She smiled to herself. It was cute. *Gods.* She thought he was *cute.* This magic clearly wanted her dead. She slipped out from under the blanket and grabbed her hair tie and her dress from the floor, wrapping up her hair as she stood.

"I'll see you again tonight?" His sleep-laced voice floated behind her.

She held her dress close, taken by some kind of instinct to cover herself even though this man had seen, touched, *tasted* every inch of her only hours before. "Yeah." She nodded. "Hopefully, I'll find some sort of an answer." She slipped into the dress, tying it and brushing down the wrinkled skirt. "What if—what if this answer isn't—"

"I meant it," he interrupted.

"You meant what?"

"When I said you're beautiful."

She blushed and turned quickly to find her boots, hiding her ever-reddening cheeks, hiding the smile she couldn't fight off. "You're quite lovely yourself."

He laughed. It was a confident, deep grumble of a laugh, and it made her thighs fucking tremble. "Never been called *lovely* before."

"That's a shame." She needed to leave before she fucked him again. It took her a moment to find her boots, to remember where they'd been tossed in the events of the night before. "I'm sure you've left quite a trail of broken hearts and bastard sons." *Don't look at him. Don't look back at him.* Her body betrayed her instantly, and her glance over her shoulder sent more fire between her thighs, electricity through every molecule of her.

That smile. That cocky fucking smile. His chest was exposed. He was propped up on one elbow, the outline of his cock just *barely* visible beneath the thick blanket. "Far less than you'd imagine, love. Not a lot of time for lovers in my line of work."

She bent over and laced her boots. She could feel his gaze burning on her ass as she teased him. She could almost see his dick twitching beneath the blankets. Fuck, she needed to *leave*. She stood back up, tossing her ponytail over her shoulder. "Well then, dear hunter, I'm afraid I must be off." As she spoke, the knots that'd formed in her stomach twisted more. She didn't want to leave. The man she should be the *farthest* from, and it was painful to leave.

"I do hope this spell—whatever it is—isn't one we must break, love." He said it so genuinely, so truly. He . . . meant it, at that moment. Regardless of whatever consequences would come, or what it meant, he meant it.

He didn't understand what he said. He *couldn't* understand what he said.

She sucked in a breath. Her heart was beating faster than she knew it could. "I'll see you soon, dear hunter."

And she left.

*****

The morning air was crisp. Autumn's cold kiss woke her up enough to keep the tears forming at bay but not enough to ease the ache.

The morning appeared mundane enough as she walked quietly through Torzen, chatting with passerby. Whispers and giggles from those who saw their dear dancer disappear with the handsome hunter the night before followed behind her. Word like that spread quickly. No matter how quiet one tried to keep it.

She knocked on the door of Morel and entered slowly, wincing at the hell about to be unleashed on her. "June?" She stepped in, closing the door behind herself. One hand wrapped around the opposite arm, and she tucked inward. She had to tell June that not only had she slept with the *vampire hunter* . . . she'd slept with him a lot.

"You didn't come home last night, Ellie. Do you understand the level of fear I— You—you need to be fucking *careful*, especially right now." June's looked up from the book in her hands and at Elle. She closed the book and her eyes at the same time, inhaling deeply through her nose. "At least tell me that it's because you finally got laid."

Elle paused for a moment. *Here we go.* "I did."

June's eyes popped open, and a smile curled on her lips. "Excuse me?" She laughed softly. "My sweet, innocent little Ellie actually got laid last night?"

She could only nod.

"Oh. My. Gods. Do fucking share who got to partake in this!" June laughed again as Elle's ears warmed. "That blond guy who watches you all the time? The girl with those blue eyes? Both?!"

Elle didn't respond at first. She couldn't. The words were stuck. She averted her eyes. June would pry this from her. She couldn't lie.

"Someone else?"

"June, I . . ." She rubbed her forehead, pressing her fingers into her temples. "It was the hunter. But let me explain."

"The—" June's voice hitched. "The *fucking hunter*?" She nearly dropped the book but managed to set it down on her table after fumbling with it for a moment. "Elle— What? No. No. You know what? Explain it then. Explain why you would *fuck* the man literally paid, trained, fucking created to *kill you*."

"It's not a *good* explanation. It's more of a question." Elle's hands fell from her head. She felt pathetic. "It's like this . . . urge." Her hands clenched and twisted where they hovered before her stomach.

"Ellie, baby, that's just what it's like being horny." June rolled her eyes. The rage that had coursed through her seemingly calmed as she continued to look over Elle. A shift in demeanor Elle had seen enough times to recognize that her presence had calmed the storm in June. "I'm sure he's packing quite a long sword, but he's also packing a literal sword. A literal sword that he uses to kill *vampires*. Which you—might I remind you—ARE."

"It's different from that. It's confusing and overwhelming . . . It's this— I can't stay away from him. Trust me, I wanted to. I know how fucking stupid it is. I know. I know. But it's more than sexual. It's so much more than that. It's like . . . He's— June, it feels like something is pulling me toward him. Like my very soul is reaching for him, and I don't understand it."

Desperation weighed her voice. She was so afraid of what it was, what it meant. "Maybe it's some deep magic, but he accused me of putting a spell over him. He feels it too." Her hands moved around as she spoke, trying to verbalize feelings that she could barely grasp. "I figured if it's magic, you could help me understand. Please."

June's eyes darkened as she listened to Elle. Her expression was cold, unmoving stone, but something in her eyes changed as Elle said the word *soul*. "It's . . . your soul?" When she finally spoke, Elle could barely hear it.

She nodded, unable to break away from watching that change in her friend's eyes.

June quietly moved toward one of the bookshelves. After searching for a moment, she pulled a book down. She thumbed through the pages, evidently seeking something specific. "Remember when I studied vampire bonds after I found you?"

"I do." She watched June's eyes scan the pages.

She continued flipping through the book quietly, then stopped, her brow furrowing as she took in what she was looking at. "For fuck's sake." She rubbed her forehead and sighed.

"What?"

"Soul bound." Another heavier sigh escaped through June's lips. "The moon bound your souls. I remembered reading about this kind of thing. It's incredibly rare and, according to everything I read, only something that happens between vampires . . ." Her gaze darted up to Elle's briefly. "A vampire's soul can be bound to another. It's like fate. You're mates chosen by the moon herself."

"*Mates?*"

"And if you choose to accept the binding and enter into a bond contract, apparently it's incredibly powerful." She stepped back toward Elle. "Already you're clearly *very* drawn to each other. Enough you'd fuck him." She placed her finger between the pages of the book to mark her spot as she closed it. "It's ancient magic. Powerful magic. And it seems that it's bound you to him."

"To him." Elle tried to swallow the knot forming in her throat. "To the man who's supposed to kill me."

~ 13 ~

CHAPTER 13

K^{IRK}

He couldn't get her out of his head. He'd been able to hold her, for one beautiful night, and it had felt like he'd held the entire world in his hands. She was stunning. She was gentle. She was kind. The way her hair fell over her shoulders, the way her hips felt against his. The way she spoke. The thought of having to leave her made his stomach turn. When he was done with his hunt, he would have to leave, move on to his next job, and he didn't understand why imagining leaving this dancer behind felt like his heart was being ripped from his very chest . . . He barely knew her, but she was the entirety of the world.

In another life, were he not who he was, *what* he was— If he were still a human man, he would marry her. He would build her a farm, raise children beside her. He would love to give her a simple and beautiful life. Take her far from the city if she wished. He would see her womb swollen with his children . . . But this, what they had now, it was doomed. Whatever it was. He was cursed. He could never give her children. He could never be a simple human husband as he so desperately wished he could be.

In another life, he was.

Still, even knowing he could never give her more than what they had, he was going to let himself slide back to her that night. She was like a drug, addictive, and he so desperately needed another taste. She was worth the heartbreak he knew loomed on their horizon. It was as if an invisible tether pulled him back to her. Could he leave it all behind for her? Give up everything for her? A woman he barely knew yet felt like without he might simply cease drawing breath . . . For a moment he dreamed of it, but then a vision of *him* flashed in front of his eyes, and he thought he might vomit.

He couldn't stay with her.

He'd taken *his* life for this.

Not yet. He didn't have to leave her yet. Not right then. He was going to hold her tightly against his chest while he could, feel her breath against his neck.

He couldn't keep away from her, and he wasn't going to until he *had* to.

*****

She managed to distract him without being anywhere near him. He had a job to do, but that seemed to be the furthest thing from his mind. He had a task. He had been paid to hunt a vampire who had murdered a man. He needed to stay focused on his work. He could figure out what to do about *her* after.

He'd gathered up his gear and loaded Love with enough for the day trip. He'd barely made it out of his room in the inn. It smelled so strongly of her, he wanted to remain and sit in the scent.

You have to work, you bastard. You'll see her again.

He led Love from the pasture, then mounted her once they'd cleared the gate. He petted her neck gently. "Heaven help me, Love."

According to the innkeeper, the ride to the castle was less than half a day on horseback.

The half-breed and Elle had claimed that the vampire who'd killed Stephan was likely one of those who resided in this castle, but Kirk would have to be cautious with such an accusation. He would need to be very considerate with how he approached it. Vampires who did not break the laws of men were protected just as much as men were, and should he make the wrong move, especially with *this* castle, he could start something far bigger than he ever wanted. If what he'd heard was correct, if this was truly where *Dae, Lord of Blood* lived, he would need to watch every word out of his mouth.

Kirk did not wish to start a war with the last great vampire lord. Dae was certainly not a male to anger.

Kirk had never met the male himself, but he had heard enough to know the danger of the castle he rode toward.

The ride was quiet enough. The road was well used. Dae had plenty of worshipers or willing sacrifices. His court was made up of enough old-blooded vampires that a steady stream of humans would have to have walked this road. Kirk wondered if any had ever walked back.

He could not understand it. Worshiping *them*. Giving yourself over to *him*. Giving oneself as food to another creature simply because of their power was a thought he could not wrap his head around. He'd fought so long to survive, to keep himself, other humans, his brothers *alive*. He couldn't understand allowing a vampire to take your life. He couldn't understand a world where one would willingly become food.

He dismounted Love as they reached the courtyard of the castle. The garden around him was well maintained, manicured, and cared for. A few human servants, likely who kept it, darted out of sight as he approached. Every bush was trimmed. Enormous, stunning rose bushes covered much of the garden, deep red, blood-red roses. He had to give the vampire credit, he kept it classic. Vines climbed up the sides of the castle, twisting and curling around the stone as though they wished to consume it and pull it under. As though the earth sought to reclaim this evil, drag it back into the dirt, back to hell. As though it wished to purge the evil just as Kirk did.

He spoke softly to Love, a command to wait that only she understood. He dared not tie her to anything should she need to run.

He strode toward the massive stone stairs that led to the main entryway of the castle. As he walked toward the top of the stairs, he tightened the tie around his hair. Large wooden doors waited for him. On either door hung a metal knocker in the shape of a demon, their faces contorted in a bitter scream, the rings hanging from their lower fangs.

He lifted the ring and let it fall against the door. The sound echoed through the halls of the castle before him. He waited a moment before he dropped it again with the same thunderous clap.

Only a few moments later, the door opened. A human woman's face appeared in the crack. She wore a simple dress with an apron tied around her waist, and her eyes were a dark shade of brown. Blond hair was tied tightly into a bun. She appeared so ordinarily human against the Gothic castle.

"Hello." She stepped back, her eyes wide, and the door opened a bit more. "Sir, you—you shouldn't be here, sir."

"I'm here to speak with Lord Dae." He kept his tone carefully controlled. This part of vampire hunting he did not excel at: politics, when hunting vampires required stepping carefully around the ancient ones and attempting to keep the powerful creatures from feeling threatened.

The woman nodded and gestured him inside hesitantly. "I'll let him know you've come then . . . Your name, sir?"

"Kirk. Kirk Smith." Kirk tilted his head slightly, trying to put the anxious woman at ease.

"I'll come gather you in a moment, Mr. Smith. Stay here." She gestured toward him, motioning he stay in the foyer where he stood.

The inside of the castle was exactly what Kirk had expected it to be. Enormous and ornate. Every wall hung with deep red curtains with golden-lined edges. Portraits and tapestries were mounted against the stone. Everything that could be was carved with intricate details. Ancient and stunning art was in every corner, in every element. Hundreds of years and so very much money had been poured into the space around him. Dae had had a long time, and a deep wallet, and it showed in the extravagant decor. Even so, with all that glittered about the castle, a darkness clung to every inch. The paintings on the walls featured gory images of demons or old vampires with stone-cold expressions. The carvings in the stone, the wood, all showed scenes of men, women, and children being torn apart. Monsters, demons, and vampires in brutal portrayals of violence. *Yet again, Dae is a male of classics.*

Centered on the wall before him was a portrait, its subject a male vampire with black hair cut clean and slicked back. His clothes fit closely, tailored precisely to him. His features were sharp and cruel. His eyes, even painted, were piercing. Kirk could only assume this male was Dae. The powerful and ancient creature who owned this gaudy house of horror. But something else caught Kirk's attention about the portrait. The features of the male, the face of Dae himself, was a face he had seen before and a face he knew.

The features matched the half-breed. Bliss's father was the devil himself. Bliss's father was Dae. No wonder he feared bringing the wrath of the castle down upon himself. He was the bastard of the Lord of Blood. He cursed under his breath. The little shit could have told him.

The human woman returned, her expression still deeply concerned. "He will see you now. This way to his study." She motioned Kirk follow her.

The hallway looked similar to the foyer, styled in the same way. He followed the young woman toward a room at the end of the hall, passing doors and other hallways that led to what he was sure were bloody horrors. She had countless small scars, teeth punctures on her neck and what appeared to be scratches, some far fresher than others. She was not only a servant here, she appeared to also be food. He wondered what she had been promised. What she believed of these creatures to be in such a place, or if she was truly there under the rules of the treaty.

The door she led him toward was already opened. The room beyond was lined with bookshelves; the books resting on them were all older than Kirk himself, by quite a margin. In one corner was a large wooden desk with a matching chair. A few bottles of wine, also clearly older than Kirk, rested atop the desk, and behind that desk stood the male from the paintings. He looked just like his portrait, nearly exactly. His hair, his clothes, every detail curated to perfection. A glass of wine rested in his hands, balanced between his fingers. His ears came to a sharp point and his fangs an even sharper one.

"A hunter. In my home."

~ 14 ~

CHAPTER 14

Dae

He turned as Isabella guided the hunter into the room. He could see hints of the black clouds that began to swirl around him in the corners of his vision. Rage twisted and burned in his blood. A hunter, in his home. But when the hunter entered, that was when his emotions nearly got the best of him. He nearly stumbled backward. He could sense it on him. A power he had not seen in many, *many* years.

Fire.

The only time Dae had ever feared for his life, truly, was when he'd stood against a fire hunter. The flames had danced around him, threatening to consume him, and he'd felt something foreign. Terror. It had burned. The smoke had filled his lungs, and it'd felt like they were going to collapse in his chest.

Isabella left them alone and Dae stood before him. *Kirk Smith.* A hunter. But more importantly, a fire wielder.

The hunter held his composure before Dae, though Dae could see the most subtle of nervous sways in his hand. "I'm only here to ask a few questions," the hunter said. "Forgive my intrusion."

He appeared as any other hunter Dae had seen before. Dressed fully in leather and strapped to the throat with weapons, spells, and a variety of tools that would make any younger vampire sweat. He was sure the hunter questioned why he did not ask him to remove the weapons, but the show of confidence, of power, not giving any indication he was threatened, that was far more important. It did not matter anyway, the fire the hunter before him wielded would remain even if the man were naked.

Dae sipped at the wine in his hand, another intentional move to show just how little he cared. "Go on with them then. Your questions." His voice gave only a hint of his feelings away, how fucking furious he was to have this *monster* in his home.

*****

KIRK

Kirk's skin crawled. This male was made of something else, something darker than any vampire he'd ever hunted before. Dae was an evil beyond what Kirk had ever come into contact with. "There was a human murdered in Torzen." His hands grew slightly sweaty. Gods, this vampire struck something in his soul he hadn't felt in such a long time. "There are no vampires in Torzen, and I have come to ask if you are aware of a vampire who may have committed this crime." *Appeal to him as a reasonable beast.* "You understand the rules and laws, and you can understand why I'm here to find this vampire and bring them to justice."

Dae sighed, swirling the wine in his hand, eyes on the liquid dancing in the glass. "I am *well* aware of the laws. I was there when they were written. But, dear hunter, it was none of mine. Hear my voice and know that I do not deceive you." He looked over the glass at Kirk, his eyes narrowing on the hunter. "I do not wish a war with humans. I only wish to spend the rest of my afternoon in peace without *you* stinking up my study." His fangs flashed as he spoke. He seemed to wish to avoid a conflict as much as Kirk did.

"Forgive me, but I must push further." Kirk dared not reach for his sword, though instinct told him to wrap his hand around the hilt for some kind of comfort. But he knew any signs of aggression and the vampire would attack, and he would unleash a fury Kirk could not stop. He could not fight the entirety of this vampire court without burning it completely to the ground. From there, it would only spiral. Vampires would retaliate. The hunters would counter. He needed this to remain entirely calm, entirely collected. *Fucking politics.* "There are no vampires within the walls of the city, and I have not been able to sense any in the woods around it. Are you *certain* none of your court would harbor the fugitive, then?"

"We have done no such thing." Dae set his glass down, and those dark shadows swirling around him grew. "I do not wish for some low-blooded vampire to dirty our name—*my name*—in this area. Pray you find the poor bastard before I do. The death you bring upon them will surely be far more merciful than my own."

*****

DAE

Get the fuck out of my castle. He'd known about the human murdered in Torzen, and it *hadn't* been one of his. He spoke no lies to the hunter. He wanted the vampire who threatened his comfort removed, quickly. It was why he'd sent Silas to hunt them, the thirsty low-blood who'd sunk deep enough into their hunger to murder a man and do it so *violently*. It lacked finesse. *And to attack someone of high enough status they've hired a hunter?* The vampire was a fool. The vampire was a fool who had brought a hunter—a fire wielder—to *his* doorstep. That vampire better pray to the moon the hunter found him first.

Dae and his court stayed out of the streets of Torzen and remained unregistered. Mutt and Clementine spent time *beneath* the city, but his people kept their distance. Having to send Silas in to hunt for this vampire was another risk that added to the list of things that made Dae exceptionally angry. Risking Silas's safety was of no consequence, but Dae had worked hard, made agreements with Torzen, to ensure they *left him the fuck alone.*

But a hunter stood in front of him. A hunter who had *no reason* outside of his word to trust him.

"May I speak with the other members?" the hunter asked. He seemed just as impatient.

"No." Dae shook his head. He sat back in his chair behind his desk and sipped his wine again. "Do you have an ounce of proof one of my people did it?"

The hunter hesitated. "No."

Dae smiled, a cruel expression slapped over his anger. "Then leave."

"My lord, I've been given information that one of your vampires may have been involved. And if I'm being forward with you, this is the only place such a vampire would be."

"Information?" Dae raised his eyebrow. "Who would send you here?"

"An informant." The hunter shifted his feet a bit. "Only said he believed it was one of yours."

"Well *he* was wrong." Dae glared. "Dear hunter, leave my home before I have you removed from my space. Only return here when you have something *real* to tie one of mine to this death, yeah?"

Smith wavered a moment. "I appreciate your time. I pray we don't meet again."

"The feeling is mutual."

*****

KIRK

The woman, Isabella, walked beside him as she escorted him to the front door. He had to ask, potentially open a Pandora's box that could ruin his life, but he had a duty. "Isabella," he started. "Are you here of your own will?" He kept his tone hushed.

She paused for only a moment. "Mr. Hunter, I am." Her voice did not falter.

"May I ask *why*?"

"It's an answer that would take us hours and a bottle of wine to unpack, sir." She laughed, just barely. "But I assure you, I am here because I *chose* to be."

"Are there others?"

"Yes."

"And them?"

"It's not my place to speak for them." The fear radiated from her voice then.

Kirk nodded. "Of course, ma'am." Whether or not the other humans were there of their own accord, Dae did not seem to be a man who would suffer his servants to share any details of his household with an outsider. Especially one of Kirk's type. He sensed quickly, should she confide much more in him, the horrors she would suffer at Dae's hands would drastically outweigh whatever life she led then.

*****

DAE

"What was a *hunter* doing here, Father?" Suho stood before Dae.

Dae's eyes moved to his son. The eldest of the bastards he'd allowed to live with him . . . the child who had survived the longest within his walls. He'd kept the information surrounding the murdered human quiet, but a hunter arriving on their doorstep made keeping it under wraps nearly impossible. "A human was murdered in Torzen. By a vampire." He rubbed his forehead, the pain behind his eyes growing only sharper. "He was here because they assumed it was one of ours."

Suho's face was nearly identical to Dae's. His blood ran thick in his house. He stood two inches taller than Dae, with broader shoulders, someone on his mother's side giving him a larger frame than his father. "And was it?"

Dae's hand paused its massaging of his temples, and he growled, "Do you think if it was I wouldn't have handled it *before* a hunter showed up on our steps?"

"Of course . . ." Suho sank back a bit. Though larger, his presence paled in comparison to the aura of the elder male. "Then—"

Digging his other hand even farther into his temples, his nails nearly cutting through the skin around them, Dae held up a finger. "Suho, I have Silas handling the issue. Leave."

Suho slipped out of the room, the pace of his steps picking up the closer he got to the hall.

This . . . is going to be a fucking nightmare.

*****

The smell of the fire wielder lingered for hours after his departure, and it gave Dae a migraine. He couldn't seem to light enough candles or open enough windows to rid the space of it.

It ached enough, he grew wearing of his reading quickly, the words seeming to worsen the throbbing behind his eyes. He stood, closing the book in his hands and setting it down on his desk. The fucking hunter had ruined his afternoon. "Isabella."

She looked in through the doorway. "My lord."

He waved a hand. "Bring me one," he sighed.

"Do you want only to feed?" She had been in his service long enough that she almost certainly had a guess of his answer. With a hunter visiting the castle, and the . . . aura he knew radiated off him at times like this, she must know he wanted one to kill.

A familiar voice came from the hall behind her. "Isabella, you already know his answer. Why pester him so?"

The male's voice was low. Dae recognized it immediately and the migraine it would bring about.

She spun around as Silas stepped into Dae's office. "Silas, you've returned from Torzen."

"Only for a moment, sweet." Silas smiled at her, the grin tainted with his cruel nature. Dae could see her shoulders tense even as

Silas used every ounce of grace he could in his voice. "Go fetch the lord what he needs."

Insufferable.

Isabella left quickly.

Dae's patience was hanging on by a *very* thin thread at this point, and the male before him, while one of his most potent tools, managed to push his precarious handle on his control closer to snapping every time they spoke.

Silas's long white hair was pulled back and swished behind him as he walked, his red eyes such a vibrant shade of crimson. Everything about Silas was slender, his build, his features, his hair even. He moved about a room with a dancer's grace, and his low voice was made from silk.

Dae admired the poise and refinement of the male, and that was where his admiration swiftly stopped.

However, Silas was a powerful weapon. Of an old and long-dead house, Silas was blessed with the power to know and manipulate minds. *Human* minds. He could manipulate a human easily, their minds nearly clay in his hands if he wished to expend the power. A vampire was far more challenging for Silas to harm. A vampire would have to be sedated, weak, or wounded. A vampire would not succumb to his power as a human would.

He could be used without posing enough of a threat to Dae to need to be removed. Silas harbored a cruelty that nearly rivaled Dae's, yet how he relieved such tension was entirely different.

Silas had his own chamber in the darkness below the keep where he . . . experimented. His experiments, while generally loud and messy, kept him occupied, and so Dae allowed it.

"What have you found, Silas?" Dae grumbled. Sending Silas to the surface world of Torzen was risky enough, but if any of his court could get in and out of the city without a human growing too suspicious, it was the one before him.

Silas's expression had grown still since the human woman left the room, his need for a mask having run off to gather up Dae's next meal. "I may have located the vampire."

And there it went, the last shred of patience of the oh so little Dae had to begin with. "And he is not knelt before me, *why?*" he hissed.

An unfamiliar expression appeared on Silas's face, one Dae did not fully understand initially. Anxiety. "How many years has it been since we've traveled the streets of the city, my lord?"

"Do not test me, Silas. If you've located that vampire, tell me why he is not bleeding before me." It had been many human years since any of his court had walked the streets. There was no need. The human cities bored him. He gathered his meals beneath Torzen and cared little for their world above. Their lives were so fleeting, so short and pointless.

"My lord." Something in that voice of silk wavered. "My lord, there is a vampire among them, I believe. *She* is deeply hidden. The spells hiding her scent made her nearly impossible to detect. I only found her because I could not hear her mind as I heard the humans around her."

Irritation pounded in Dae's head, his migraine deeply embedded now. "A vampire in hiding is *not* uncommon, Silas. For the love of the moon, if you do not tell me what you are avoiding, I will remove your head and mount it to my wall."

He was not joking.

"I believe she's *of Bone.*"

Silas ducked as Dae launched a wine bottle at his head. He swallowed hard.

Dae's voice rattled with rage. "OF *BONE?* And it's not here?!" He had yet to unleash himself only because of Silas's usefulness. Any other creature would have been torn to shreds by now. His voice lowered, and he spoke through clenched teeth. "Tell me *why the fuck* an heir of Bone is not *here. Now.*"

"She was never alone. Apparently the human she's parading around as is quite famous in Torzen . . . and she was guarded. A mage like a guard dog had wards *circling* her."

A detail finally registered through the rage coursing through Dae. "*Her?*"

"A female of Bone. I'm nearly certain of it."

"Send Mutt—"

"Sir," Silas interrupted, then took a step back, his body growing rigid, "allow me. It will take finesse to get her out without a fuss. Without damaging the fragile reputation that brings us such comfort here."

"Then *fucking* go."

"Yes, sir."

*****

THE MOTHER MOON

The stars danced excitedly around her. Another sibling would soon join them in the sky. Their baby brother. They sang as they swirled about, announcing with excitement the arrival of another of the moon's children. Against the blackness of the sky, the stars shone brightly, their golden, white, and blue light emanating from them. The earth below watched breathlessly as the skies proclaimed their joy.

The moon birthed a boy, but he was not like his siblings. He was not like the stars. His form was different from theirs. The singing of the stars quieted as they took in the new creature. They flitted about him, curious and confused.

The moon held him in her gentle glow. She spoke after observing her newest babe for a moment. "Your new brother is special. See his hands and feet. He is meant to walk on the earth. See his face, his eyes, he is meant to see beyond our sky. See his ears, his mouth, his teeth. He is meant to hunt and sing."

"We see, Momma," the stars chattered softly.

"He cannot stay with us."

"But Momma," the stars protested, "we love him. We do not want him to leave us."

"I know, my children. I too love him. But he is not yet meant for the sky. Someday he will return home and he will dance with you, I promise."

She wrapped the babe in moonlight and gently laid her new son onto the earth below her. A tear fell from her beside him. and a lake was formed.

Vampires often traveled to that lake. To honor the moon. Even after the story had shifted to legend, and time had blurred the truth.

~ 15 ~

CHAPTER 15

KIRK

He walked down the stairs outside the castle, cursing an-other roadblock in his hunt. *But it prolongs my time here. With her.* The moment he allowed thoughts of her in, they consumed his mind again. He mounted Love and rode back toward Torzen, every thought wrapped up in that dancer, between her thighs, where he longed to bury his face.

She obliged him when he'd asked to learn of her, and she'd shared such simple things about herself. Each detail he'd lapped up like a man dying of thirst. She loved green. She preferred mead to wine. She longed for a life outside of a city . . . He shifted in the saddle and begged his cock to obey. The ride back would batter his poor manhood to death if he couldn't keep it under control.

He wondered if she'd learned what had drawn them together with such intensity. He racked his brain for answers, but he'd never paid attention when they'd taught the young hunters of magic. He had been a reckless child who had only wished to hone his sword. He'd been a powerful hunter prodigy—a selfish young asshole who had thought himself invincible and untouchable and entirely exempt from the need to *study. Theon could have figured it out.* He sucked in a breath as Theon entered his mind for only a moment. A flash of the look that had crossed Theon's eyes as Kirk had plunged his blade into his chest . . .

At least it cleared her from his mind for a moment.

Torzen slowly came into view, and as the chaos in his mind cleared, a singular thought entered again. He was drawing near to *her*.

*****

ELLE

In another life, she would have begged him to take her away with him. She would have begged him to run away with her to wherever life took them. But she could not beg him to do it. She was not a human. She *wasn't human.*

The man she desired with her entire soul didn't know that he'd bedded a vampire. He didn't know that the vampire he'd shared his bed with had a bounty on her head that could furnish enough gold for him to live comfortably until the end of his human days. That *she* was the very murderer he then hunted. That she had killed Stephan. That she had killed Alder. She was the reason he had been brought to Torzen in the first place.

She *longed* to tell him. To beg his forgiveness for lying. She would kneel before him and plead if she had to. He was her soul-bound mate. He was the fate the moon had woven into the fabric of her being. *Why is the moon so cruel?* The moon choosing a vampire's mate was rare, sacred, a blessing from the mother of vampires. Yet it felt like some cruel joke. A vampire hunter bound to a vampire. As a man, he was incredible, but he was all that she should fear. She did not wish to question the moon, curse the moon's gift, but how could this have been the fate the moon chose for her? How could the moon, who was supposed to love . . . protect . . . guide her, bind her together with a man designed to kill her? *Maybe the moon wishes to send me back into her embrace swiftly.* Fear coursed through her.

The last time she'd thought herself in love, it had nearly ended with her death. She'd told Alder of her nature, and he had tried to kill her. And she *had* killed him. How could she expect a better outcome with the hunter? The hunter who could kill her in a moment. In an instant. How could she expect him to agree to love a monster when she was the very thing he hunted to every corner of the earth? When she had murdered two men? They were doomed. She knew they were doomed. She had such a short time to decide what to say to him. He would return soon.

If she told him what they were to each other, he would know. Humans were not bound as vampires were. The moon did not interfere with men . . . except clearly this one. To tell him was to allow him to know her nature. He would know she was a vampire.

He would not rest until he figured it out. He was *going* to figure it out. If she waited too long, if she stalled, he might convict an innocent vampire, bring death to another, stain her hands with more blood. He would kill *Bliss*.

She had to tell him. He would not be able to cease questioning the draw between them, even if she lied that she could not find answers. How could he not?

But . . .

What if he were to stay with her?

She let her mind slip into the dream for only a moment, romanticizing the thought. The thought of him choosing to remain at her side, accepting the moon's bond . . . She let herself get lost in the romance. What if they could fall fully for each other? If Kirk could accept her as she was?

What if he could love a monster?

*****

As she walked toward the Stag, she rehearsed the conversation in her mind, playing through every possible scenario. She wrestled relentlessly with the conversation she was about to have, the conversation that could be the last conversation she would have with . . . *anyone.*

"Ellie." June had grabbed her arm. "Don't you fucking dare risk your life for this."

Elle glanced at June, pushing through her sadness to smile softly. "I have to go to work."

"Elle." June's grip tightened and she shook her head. "You cannot. Don't let him anywhere near you, understand?"

"I'm going to work. He will be there."

"Elle."

"Let me decide, June." She leaned forward and gently kissed her cheek. "Let me decide what to do." A tear rolled down her face. "It's . . . so much more than just . . . I'll see you in the morning, okay? We can talk over breakfast. I think I'm getting hungry again."

June's brow furrowed and her tone wavered, and Elle swore she almost saw a tear at the edge of her eye. "In the morning."

She stumbled once in the dance that night. She winced as she stepped off the stage. Were she a human, it would have ached the next morning. She rubbed her sore muscles as she walked to her dressing room, her hands torn fresh slowly beginning their healing as she walked. She could feel him nearby. Her heart raced, chills raised the skin on her arms, and her stomach twisted. She stood before the door of her dressing room. He was in there.

She opened the door, and there he was. Gods, he was breathtaking. Her heart jumped into her throat. "Kirk." She stepped into the room, grabbing a rag and wiping the sweat from the back of her neck. *My hands healed enough. He won't ask questions.* She tried to keep her composure, but the scent of him made her knees weak. "Did you learn anything today?" she asked, trying to put any amount of a casual air into her tone.

He leaned against the wall, his arms crossed. He shook his head and pushed off the wall. "I cannot prove it was any of the vampires in that castle, which brings me back to nearly zero." He rolled his shoulders. "But because of this *spell* over me all I could think about was seeing you again." He touched her back, his fingers delicately running over the exposed skin. "Holding you again." His voice dropped. "Tasting you again."

The fire between her legs roared. She pushed herself to walk over to the vanity and sit on the stool before it. She began to pull the pins from her hair. "I . . . understand." She looked at him in the mirror, their eyes meeting through the reflection. "Kirk . . ."

He stepped up behind her, and one of his hands gently wrapped around her neck, raising her face to meet his. The calloused skin of his hand against the silken of her throat. He leaned forward and pressed his lips against her forehead. "Yes?"

Her heart jumped into her throat. "Let me get changed first." Her neck arched at his touch, pressing even farther into his grip. "Then we *have* to talk."

"Like we talked before?" His blue-gold eyes twinkled.

She laughed, hoping he couldn't hear the nerves in her voice. "Maybe a *bit* more talking this time."

His hand slid from her neck, lingering on her collarbone, his fingers teasing the edges of her breasts before he let her go entirely. "Of course."

Elle stood and stepped away from the mirror, motioning Kirk close the door. As he did, she pulled her dress from where it hung on the wall. She slipped out of her performance attire.

He returned to the wall, leaning back against it and crossing his arms.

She did not face him as she dressed, but her eyes darted to the mirror. His eyes rested with such intensity on her. Her dress was a simple thing that tied in the back, and she turned to him as she pulled the bow taut. She nodded toward her cloak, sparing a quick glance at the thick bulge in his leather. He'd enjoyed watching her change.

He grabbed the cloak from the hook beside the door and wrapped it around her.

Looking up, she examined those eyes a moment, as if she could know by looking into the swirling oceans before her if he could love her or if that sword hanging at his hip would run through her neck this eve. She pressed onto her toes and kissed him, pulling his head down toward herself. "There's a food cart that's still open this late. You should eat, and then we can talk."

*****

The man sold skewered meat that he cooked over a fire contained in a metal pot behind his cart. Elle paid him for a single skewer and proceeded to hand it to Kirk. "I've already eaten tonight." She'd tried to stomach human food a few times after she'd killed Alder. Food that she had used to find some joy in, but it all made her sick.

He took it from her. "Thank you, Ellie."

Ellie. "Have to make sure you've eaten." She winked at him. "You'll need your strength."

Kirk laughed so hard he nearly choked on the bite he'd taken. "Gods damn it, you're going to be the death of me."

Oh no, dear hunter, you're going to be the death of me.

They made their way toward the inn. She asked him about his hunts as they walked, keeping her nervous tone at bay, learning more about the man. She wanted to postpone it, what would be their end. What would be *her* end.

The stars danced in the sky above them, and the moon lit their path. She stopped a few yards from the door. Faint music and the sound of patrons laughing and singing floated from inside on the cool night air.

Kirk glanced down at her as she stopped. His hand was tangled in hers. She saw adoration in his eyes.

She stepped a few paces forward and turned to face him, his hand still held in hers, their arms extended between them. "Come."

Her pull was light, but it seemed to catch him off guard a bit, and he stumbled toward her.

She grabbed his other hand and started to tug him into a spin. "Dance with me, Kirk." As hard as she tried to hide it, there was a hint of desperation in her voice.

He seemed unsure at first, hesitant, his lumbering form apparently unaccustomed to such delicate movements, but then he melted. He squeezed her hands and pulled her even closer against himself. His hands moved to the small of her back, her head coming to his chest. "As you wish, Elle."

They danced together underneath the moon for a while, swaying to the muffled music. He lifted her chin with a knuckle and bent over to kiss her, pressing his lips gently to hers. She kissed him back, her hands gripped tightly in his shirt, her mouth captured by his.

She knew he was able to sense her fear. Sense her hesitation. He had to feel it. That something was wrong. That that night . . . that that moment . . . it might just be their goodbye.

*****

Elle let out a small squeak when he pinned her against the wall in his room. His hands carefully took off her dress, savoring every moment as the fabric slid from her shoulders and piled onto the floor. His hands followed the dress, gently running over each newly exposed stretch of skin, taking in every single inch of her. She watched breathlessly as he knelt before her.

Her hips pressed into his touch.

He pushed her back against the wall. "That tease as you made me watch you change . . . You know you're simply wicked, my love."

My love. Could I truly be?

She smiled down at him, her hand moving under his chin and just barely tilting his face up toward her own.

He started to kiss her neck, then his lips drifted to her collarbone. They grazed between her breasts, down her stomach. Every kiss was gentle and delicate, a stark contrast to the beast before her. Those taunting fingers played near her entrance, slipping through the puddle that ran between her legs. When he finally gave in to the pleading pressure of her hips, and his fingers slid inside her, she moaned, her head pressed back against the door, but not before she caught just a glimpse of his smile.

His fingers curled and thrust, drawing her pleasure from her, while his kisses continued to cover every exposed inch he could reach.

When he pulled his lips from her, the exposed skin went cold with the sudden chill against her dampened flesh. His eyes gazed into hers as he slipped his hand from between her legs. With his other hand, he gently grasped her chin, pressing on the sides of her jaw to open her mouth just a bit wider than it already was. Then he slipped his fingers between her lips, leaving her own taste on her tongue.

He stood slowly as she sucked on his fingers. Her eyes rose with him, praying that he understood her signal that she would *gladly* do the same to his cock. Gladly fall onto her knees before him . . .

She began unbuttoning his shirt, pressed close as she fumbled with the buttons. One fell onto the floor when she tore it from the fabric. "Sorry, I'll—"

He kissed her, wrapping her up in his arms, his shirt barely hanging on.

She understood the command to stop speaking and ripped the rest of the fabric from his arms. Her hands moved to his belt buckle. She could feel his cock straining against the leather, and for *fuck's sake*, she wanted it freed.

As the buckle came loose and his pants dropped onto the floor, she pressed her chest again against his. Their bare skin could only get closer if they became entirely one. Her hand slipped down.

Each of their mouths was captured in the other's, and his hands were tangled in her hair. He moaned softly into her mouth as her fingers wrapped around him.

She stood on her toes to get close enough to reach his lips, stretching as tall as she could to minimize how deeply he had to angle himself to kiss her. She knew he would only be able to bend as he did for so long before his back gave out. His hand moved to just between her neck and her shoulder, his grip tightened, and he pulled his head back from hers. "I thought we were going to—" She pumped his cock just once, and his voice hitched. "I thought we were going to talk, Elle."

She shook her head. Her finger moved to his lips. "Bed."

He smiled softly, perhaps remembering as she was the first time she had commanded him thus.

She pushed his chest, shoving him toward the bed. "Lie down."

He stepped backward, then let himself fall back onto the bed. "Yes, my love."

Elle crawled over top of him and straddled his stomach. His erection pressed against her ass.

She felt his dick throb against her. Wet heat between her thighs and his stomach taunted them both. The look in his eyes seemed to express a deep desire they shared, to let that warmth between them wrap around his dick. She leaned forward, her hands on his chest, and started to kiss his throat.

He moaned softly into her ear, "My love . . ."

Her teeth scraped against the side of his neck, and she let a breathy moan slip into his ear. She slid down his body, her hips shifted, and one hand moved to guide him in.

"Elle," he moaned. "Elle . . ."

She rocked her hips against him, and she smiled, her own breath hitching as he filled her. "Kirk."

~ 16 ~

CHAPTER 16

SILAS

There she was. That void of a mind. A vampire. She was *so very well* hidden. It was extraordinary. He'd never encountered a vampire so well disguised.

Disguised so well that as he watched her exit through the back door of the Stag, she was arm in arm *with the fucking hunter.* Even a vampire hunter couldn't see through it. *Truly impressive and confident. And stupid.* To trust in a ward enough to sleep with a vampire hunter . . . It was evident she was indeed what they suspected, a *powerful* royal. The old House of Bone had held powers beyond even those of Dae. Of Blood. It was why he had eradicated the family. Why Dae had killed every one of them. Or he'd thought he had.

This girl was a master of deception. She moved and spoke with flawless innocence. Silas smiled to himself as he stalked the shadows behind them. He wondered if Dae would let him inside her head. While he couldn't control vampires, couldn't read their thoughts, he could still enter their minds given they were sedated enough, root around, do some damage, and he found her mind so very . . . intriguing. He wondered what it tasted like. Such cunning. The flavor of her had to be exquisite.

He'd likely spend little time with a female of Bone. Dae would have plans for her.

Silas almost laughed. The tiny vampire he followed was so very unaware. She might assume the greatest danger to her was the man she was dragging toward an inn, the hunter, but he should be the *least* of her worries. If she was truly what they suspected., the last heir of Bone . . . What Dae would do with her, *to* her. She'd wish the hunter had killed her.

~ 17 ~

CHAPTER 17

KIRK
"Elle." He lay beside her, his hand on her hip, his other arm tucked beneath his head. "Did you find anything out?" His thumb gently ran over her exposed skin, caressing the soft flesh of her side. "About whatever . . . this is?"

She shifted nervously beneath his hand. Her eyes would not rise to meet his. *So she has, and she doesn't want to say.* Whatever she'd found, she was afraid to share. It hurt him. It hurt when she became so nervous around him. It hurt when she seemed to feel fear in his presence. What else was he to do to assure her? He couldn't understand why she feared him. His body ached for her. He would do anything to keep her safe, to keep her happy, to protect this beautiful being beside him. What could she have possibly found that would make her *fear* him? She felt as he did. She had to understand the intensity of the yearning. How completely overwhelming it was.

"Elle . . ." His hand moved from her hip to her chin, raising her face to meet his. "Tell me, what have you found?"

She started to cry. She sat up, wrapping the blanket around herself as tears poured down her cheeks.

He pulled himself to sitting, his hand reaching to her. "Ellie . . . Elle, what is it?" He wiped a tear from just below her eye with his thumb. "Is it some kind of curse? If it's a curse, it's fine . . . We can figure it out. This is the best I've felt in my entire life. Being near you is the best feeling I've ever known. Please. Please tell me what you learned."

She hesitated. Her green eyes searched his for just a second. "We're . . . bound, Kirk." Her voice was small at first. The tears poured with even more intensity as she spoke. Her voice rose slightly, desperation and fear in her tone. "We're bound. Soul bound. Our literal souls are woven together by the moon herself."

His head was swimming. He tilted it slightly as he tried to understand what she meant. "Bound? By the moon?" His hand dropped from her face and ran through his hair, his mind racing as he tried to sort through it. What it all meant. "Like . . . in vampire lore . . . ?" He'd heard of soul-bound mates. He'd been told about it. But it was vampiric. Old vampire magic. Legends.

She nodded, her breath shaking. "Yes. Yes exactly that, Kirk."

"Forgive me, but I'm confused." *A mate. She's my mate. My mate.* His eyes searched her face for anything. *How can we be mates? How could that be? She's my mate. My mate, my mate, my mate.* "But, Elle—Elle, we're not—" Her expression shifted. Her face changed as he was about to say, *We're not vampires. We're human.* But he wasn't human. He was some mutated version of a human.

But then he knew.

Understanding settled deep in his stomach. It wasn't because *he* wasn't human that her face changed. It was because she wasn't either. "Elle . . ."

She pushed farther away from him, nearly off the edge of the bed. Her weeping doubled her over herself. She pulled the blanket tighter around her shoulders, and she crumbled before him. "Forgive me. Forgive me. Please. Please forgive me, Kirk. Please."

He didn't want to believe it. He didn't want to accept it. "What are you saying? Elle. Elle, tell me what this means. Tell me what *you are.*" His throat threatened to seal shut. His palms grew sweaty. *She can't be.*

Through her sobs she spoke it, the words that he could barely process the meaning of. "A vampire. I'm a vampire."

His stomach bottomed out. "Your teeth. Your eyes. You don't look or smell like one. I don't understand." *No. No. No.*

"I'm a vampire." She shoved off the bed, stood at its edge, the blanket still wrapped tightly around her. "I'm so sorry. Please forgive me. I'm *begging* you to forgive me. I didn't know—I didn't know the moon bound us. You understand why I didn't. I'm sorry. I'm sorry." She stepped back again.

So this is why she fears me. Because she should.

He was frozen on the bed as she backed away from him. He was frozen, watching those green eyes full of a fear he'd seen so many times before, the look he'd seen on the faces of the vampires he'd killed. Nausea swept over him. Instinctively, his eyes moved to his sword. But he couldn't hurt her. He could never hurt her. He could never kill her . . .

But he didn't have to. She was just a vampire. He could love a vampire. He could. She wasn't—

No.

Kirk did not realize until then that the world could fall out from beneath his feet even farther. It couldn't be that she . . . She couldn't be the one who'd killed Stephan. She couldn't be. She was kind. She was gentle. She was delicate and caring. She wasn't. She wasn't the one who had murdered a man. She couldn't be the monster who'd torn his heart from his chest . . .

"Elle." His voice hitched. *Tell me you aren't.* "You didn't kill Stephan, right? Tell me you didn't. Please." His voice rattled as panic began to settle in his core. "Please tell me I'm not here to kill you. Elle, tell me I'm not here to *kill you.*"

"I-" She froze. He could see her entire body shaking beneath the blanket. "I did."

His heart stopped for a moment.

"Please understand, Kirk. Please. He slit June's throat. He was going to kill her. I had to. I had to protect her. Please, Kirk. It wasn't about food. It was in defense. Please. Please please please believe me."

No. "You've lied to me since the moment I met you. How could I believe you now?" His words were cold. He couldn't breathe. His stomach twisted into knots he wasn't sure would ever come undone. Betrayal had settled so deep into his heart so fucking fast he didn't know if he could ever dig it out.

Of course, she had lied to him. Of *course*, she had. He was there to kill her. *Why would she have been honest with me?* The thought whipped through his mind, Would he have been able to kill her? His eyes dropped to his hands, hands that knew the feeling of her skin. His muscles tensed at the idea of those hands dripping with her blood. He could never.

Even then, as he reeled from her lies, he only wanted her in his arms. He only wanted to pull her tightly against his chest. Even then, as his gaze rose back to hers, as he stared at her, he wanted to jump from where he sat and wrap her up in his arms. He wanted to hold her. He wanted her to feel safe. Protected.

But he couldn't move. He could only stare at her. The shock rendered him immobile. He could only stare at the *vampire* in front of him. The conflict waging war in his mind was threatening to take his consciousness from him. His head throbbed. Pain shot through his chest like a blade driven into his heart. *What the fuck am I supposed to do?*

"Are you . . . going to kill me?" Her voice was small. Her eyes darted to his sword.

He bent forward, his hands tangled in his hair. "No." He couldn't look at her. It hurt so deeply. Everything hurt so fucking deeply. His heart screamed at his limbs to stand, to scoop her up and kiss her. To comfort her. To promise to protect her and love her and fuck her for the rest of time. Tell her that they could figure it out together. But every limb felt like mush. What wasn't numb was in so much pain he felt like the world was collapsing in on him.

He heard the blanket drop, heard her hurry into her dress. He still couldn't look up at her. His soul screeched. *Beg her to stay. Grab her. Hold her. Love her. Fucking stop her from leaving, for fuck's sake. Stop her. Stop her. Your mate. Your mate. Your mate. Don't let her out of that door. For the love of the moon, don't let her walk out of that fucking door. Your mate.*

But his mate had lied.

"I'm so sorry." Her voice was barely above a whisper.

He heard the door close.

And he let her leave.

~ 18 ~

CHAPTER 18

ELLE
She ran as soon as the sting of the night hit her face. She wasn't sure where she was running, but at that moment, she didn't care. Parting from him had hurt before, but this, this was excruciating. Like something was ripping her heart from her very chest. The cold air bit against the tears pouring down her cheeks. The streets were nearly empty, but she didn't run deeper into the city, not even toward June. Her feet were headed toward the outskirts. Toward the woods around Torzen. *Just like last time. You can't help but run away from it all. Because you're a fucking monster. You're a fucking creature. You're a monster born of the darkness, and you're doomed to return there. Again, you run into the woods and beg death to take you away because you're a monster and a fucking coward. It's where you belong. You cannot know love. Even your mate. Even your mate. Your mate. He cannot love you.*

Your mate.

Her thoughts spiraled out of control, and she did not sense the monster in the shadows behind her. The monster following her.

She ran through alleys and backstreets. She tripped, her steps unsure. She stumbled to her knees, hunched over. Her arm wrapped around her waist as her chest heaved with the sobs she could no longer contain. She could not catch her breath; she felt like she was going to vomit. Her throat burned as the emptiness in her stomach threatened to turn her inside out.

Then she heard footsteps behind her. She shoved herself to her feet and turned to face whoever approached. She assumed some guard. Someone who had seen her running and came to offer help. No one could help her. Nothing could help her.

"I'm alri—" She paused when she saw the male approaching.

He was unfamiliar, tall and slender, with white hair falling past his shoulders in a ponytail that swished with each step. The jacket he wore appeared expensive, fitted to his toned torso. His steps were quiet and smooth, and *inhuman*. His eyes were red, almost black in the night. White fangs glinted in the moonlight when he smiled. "Hello there."

She stepped back. Instinct told her feet to move, screamed at her body to run. "You— You're a vampire . . ."

"As are you." He stepped closer to her steadily, ever closer. "Truly an incredible feat to appear so fully human. I'm genuinely impressed."

"Who . . . are you?" Fear numbed her legs, and her feet grew heavy, all but cemented to the ground.

He was directly before her then. She could nearly feel his breath. "Who I am really isn't important, princess. *You*, however. Who *you* are is very important."

He grabbed her arm. His other hand rose.

She felt a sharp prick in her neck.

Then everything went black.

*****

She opened her eyes. Elle winced as her head throbbed, and her hand moved instinctively to touch her aching forehead. She was lying down . . . draped over velvet cushions on a small settee. She sat up slowly and glanced around.

The room was large. Bookshelves lined the walls. A desk was in one corner . . . She shoved herself up as she saw him, a male seated behind the desk.

"You're awake." His voice sent a deep chill down her spine.

She stood, unsure what else she was supposed to do. "Who . . . are you?" Her knees wobbled. Whatever they'd used to drug her was not fully gone from her system.

He stepped around the desk. His clothes were tailored tightly against his body. His hair was slicked back, his eyes a shade of red darker than she'd ever seen before, his features sharp, and his eyes narrow. His hand moved over his heart in a gesture of mocking shock. "You *really* don't know?"

She shook her head, but as she looked at him, she realized she knew that face. She knew his face well. It was Bliss's. Which meant the male before her . . .

"My dear girl." He stepped toward her. "I'm the Lord of Blood, and you've lived in my shadow for a few years now."

She felt something in her blood, like a phantom grip around her veins. " . . .Dae."

He smiled when she spoke his name. "Welcome to my home, little princess." His strides were confident, deliberate, each closer to her, each movement only driving that fear deeper into her bones. "What a blessing from the moon to have found you."

Elle desperately wanted to take a step backward, but as she tried, she felt that ghost grip on her blood tighten. She knew if she continued to move, if she moved at all, it would constrict. It whispered through her body of promised pain. "Why would you look for me?"

When he reached her, he grabbed her face and lifted her gaze to meet his. His nails dug into her cheeks as his grip tightened. "You're unaware of who you are, darling?" His eyes stared into hers. It felt like he would stare through them. "Your parents went to such ugly lengths to hide you. I can't say I'm not impressed. Eighty years you've hidden from me, only to show up on my doorstep. The moon clearly sent you here as a little gift."

She tried to pull away, out of his grip, but his nails dug in deeper. Blood dripped down her cheeks. "What are you talking about?" She couldn't control the shaking of her voice.

"A daughter." He turned her head side to side, his eyes moving over her face, analyzing it, hungry. "A female to carry your family bloodline."

Her stomach dropped. "What . . . ?"

He ripped her forward and dug his teeth into her throat.

She screamed.

His hand pressed against her collarbones as he bit down on the column on her neck. His other hand wrapped around her back and pulled her against his body. He sucked at the punctures he'd created, and his nails dug into her chest. Black clouds swirled around them, and something seared into her skin. Dark magic coursed through her. Something *evil* entered her. Something dark and cruel. Phantom chains wrapped around her heart and her mind. Chains constricted her soul.

A curse. He had cursed her. He was binding her to him. Her screams continued. Her knees buckled as the curse took hold. His claws dug into her back to keep her standing as he drank from her neck. He ran his tongue along her wounds, lapping at the blood like he was starved. The magic was driven into her chest.

He cursed her.

And she became his.

Part 2

Lost

~ 19 ~

INTERLUDE

June stood, placing the bunch of herbs in her bag, and she wiped the sweat from her forehead. She had been out for most of the day, collecting what she'd been running low on. She'd been busy foraging late into the afternoon. It was near time to return. The woods were dangerous at night, and she didn't feel like running into something in the dark.

She began her trek back home. She'd gotten farther out than she'd initially thought. She'd been so caught up chasing mushrooms that she'd lost track of how far she'd been wandering. Something caught her eye, a movement in the brush. It was slight, but it didn't seem like an animal. Something immediately felt off. A knot formed in her stomach. As she decided to investigate, she drew her bow, an arrow ready for whatever she was approaching.

Then she came upon it. It was a person. A girl, lying on the ground. She was hardly even conscious. Her clothes were torn, barely hanging onto her body, and what was there was entirely stained with blood. The blood was dried, old. It had been there for a few days at least. The girl's face and hands were covered in the same dried blood. She was thin, her ribs visible through the tears in her clothes. Her hair had been braided, but it had almost entirely unraveled. Under the blood, she was bruised and cut. It appeared as though she'd been badly beaten; though there was far too much blood for it to have only been hers, no matter how severe the beating.

June lowered her bow and dropped to her knees. "Oh my gods . . . oh gods. Hey . . . hey, hey, what happened?" She lifted her, holding her up and trying to get her attention.

The girl in her arms didn't respond at first, just lay limply in June's grasp.

June looked the girl over. There were no large wounds. There was a large gash in her shirt, a scar on her stomach underneath, but it appeared to have been healed for years. The girl was cold to the touch, her breathing faint. June sighed. "Listen, I'll get you back to town just . . . hang on. I'll get you help." With no obvious wounds to treat, June was unsure how to use her magic to help. What could she do if she didn't know what was wrong? She needed to get her back to town and maybe she could figure it out. Maybe one of her books might have an answer.

The girl spoke softly, her eyes still closed. "Leave me . . ."

June looked down at her, surprised by the faint voice. "I'm getting you help. What happened? What's going on?"

"I'm . . . vam . . . vampire . . . Just . . . let me die here . . . please . . ."

June froze for a moment. She remembered learning about vampires from her mentor. She'd learned about their healing powers, their history. She knew they could heal quickly, but they needed human blood to replenish their strength. Vampires that went too long without feeding would grow crazed.

But this girl didn't look like a vampire. She didn't have fangs or red eyes, the two initial signs of a vampire, what anyone would look for to identify one quickly. She was pale, sure, but June had assumed the coldness of her skin was simply from being nearly dead, blood loss even, not being a . . . vampire.

So this girl needed blood. That was what she needed to stay alive. June's mind was running through the scenario quickly—she found a vampire in the woods, the vampire was nearly dead, she had clearly been very hurt, she had someone else's blood on her, and she sought death . . .

This vampire had been attacked, and she did not seek to be saved.

June sighed. "No. No, I can't let you die here." She knew, she knew her teacher would want her to save her. Vampire or not, this girl needed help. June wasn't going to deny that help. She wasn't going to let her die out here. This decision came with the understanding of what she had to do.

This vampire needed human blood. She was within hours of death without it. June hesitated, fear racked her body as she considered it, giving this vampire her blood.

But the choice was made for her. June barely understood what was happening before she felt teeth digging into her neck.

The girl had lost control. She couldn't fight it. She smelled human, smelled blood, and June was right there. A vampire gone too long without blood would lose control of the urge and attack, too weak to fight the desire. It was a survival instinct, their body doing whatever it needed to carry on. So this girl plunged her teeth into the side of June's neck.

June gasped, but she didn't pull away. Pulling away would only cause the wound to tear further. June was shocked by how weak this girl was. She had grabbed June's arm as she bit down, but both her grip and her bite were feeble.

She fell back off June after a moment. Her eyes were open now and full of fear. June's blood dripped from her mouth, streams running down her chin. Her teeth were stained red. "Please. Please run. Dear gods, run before I hurt you again." The girl's voice shook, and she shoved away from June.

June looked into her eyes. They were bright green. June could see magic alterations in the color. So that was how she'd hidden the red. Those eyes were full of panic and pain. The girl's desperate pleas only pushed June's heart further toward her. This girl was not a monster. She was starving and frightened. Warm blood ran down June's neck from the punctures. The girl's teeth were dull, so the wound was messy, ripped open instead of pierced. June pulled a piece of cloth from her pack, pressing it against her neck as she stood. "Can you stand?" Her heart ached as the pitiful monster shook before her.

The girl stared at her, her expression unwavering, then she nodded, tears welling up in the corners of her eyes. She shakily attempted to stand, but quickly stumbled. She wasn't nearly strong enough to move on her own yet. June's stone heart softened, warming enough that her expression must have calmed the girl's fear just a bit. June's words were deliberate, sure. She was not afraid of her. She was not looking at her with hate, but pity ... and care.

June's gaze was gentle as she offered her hand. "I'll help you." She took the girl's arm and pulled it over her shoulders. "Lean against me ... Promise not to bite?" June smiled softly.

The girl pulled away.

June pulled her back. "C'mon."

$$\sim 20 \sim$$

CHAPTER 20

JUNE
Elle didn't come home. June tried to sleep. The half-breed lay beside her and tried to take her mind from the thoughts that tormented her, but he could only give her a moment of distraction. Only a brief reprieve from the nerves that threatened to consume her. Elle was okay. Elle *had* to be okay. Now that she knew Elle and the hunter were bound by the moon . . . Of course, Ellie would tell him. She wouldn't be the Elle June knew and adored so deeply if she didn't.

June, however, *hated* that idea. If Elle hadn't returned by morning, she would go search for her. She would give them the night. Elle had asked that of her. She would *only* give them the night. Any longer than that, and she would find that hunter, and the moon help him if he'd so much as laid a finger on Elle. If he'd dared touch her, no one would be able to identify the ashes.

She awoke. Bliss was wrapped around her like a blanket, his breaths heavy against her neck. She was thankful for him, the little bastard. At the end of the day, she would not have survived that night alone. She shifted in his arms. "Bliss, I need to get up."

He moaned and pressed his face deeper into her neck. "Rest a while longer with me," he cooed.

"I have to find Elle. I can't— Not until I *know* she's safe." June sat up, and his arms fell from around her.

Bliss sat up beside her, rubbing his eyes and yawning softly. The pattern of the blanket he'd curled up with was imprinted on the side of his face, and his hair was still tangled from the activities of the night before. He kissed June's nose then slid out of her bed, his body fully exposed to the morning air.

June's eyes ran over him in the light of the sun peeking through the window as he stretched and scratched his head. He was covered in tattoos, his arms and back marked with a variety of black symbols and pictures etched into his skin. A few deep scars ran down his back. Some from fights he'd lost. Some from times he'd gotten his drunk ass in trouble he couldn't quite get out of. One . . . One scar from when he'd been left for dead. When an assassin had assumed Bliss and his mother were *both* dead on the floor of their home.

"June."

There was anxiety in the soft voice of her lover, and it shook her from her thoughts. "What?"

"There's a note on the floor." It rested just inside the door. Someone had slid it through the doorframe. He bent to pick it up and handed the paper to her.

She felt the weight of his eyes on her face as she read it. He'd never learned to read. June had tried to teach him a few times, but he had struggled, grown frustrated, and every time they wound up just fucking instead. Her hand slid over her mouth. She couldn't believe what she was reading. Something was wrong. Something was very very wrong.

"What is it? What does it say?"

June's hands trembled. "No. No no. NO." She shook her head. "She wouldn't. She *wouldn't.*"

But she had.

"June . . ." Bliss walked toward her, his hand stretched out in her direction. "What does it say?"

"She left." She kept shaking her head as she read the note over and over and over. "It's from Elle . . . It's her *fucking* handwriting. She left. She left to protect me. To protect that fucking hunter. Because she's killed two people now. She's fucking running again. She's fucking running." Her eyes met Bliss's. Desperate tears streamed down her cheeks. "She *fucking left.*"

In that moment, it tore from her. She doubled over in her bed, her hands crumpling the note as she grasped it. "NO!" June screamed. "No, Elle, don't do this! *Please!*" She looked at her arm. It shook violently. *No no no no no no.* Their mark. It was gone. Their mark was gone. Elle had broken their bond.

Elle was gone.

She tried to catch her breath, hunched forward and panting. "That fucking hunter." She looked at Bliss as she desperately tried to regain even an ounce of her composure. "He must have said something. Threatened her. Something. That's why she ran. That's why she *left me.* Because of him. It has to be." She threw her legs off the side of the bed and hurried to get dressed. "C'mon. I'm going to find that bastard, and then I'm going to find Elle."

It was her fault. She had forced Elle to confront Stephan. She had started this entire mess. The hunter was here because she had started a fight that *Elle* had to finish. Elle had protected her. This was all because of her.

She had to get her back.

June,

I'm sorry. I really am. It's not safe for me to stay with you anymore. After Alder. After Stephan. I'm a danger in your life. In Kirk's life. Believe me, June, I've never wanted to part from you. Never. But I have to. For you. For Kirk. Our bond will break. I will disappear. Your life can continue on.

Tell Bliss you love him. I know you do. You know you do. He's an idiot, but he's ours.

June, I love you. I love you more than I could ever express. More than I could ever say, which is why I have to go. It's why I have to leave.

I'm sorry.

Don't look for me.

I love you,

Elle

$$\sim 21 \sim$$

CHAPTER 21

KIRK
He had not slept after she left. When he caught a glimpse of himself in the mirror, he winced . . . He looked like hell. He felt like hell. He stumbled out of the bed and got dressed slowly. Gathered his gear and began to pull back his hair, running his fingers through it and tying half of it up to keep it out of his face. With his sword strapped to his belt, his hand resting on the hilt for a moment, he looked once more at the mirror. He needed to find her. He needed to talk to her. They could figure out what to do. What they could do. Together.

He'd rolled it over in his mind for the entirety of the night, and what he knew was that he could not lose her. It was all he knew. He knew he needed her. He needed her with him; he needed her beside him. He could figure out what to do about her bounty, what to do about her being a vampire, but he knew he couldn't lose her. If he hadn't already.

He needed to find her, and so he began his trek. It was too early for her to have gone to the Stag. She'd likely returned home. He just hoped he wasn't too late. He'd have to deal with that mage, who'd likely try for his head. He prayed his silence the night before hadn't taken her from him. They were bound. She was his mate. The moon had bound their souls together. She felt as he did. He knew that. That was why she'd risked everything. Why she'd stood before him and told him everything.

She had chosen to give him everything he needed to kill her.

He had to make it right. Make up for his silence. Make up for his fear. He would give her everything. He could figure out the details. He only knew he needed her.

He continued through the streets toward where Elle and the mage lived. His steps grew more and more hurried. He just wanted to see her. To talk to her. To fall on his knees before her and beg for her to figure it out beside him. He had no plan. Nothing. His mind had been so wrapped up in her, the logistics of it all would have to come later. This primal need of his soul to be near to hers— He'd give up everything for her. *Everything.* He only wished he'd been able to speak it the night before. Before she'd left. Before he may have hurt her enough that she was unable to forgive him . . . He prayed she could forgive his silence, the harshness of his few words. All of it.

A hunter mated to a vampire. It was unheard of. There weren't even records of a human who'd been mated to a vampire . . . not in this way. Plenty had loved. Plenty had *procreated*. But never had there been a couple *soul bound*. Not by the moon. Kirk had never believed in the moon as the vampires did. Yet there she was, deeply intertwined in *his very soul*.

He wondered if he felt it all so strongly because of his humanity, whatever little of it was left. He could never have explained feeling as he did within mere moments of meeting, but if their souls were bound, it meant what they felt for each other was so far beyond human emotion, so far beyond vampiric emotion. It was a connection by and of the gods themselves.

What had he done to deserve this gift of the moon? What had she done to be cursed with *him*? What if he had already ruined it?

Elle. He had to find Elle.

As he neared their home, he saw the mage walking toward him. When their eyes met, fire burned in hers, but behind that fire, her eyes were red, her cheeks puffy. Something was wrong. The mage had been weeping, and as her eyes locked onto his, he felt like the earth dropped out from beneath his feet.

She walked directly to him. Her hand wrapped around one of the straps across his chest, and she pulled his face down toward her own. Her eyes narrowed into a glare. "What did you say to her? What the fuck did you do?!"

He swallowed. Had Elle not gone home? Had she not returned to the mage? *Don't panic. Not yet.* "I'm trying to find her. I didn't say anything, and I think that's why she left. Is she not with you? I need to talk to her. Please. Mage, where is she?"

"She fucking LEFT, you bastard!" June's grip tightened for a moment, then she released him, shoving him backward. Her other hand reached into her pocket and pulled out a wadded note. She shoved the scrap of paper into his chest, and he stumbled back a step. "She left last night, and this was under my door this morning."

He delicately unfolded the paper. Running his eyes over the page, he read through Elle's words. "She ran . . ." There was a knot in his throat, and no matter how hard he tried, he couldn't force it away. "I'm . . . too late. I couldn't stop her . . ."

"You're the fucking reason she's gone! You're the one who sent her away!" June hissed at him, her words daggers that she fully intended to harm. "This is *your* doing. You and that fucking cursed moon took her from me!" She started to shatter before him, tears falling again from her eyes. "Don't you dare go after her. I'll fucking kill you in an instant if you go anywhere near her again. Don't fucking touch her."

"I'm not going to kill her, June." His tone was hushed and his eyes darted around them, the passerby distanced enough to not hear his whispers. "I could never. I could never."

June shoved him.

Fuck. This mage was making a scene. This needed to get resolved quickly.

"Fucking leave. Now. You've done enough fucking damage."

"June," he pleaded, "where might she have gone? Please. I *have* to find her."

"I fucking told you. Don't you dare go after her. I'll find her. Myself. Leave her alone. She left. She's left you behind. She's chosen to stay away from you. So *you* need to leave her the fuck alone." June stepped toward him again, her hands balling into fists.

His voice shook. "She left you too."

June raised her fist to strike him.

He caught her hand in the air. The folks walking stopped.

She gritted her teeth, her fist shaking in his hand. "She wouldn't."

"Clearly, she did." He was cold. It hurt too much. It hurt too fucking much. "Let her run then, and we can talk *in private* about the rest."

*****

He stood in Morel, staring at the mage who glared at him, her arms crossed and her eyes narrowed.

"What are you going to do then? You know what she is. You know what she did. She's run away. If you fucking try to hunt her—"

"I've told you enough times, mage, I refuse to harm her. But that doesn't change the fact that I have to do something to *complete* my job here." He paced slowly. He couldn't let it hurt yet. "I'm going to speak to Gen."

"And say what?"

"I'm going to tell him I killed her." He hitched on the words. "He will believe me. My vampire hunts don't usually leave much behind . . . and that will clear her bounty. No one keeps looking for her. She'll be free to run without hunters after her. She can hide. She can be free from all of this. Including me, as she clearly wishes to be." It burned to say. It hurt.

It can't hurt yet. Not yet.

He saw the fire in her eyes flicker. "Both of her bounties."

"Both?"

June nodded. "She killed another man in defense once before. A lover who tried to kill her. It's why she moved here in the first place. Clear them both."

"I will do that." He . . . truly did not know her. "I need something of hers. To burn."

*****

"The dancer?" Gen's eyes were wide as he rubbed the back of his head. "Gods-damn. You really couldn't tell she was a vampire."

"She was using powerful magic to hide herself. I've never en-countered a vampire so well disguised." That wasn't a lie. She'd had him entirely fooled. *It can't hurt yet.* Kirk's eyes moved around the room, visions of her dances flashed in his mind as he took in the empty stage. *I wonder if she'll dance again. I . . .want to see her dance again.*

"And do you have anything left of her? A body I must dispose of?" Gen's shock had seemingly already passed, his eyes darting back and forth as he ran the numbers in his head of his losses with-out the Stag's main entertainment.

Kirk reached into a leather bag at his hip and removed the scrap of her cloak. A tear had escaped as he'd burned it. He held the rest of those tears at bay then as he looked at it again. *Not. yet.* The flames from his hands burned away a memory of her, and his soul burned with it. "This is all I have. She was powerful. Power-ful enough to hide with spells like those. There wasn't much left of her other than ash." He dropped the fabric in Gen's hand. A flame danced across his fingers as he pulled his hand back to reinforce the point. "Even vampires burn."

But the thought of her burning drove his stomach into his throat.

"It's scary knowing she was hiding under our noses." Gen twisted the fabric in his fingers. "Who knows how many of us she might have attacked."

None.

"And such a pity to lose my best performer." He sighed heavily. "But I appreciate your work, good hunter." He took in a deep breath, his eyes closing a moment. "Collect your payment from Lynn. And please"—he gestured to the bar—"another cup of mead. On the house, for all your work for us."

Kirk needed a barrel of mead to drown these feelings. After he'd collected his pay, he began his walk back to the Sunflower. It was over. He had completed his job in Torzen. And he had lost everything.

She had made the decision to leave.

He had waited and let her leave.

As soon as he entered his room in the inn, he sucked in a sob. *Now. Now you can let it hurt.*

And fuck, it hurt.

I could tell
Love was Always
about going
back into
a tamer,
she never
let me
Braid
her
hair
my girl

~ 22 ~

CHAPTER 22

KIRK

Kirk tossed his bag over Love's saddle and petted her neck gently. "Ready to go home, Love?" His voice was hoarse. He hadn't slept that last night in the Sunflower. He hadn't been able to pull himself from wrestling with his own twisted feelings. He would have to ask Bran about the moon bonds when he arrived back at the hunters' keep. Bran had studied vampiric lore enough, maybe he knew of a way to unchain his heart.

But Kirk didn't want to.

Vampires truly were cruel. To curse him with such pain and torment that he feared losing it because it would mean he had lost her entirely.

Did she feel as he did?

Could she feel as he did and leave?

But he'd let her go.

He'd watched her walk out.

He rubbed his forehead. It all made his head ache terribly. His chest pounded. His body tried to reconcile emotions beyond a man's understanding. They threatened to tear him apart.

He would pick up whatever job he could next. He needed work. Something he could focus on. Something he could put the *entirety* of his mind toward. Just for a while.

He rode out of the city and passed the forest that lay before the Red Castle. Something in their bond pulled as he rode past. *So that's the direction she traveled.* He sighed and urged Love on, away from that tugging.

Away from her.

Like she wanted.

*****

His journey back to the hunter's keep was unhindered. He camped at night as he had every night before. He slept inconsistently, and his dreams were consumed with the few days he'd spent knowing his mate. Most men could go their entire lives without *knowing* with certainty who the love of their life was. He'd had the luxury of it. And then . . . having lost her, he nearly wished he could have continued in ignorance.

As he approached the keep, some sense of familiarity cleared part of his mind. He knew this place, and it meant going back to a simple routine. He tried to take comfort in the known.

Bran was in the courtyard training the younger hunters when Kirk rode through the gate. Bran nodded and waved, then crossed his arms over his chest. "Good to see you back."

Kirk slid off Love's back and walked with her toward the stable. "How's training the young ones?"

"Well enough." Bran's good eye searched Kirk's face. One dark brown eye analyzed Kirk, mismatched with one milky white. A scar ran through the side of his face from his forehead, through his eye, splitting apart at his lip and revealing some of his teeth where flesh should be. Bran was a man who'd seen hell and lived to tell the tales. A hunter himself who had served his time and now trained the young ones. "You look weary Kirk."

Kirk sighed and urged Love into her stable. "I am weary, old friend." Kirk felt the digging gaze, knowing well he could hide little from the man who had nearly raised him.

"Tell me of it?"

Kirk shook his head. "Let me take a bath and eat first. You finish up with the children."

*****

As soon as Love was tended to, Kirk found his way to his private quarters, his minimal possessions in a simple room. But a bath . . . that would be like heaven itself. His body ached, and he smelled like death. Days camping did not leave him smelling like a spring day. He prayed a bath might soothe the tensions of his soul.

He tossed his things onto the bed and stripped, his clothes peeling off after being stuck to him by sweat and dirt and blood. He would wash them later.

But even the warmth of the bath could not ease the pain. Washing helped him feel less like an animal, his muscle aches were soothed slightly, but his chest still weighed heavy. He grumbled as he tied up his hair and dried off. Now in a clean shirt and pants with his sword in hand, he headed for the courtyard. He needed to blow off some of this energy.

*****

The wooden practice dummy wobbled as Kirk hacked at it over and over with his sword. He heard steps behind him, his instincts still alerting him to an approaching presence even through the fog that had settled over his mind.

"I thought we were going to speak after you settled in." Bran spoke as he approached, his voice slightly raised to alert Kirk he was behind him. "I've known you long enough, and your patterns are predictable. You're here because something weighs heavy on you."

Kirk did not reply when Bran spoke, he simply turned to face him, watching as his mentor took a guarded step back.

"What happened on the hunt, kid?" Bran pressed.

Kirk sighed and hung his sword as his side. Beads of sweat dripped down his forehead. "The vampire. She—" He looked at Bran a moment, unsure what to say, how to explain what happened when he barely understood it. "She was soul bound."

Bran crossed his arms. He'd gotten grayer.

Every time he saw Bran again, he seemed to have aged years. Those young ones must have been making his life hell. He'd sure made Bran's life hell when he was young.

"Okay? So the mate showed up?" Bran's brow furrowed. "Did she have kids or something? I know it's hard when they have kids—"

"She was bound to *me*." Kirk's voice caught in his throat. The words barely crept out. "She was *my mate*."

"Y-you?" Bran's eyes widened. "The vampire was bound to *you*?" His arms slowly fell from where they were crossed, one hand digging through his hair. "How is that possible? I've never heard of a vampire mated outside their kind—" He looked at Kirk. "For the love of the gods, tell me you didn't let her drink your blood. Kirk, you didn't accept the bond?"

Kirk shook his head. "No . . ."

"And you killed her?"

Kirk paused for a moment. "I did."

Bran grabbed Kirk's shoulder and squeezed tightly. "Not many men could have resisted such a monster. I'm so happy you did. For fuck's sake, I'm so glad you did." He sighed and let his hand drop. "This is why you seem so upset. Of course. Mated to a beast. Thank the gods you had enough sense to kill it before you bound yourself to it. She likely promised you power. That's how the bonds work. Power for blood. But you'd have been bound to a vampire. Souls tied together. Bound to a fucking monster. You'd be nothing but food." He huffed. "I've read once a vampire couple binds, their very lives become entwined. Thank fuck you killed it."

Kirk squeezed the handle of his sword until his fingers turned white. *But I didn't. I tried to run back to her. I . . . still would. If she walked through that gate, I'd collapse before her.* "Bran, it's heavy on my heart. Please. Let me process it for a while."

Bran nodded. "Of course. The magic is strong." He tapped Kirk's shoulder then stepped away. "I'd like to ask more questions soon though. Document this. The first man mated to a vampire. It will go down in our history, Kirk." He smiled softly. "Like you needed *more* of an ego." He laughed. "Our first fire-born in years is also mated to a vampire. Gods. You'll think you're a god."

"I'll keep my feet on earth, Bran. I've learned not to let my ego get out of control. A certain someone beat that out of me long ago."

Bran smiled. "Good. Rest, kid. You've had a rough go."

"I will."

*****

Kirk remained quiet over the next few weeks. He trained. He barely ate. He spent hours in the library, searching through the books about vampiric history, studying how their bonds worked.

But the moment a job request came in, he jumped to take it. To get back onto the hunt. He needed a task, and that was what he was trained for.

He'd been raised since he was a child to be a hunter. It was what his mind and body knew better than anything else. He prayed he could find peace in the familiar work.

Kirk had been sold to the hunters at eight years old. His family needed money, and when his father had heard that a pair of hunters were looking for young men, he was sold quickly in exchange for enough money to feed his siblings for a few days.

Bran had been one of the men who bought him. He was younger then. The scar revealing his teeth was already present, but his hair was darker, his good eye brighter.

Both the other man with Bran that day and the other child they'd purchased were dead now. Arthur, he'd been an old man when he and Bran had come across Kirk, an angry old bastard, bitter after a lifetime of hunting. He'd passed from pneumonia a few winters ago. Arthur had raised Bran in the same way Bran had raised and trained Kirk.

The other child purchased on that same journey had been only a year younger than Kirk. Both had been trained by Bran.

Theon.

The other child.

Had died by Kirk's hand.

Bran refused to sit down for
an entire portrait, except for
the fifteen
minutes he
sat he just
scowled
the whole
time,
refused
to smile

~ 23 ~

CHAPTER 23

KIRK
He thanked the gods and the moon for another job. The thrill of a hunt had long since died. But the distraction, the focus of it, that had remained, and the moon knew he needed something to occupy his mind. When he was a younger hunter, there had been a rush in the chase of a vampire, now it was routine. And routine was exactly what he needed.

Every night, he dreamed of her. He'd wake up swearing he could smell her, feel her, taste her. But every time he opened his eyes, he only felt that emptiness in his soul that she was gone. That'd he'd held the entire world for two nights, and he'd let it slip through his fumbling hands.

He buckled into his gear and packed a bag, his hair pulled into a small knot. His steps through the halls were deliberate, focused. They had to be, or that shadow on his heels would consume him.

He passed Bran out with the young ones again in the courtyard as he made his way to the stables.

Bran glanced up, his coaching paused. "Travel safe, brother."

Kirk nodded and waved. "Give him hell, young ones."

Bran sighed. "Give me an ounce of hell, and you'll have a face like mine, ya hear? Little fucks, don't listen to him." He grumbled and waved flippantly at Kirk.

Kirk laughed softly, though the smile vanished the moment he was out of view. He couldn't fake it a second longer than he needed to.

Once Love was ready to ride, they were headed for Draxmont. A vampire had kidnapped a woman and killed a man. It was a over a week's ride away, and he needed to move swiftly if there were to be any hope that the kidnapped woman might still be alive when he got there. A vampire bold enough to commit crimes like those likely wouldn't have enough control to leave her alive long.

Riding swiftly, he pushed Love toward her limits, only stopping to rest for her sake. He would have pushed himself much harder if not for her.

He made it to Draxmont without much trouble. He'd visited the city before. It was much smaller than Torzen, farther from the travel routes that brought in most of Torzen's gold. Draxmont was mostly a farming community, shepherds specifically, with rolling pastures and fields in all directions from the city. Generally green and flowing, but as winter had rolled in, now white with a thick layer of snow. As he approached, the smell of sheep accosted his nose. In the near distance, sheepdogs barked as they corralled their herds.

A few dogs barked at him as he approached, and a few shepherds waved.

He nodded, most of his face was obscured by the scarf wrapped over it to shield it from the harsh weather. He was no stranger to wary eyes watching as an unfamiliar face rode into town. *Find the local lord, get on the trail, find the girl, kill the vampire.* Kill the vampire. *Elle.* He was supposed to kill Elle.

He could never kill Elle.

As he rode, a flick of black hair caught his attention, and his head whipped to the left. His heart leaped into his throat. A shock ran through his spine to his fingers.

It wasn't her.

Of course, it wasn't her.

For fuck's sake.

The local lord set him on the trail. The male that had been murdered had been the brother of the woman taken. Murdered just outside the eastern border of the city. When it'd been discovered that their home had been torn apart and the sister was missing, a search party had been formed but had come up with no trace of the missing girl.

The lord had clearly written her off as dead, rightly so, but nonetheless, his city was in distress. A vampire was taking young men and women from their homes, and until said vampire was removed, the people could not find rest.

Kirk was hired to find and dispose of the threat. He was to bring a sense of peace, true or illusionary, back to the people of Draxmont.

He set off on the trail. A quick overview of the scene, a quick run through the house, and then he started through the fields, following the lingering scent of vampire. It was subtle, but death, blood, it stayed on the air behind them. *Except her. She smelled of honeysuckle.*

Love knew the scent. She'd been trained to follow it. Her senses were even further honed than Kirk's. She trudged through the snow, her nose hovering just above the ground before her. Kirk's eyes surveyed the rolling hills. *A cave. A building. Something, somewhere to hide and finish off the girl.*

Wherever the vampire lurked had to be hidden enough the human search parties could not locate it. He'd seen parties of six men torn to pieces by vampires; the group was lucky to *not* have found their target.

It was almost comical to consider Elle taking down six grown men . . .

But she ripped a man's heart from his chest.

He searched for magic. Searched for any wards and shields that may have kept the creature's whereabouts hidden.

The sun hit it just right. What he had assumed was a large snow drift shimmered in the light and reflected just the faintest magical aura on the face of the drift.

It wasn't a drift. It was a cave.

Found it.

~ 24 ~

CHAPTER 24

K^{IRK}
He dismounted, speaking in an ancient tongue a command for Love to stay put unless she needed to escape.

She nuzzled his shoulder and huffed. A reply he knew well and had begun to believe meant be *safe and come back.*

He petted her nose once, then drew his sword and began his descent upon the hidden cave. Unsure how much the vampire had or had not seen of his arrival, he moved in at an angle. It was possible the vampire sensed him, though it was unlikely. In their creation, hunters became nearly undetectable to a vampire's sense of smell. However, he'd also heard rumors that *turned* vampires had begun to evolve in new ways. New senses. New magic.

Turned vampires had come up more often in his travels lately.

In the old days, a human-turned-vampire was rare. Vampires worked to keep their bloodlines "clean," and vampires bred like any other animal to add to their numbers. A human turned into a vampire was considered to muddy the waters. Though the females surely would have aided them in their issues bearing children. Female *born* vampires struggled to conceive with vampire males, but any combination of a human-vampire mix seemed to be able to breed like rabbits.

The rise in turned vampires truly marked the decline of the age of the old vampire houses. The concern with bloodlines had lessened. The willingness, or desperation, to turn men into beasts was changing. Though a turn meant the new vampire was no longer food . . .

The turn required a spoken spell before a vampire consumed the blood of the human, then the human had to consume any blood, and quickly, or their mind would collapse with the change. It was all a nasty business. Ugly and brutal.

Much like Kirk's transformation had been.

It was all so complicated. The genetics, the politics. It'd frustrated him when he was a young hunter trying to understand it all. It seemed to complicate what his mind had wished would be simple—kill the monsters. But when monsters were mixed with humans, that simplicity swiftly vanished.

Kill Elle. I was supposed to kill her.

But vampires had complicated his life long before Elle. Never worse than Elle . . . but the damage done had been plenty.

When *he'd* been turned.

And Kirk had killed him.

Focus, for fuck's sake. He continued his approach, the shimmering of the magic veil over the mouth of the cave growing more and more obvious with each step. It was enough to have hidden it from the eyes of men, if they weren't looking too hard or didn't know what it was they searched for. But he was looking for it, and it was almost comically easy to see once observed. This wasn't a highly powerful vampire. Or at least, they'd not chosen to focus their magic on the wall.

They could always be powerful enough they didn't feel the *need* to hide well, but that seemed unlikely since it had tried to hide in the first place.

He wasn't immediately attacked as he approached. It hadn't seen him. He stepped through the false snow and into the mouth of a cave. The cavern ran deep; it was incredibly dark.

Vampires could see clear as day in the dark. A trait that hunters had bred into their own to keep up with their prey.

He stepped cautiously inward, his sword gripped in his hand. He listened intently for any sign of the vampire, of the woman it'd taken, anything.

Sounds came from deeper in the cave. A voice, muffled sounds, footsteps. But none of them clearly human or vampire, which only confirmed his worries. Until he heard a cry—a very human cry. She wasn't dead. Not yet.

He ran.

Between steps, he ignited his sword.

Even vampires burn.

Even Elle would burn.

The vampire's head whipped around as Kirk rushed toward them. A female with black hair. She was taller than Elle. She had red eyes. She wasn't Elle. She wasn't Elle. His mate. It wasn't his mate.

But he hesitated.

He *fucking* hesitated.

And the vampire killed her.

The girl in the vampire's grip died because he hesitated. Because of Elle. Because he couldn't shake her. He needed her. He needed her. He needed her. His mate. His Elle.

He screamed as he brought his sword down on the vampire, driving it into her shoulder.

She screeched as his blade, enchanted and aflame, tore into her.

The girl she'd killed fell into a pile on the floor, her body entirely limp as a pool of blood spread from her.

The vampire collapsed to her knees. Her eyes lifted to Kirk's as he raised his sword.

Those weren't Elle's eyes.

He brought the sword down swiftly against her neck, some of her hair falling as he cut it in the swing. The flames of his sword burned flesh as he separated her head from her shoulders.

The head rolled toward him.

Quickly he knelt beside the human girl, checking for any signs of life, but she was surely dead.

Her eyes were green.

Like Elle's.

What if another hunter had gone after her? What if another hunter had taken Elle's head? What if someone touched her?

He stood and lifted the human girl gently. He had work to do. Get the body back. Burn the vampire to nothing but ash.

He set the girl farther in the cave so the fire he was about to set wouldn't touch her. Her family could bury what was left without his fire damaging her corpse. He'd had families ask him to cremate bodies before. This family might with the pieces of the girl he'd failed to save . . .

He walked back to the vampire and picked up her head before setting it on top of her body, then he did a quick search to make sure there wasn't anything on her that need not be burned.

Then he retreated a few steps, and flames began to dance around his hands.

Even vampires burn.

*****

He rode Love back into town, the body of the human draped over her back. A successful hunt by the expectations they'd set. Bringing her home alive would have only been a bonus. But her death hung heavy on Kirk's heart. She didn't *have* to die. He cursed his own inaction, his own inability. He had to break away from this. Break away from *her*. It was going to kill him.

The family wept at the sight of her as he handed them the body. He was used to this. He'd done this so many times. But this time hurt so much more. He took half of his pay and handed it to the girl's family, and he left town quickly. Normally, he would have treated himself to a mead, stayed in town a night, and enjoyed a local drinkery. But he wanted to distance himself as much as possible. He needed to be in the woods. Try to clear his gods-forsaken head.

She killed to survive.

He killed to protect.

What made them different?

They weren't different.

He made camp once he and Love had made their way into the woods and away from the open pastures, back where he was most comfortable, tucked in the trees.

Sitting beside the fire he created, he stared at the flames dancing in front of him. He got lost in the flickering colors and floating embers. Maybe he'd need magic to break free from his longing. A spell or a mage to release him from his desperation for the vampire. For her. Elle.

His mate.

Humans weren't meant for these kinds of emotions. Human souls were not strong enough to process something so . . . consuming . . . These were emotions of ancients and gods. His mortal soul could not take much more of this.

He wanted her.

He needed her.

After tossing and turning and cursing the moon, he finally fell asleep beside the fire. Finally let rest take him, but it was short-lived.

He shot up. His hand grasped at his chest desperately. His nails dug into the flesh above his heart. *Elle.*

Elle.

Elle.

Elle.

My mate.

The nightmare he'd woken from had been vague. Dark and violent. He'd felt fear unlike any he'd felt before. A fear that every inch of his body was in danger. That was *her* fear. He knew so assuredly that he'd felt *her* fear. He'd been trapped in shifting nothingness while unfamiliar hands grabbed and pulled and tore. While someone else ripped at his . . . *her* very flesh. It was disorienting and unsettling. He couldn't understand where he was, what was happening to him, but he knew he was *afraid.*So fucking afraid. He knew, to his horror, that was how *she* felt . . .

An unfamiliar female voice spoke softly into his mind, just barely audible. *Save her, hunter. Save my child.*

Sweat rolled down his back and his chest, beads running over his muscles, soaking into the fabric of his shirt. He closed his eyes to focus on the breaths that staggered from his lungs.

In. Out. In. Out.

She was in danger. She was in so much danger. And she was afraid. So fucking afraid.

He had to find her.

He had to find Elle.

~ 25 ~

CHAPTER 25

JUNE

June had become a husk of herself. Even with Bliss spending every moment he could trying to comfort her, bring back her light, she'd lost her best friend, her sister. Her ability to deal with the customers of Torzen was slipping, her patience and grace waning *quickly*. She'd relied heavily on Elle's gentle soul to ground her own. She hadn't even realized how deeply she'd come to need Elle. And now she was gone.

It never sat well with June. Elle's leaving felt forced, felt wrong, but she had no idea where the girl had gone. She started researching tracking spells, but she'd wavered on using them once she'd learned them. Elle had *gone*. She had *chosen* to leave them behind for their safety. Would finding her, risking herself and Bliss, only push Elle farther away? Would hunting down Elle, whose bounties were finally cleared with her "death," only endanger Elle more?

Could June give Elle up, or would she have to find her . . . whatever the consequences may be?

Then June heard the rumor. The hunter was spotted riding back toward Torzen. It'd been nearly three months since Elle left.

Had he been as tortured as her? Had the mate of *her* Elle suffered as she had being parted? She'd continued to kindle the flames of her anger toward the hunter. She dropped so much of the blame onto his shoulders to lighten the load she placed on her own. But if he was returning . . .

If he was returning when there was no word of vampires in or around Torzen, was he coming back for Elle? How could he not be? How could someone mated to her not *run* back to her?

So when the hunter darkened her door, she was not shocked. She crossed her arms as he walked across the threshold of her shop. Trying to hide just how much of a mess she was inside, she kept her expression carefully stony.

He looked like shit. Absolute dog shit. The blue of his eyes had dulled. Weariness weighed his face and shoulders. His hair was messily pulled back. He closed the door behind him and scanned the room, verifying they were alone. "Mage."

Her posture did not shift, if anything, somehow she grew stiffer, but she gave him a single nod in greeting. "Hunter."

"She's in danger." He spoke softly.

No. Fear. True and deep fear took hold of her. Reason left her. He was her mate. He would know if Elle was in danger. "Then where the *fuck* is she?" she hissed, her voice on the verge of cracking even as she tried to keep her panic inside.

He shook his head. She swore she saw tears on the edges of his eyes. "I don't know. I don't know. I can't find her. Help me. For the love of the moon, help me find her, June."

*****

The hunter reminded her of her own reflection. They both had lost themselves when Elle left them. She could read it clearly on his face. He'd grown thinner, as she had. He looked as desperate as she felt. He'd told her of his nightmare, of the feelings he knew were real, were Elle's.

Bliss had joined them in Morel as they discussed the months they'd been separated and what they would do next.

June cursed her hesitations. She could have been looking for her; she could have been *searching* for her. She had felt in the pit of her stomach that it wasn't right. That Elle hadn't left. That something was wrong with the girl she loved. When she finally spoke, even her cold tone shook just a bit. "I've learned tracking spells, you're bred to track vampires. We start searching for her. We find her. We *fucking* find her." Her bitterness toward him seeped to the surface again. "And then you stay the fuck away from her."

Kirk lurched forward. "No. No, I will not let her out of my sight again, mage."

She glared at him, anger keeping the tears at bay. "No, you fucking won't. You're the reason I lost her. You are the reason she's fucking gone. You stay the fuck out of her life. Help me find her and disappear. That's what's best for her. Reject the bond, and leave her alone forever, you fucking—"

Bliss grabbed her arm. "That's not your decision to make, babe."

She whipped around, her eyes piercing through him. "He may be her mate, but she was mine for years before he was a part of the picture. And I cannot trust him anywhere near her. I have to protect her. I failed her enough as it is."

He squeezed gently on her bicep. "It's not yours to decide." His hand moved to her cheek, and he pulled her forehead against his lips. "It's for Elle to decide. You . . . you do not understand what a bond with a mate feels like . . . It's for her. All we need to worry about right now is finding her. Getting her safe, okay?"

June's shoulders softened as her lover's lips pressed to her face. "I cannot ask you to leave your home and die for her, Bliss."

He laughed softly, kissing her forehead again. "My home has been at your side for a long time. I'd follow you to hell."

She sighed and rubbed her forehead, glancing back over at the hunter. "Where do we start?"

"We start by tracking her. Finding her. Bringing her home." Kirk stepped toward the table where they'd laid out a map. "After we've found her"—he pointed—"here, Spiritmire. I've traveled to this city before. If we can find her, we can take her there. It's far enough away she won't be found. There are plenty of small farms secluded enough she would never have to speak to another human if she didn't wish to. I've dreamed of retiring there."

"I didn't know hunters retired," June said, looking at the city beneath his finger, then up to him.

"They don't. Why it was only a dream."

June knew as well as he did that hunters didn't retire. Hunters died. They didn't marry, they didn't settle down, their lives began and ended with their hunts. They were created, mutated, and formed for a purpose, and that purpose became all they were.

Kirk spoke softly. "I'd never considered a human life. It was too painful. But now . . . with her . . . those dreams have resurfaced. I want a simple life beside her, mage. She described it to me once, and it's all I can see. A farm, beside her."

~ 26 ~

CHAPTER 26

KIRK

He let hope slip into his heart again. When they found her—if she would have him . . . if she could forgive him—he would buy her a farm. He would build her a home. They could have a simple life. They could have everything. Everything but a child. But he would provide everything else. Once he found her, he could offer it to her. He would drop onto his knees before her and offer her the life she'd described.

Except children.

It was part of the mutation. When hunters were turned into the creatures they were, the ability to sire children was taken from them. Kirk had lived long enough as a hunter that he'd long since given up on the prospect of it. Why yearn for something that he could never have?

The mage was describing to him the spells she'd learned for tracking. They were powerful. They might just lead them close enough to Elle; his hunting skills could handle the rest.

They just had no idea what kind of monsters had her. What kind of danger they were running into to save her.

The three of them would conquer hell for her, but they needed to be prepared if they wanted a chance to bring her home.

It was already growing dark, so they agreed to set out in the morning. None of them anticipated much sleep, but they would need daylight, so they had to suffer one last night before they

177

could begin their hunt for her. Before they could find her and bring her back.

Kirk thanked the mage quietly, his eyes lowered and his voice rough as he tried to reconcile waiting even one night. He'd *never* felt fear like the fear he'd felt from her. Still it lingered on his soul, like a taste on the back of his tongue he could not wash away. This looming shadow of *terror*. He had to find her.

June and Bliss went to pack their things, gather what they needed and what they desired to take. They all knew . . . they wouldn't be returning to Torzen. This was the last June and Bliss would be in their *home*. June gathered and packed components for the spells to find Elle. Get them closer to her at least. Kirk's bond would help.

Kirk excused himself to let them pack, gather their entire lives, mourn if they had to.

He walked back toward the Sunflower. The memories of walking beside Elle were heavy like boulders on his back. If he couldn't find her, or break this bond, he would be crushed.

He was going to crumble beneath this weight.

Kirk stepped into the room at the inn, his shoulders slumping as he looked at the bed. Sleep would evade him. But maybe a bath . . . Maybe it could ease even some of the tension in his shoulders. Who knew when he'd bathe again after they set out to find her. To bring her home.

Home. He would be her home if she allowed him. If she could forgive him. If she could accept him.

He slipped out of his leathers and heated the water as he had once before, then slowly lowered himself into it, his back and shoulders aching as the warmth soaked through the muscles.

He leaned his head back and ran his fingers over the hilt of his sword. He had every part of the design memorized. Every curve. Every line.

Then the door to his room opened.

He stood, his sword in his hand in an instant.

A figure stepped into the room, a hood over her head. She pulled the hood back and looked at him with fear in her bright red eyes.

Her face was familiar.

She was one of Dae's bastards.

She held up her hands defensively, the universal signal that she meant no harm. "Stop!" Her hands shook. "I'm here about your mate. She needs help. I need your help to get her out."

He nearly dropped the sword. "You know where Elle is?"

Part 3

Within The Devil's Walls

$$\sim 27 \sim$$

INTERLUDE

"**N**o. NO!" *Kirk's young hands trembled profusely and tears burned in the corners of his eyes are he stared at his friend, his brother.*

Theon smiled sadly. "Kirk . . . please understand."

"You can't— You didn't. WHAT THE FUCK WERE YOU THINKING?"

They were nineteen.

Theon had just come back. He'd been missing for days. Kirk had lost him during a hunt and had been searching desperately for him. His friend. His brother.

And there Theon was before him.

But he was a vampire.

Theon had become a vampire.

Bran was behind Kirk, his own sword drawn.

Theon had had the balls to come back to the home of the hunters. What had been his home. But it was no longer. It could never be his home again. He'd turned. He'd fucking turned. Why had he returned knowing they would kill him? Had he truly thought he would find an ounce of understanding in the men who trained every day to kill their . . . his kind?

Kirk's heart shattered with the betrayal as he stared into the eyes of one who had become his brother. They were now . . . red. They were fucking red.

Something inside Kirk broke.

Bran's command was clear. "Kill him, Kirk!"

Kirk's hand shook around the sword he carried. This was a test. A test of his loyalty. Of his skills. His friend had betrayed them. His friend had become one of them, and now he needed to end it. He had to end Theon's suffering.

Theon shook his head, his hands raised. "Kirk, I can't fight you. Just listen to me, please. Kirk—"

"Kill. It. Kirk."

Kirk raised his sword.

Theon stared at him with tears in his eyes. Red eyes. "Please listen to me, Kirk."

Kirk shook his head, tears streaming down his own cheeks. "I'm sorry."

And he brought his sword down.

~ 28 ~

CHAPTER 28

E LLE
The night she was taken.

She was escorted to a room. She had assumed it would be a dungeon cell at first. She hadn't expected a bed, a proper room. She had been taken. She had been cursed. By the Lord of Blood. Dae. She was his prisoner, locked in that room.

The mark seared into her chest burned.

The carvings in the frame of the large bed in the corner were intricate. Dark red bedding draped over the mattress. The colors matched the canopy that hung over the top, deeply swooping down in the middle. The art lining the walls was nearly as old as the castle itself. Images of vampire history, vampire lords. Dae's face was in some, what appeared to be his ancestors were in others. A large mirror and a vanity occupied the opposite side of the room from where she stood. Under different circumstances, she might have considered the room beautiful, she might have admired it. She would have studied the art with eager eyes. It was her people's history that surrounded her. But she couldn't see anything beautiful in the room, not as things were then. It was a prison. A beautiful cell. Magic wards locked every window and the door. She was trapped.

She could only leave when *he* allowed.

But he was worse than her prison could ever be. It would be better to die in that room.

After the curse had been sealed, after she'd become his, he'd simply had servants drag her away. The punctures on her neck had already begun to close. She'd fought the servants at first, shoved against her captors, but then, when the curse had sealed, she'd felt that power, that phantom grip around her blood. It had become stronger. As she'd fought, searing pain had twisted through her veins, and she'd crumbled. They'd pulled her to her feet, wrenching her off the ground as she writhed. A sharp glare from Dae had made it clear, if she continued to resist that pain would continue, that pain would increase. Tears had run down her cheeks. She'd tasted her own blood in her mouth . . .

Then she'd been taken to that room.

The room was one of their *spare* rooms in the castle. For a moment, she wondered how grand the main rooms were, quickly praying that she may never come to find out.

Dae's power was great enough, he hadn't needed to be present to set the spell that locked her in the room. From where he was in his office, he'd simply . . . created it.

The fear in her stomach weighed heavy; the realization of what had just happened pounded in her heart.

She knew of curses; she knew well of being bound against one's will. Only ancient vampires, vampires with incredible amounts of power, could create such bonds and maintain them. His words echoed in her mind. *The bloodline.* She didn't know what bloodline he referred to. She had no idea where she'd come from. As a babe, she'd been dropped off with a couple. A human man and his vampire partner. They'd raised her, unaware of her history themselves. She wondered if she'd read of the bloodline before, who she was that her lineage mattered to Dae. Who exactly had left her in the care of the males who'd raised her. But Elle's curiosity was quickly outweighed by dread. Somewhere she knew that whatever his intentions around her bloodline . . . she would hate finding out what he meant.

She wondered what June thought. Where June thought she was. She prayed June was safe. Kirk was safe. She wondered what Kirk thought. She'd run away, and now she'd vanished. He might assume she'd run from him. Of course, he would assume it. He would leave town. He would forget her completely . . . maybe. Thinking of him made her soul ache, made her stomach twist. It hurt to think of him. It hurt to feel the void where he should be at her side.

The door opened and she turned.

The male who'd taken her stood in the doorway. "I need something from you. Come." He walked toward the vanity. In his hands were a paper and a pen, ink balanced with them. "You can write, yes?"

She stared at him, unable to will her feet to move, unsure if she wanted to in the first place. "I-I can."

He sighed and gestured her over again. "Now. Come here *now*," he growled. "I need you to handle this quickly so I can return." He laid the paper on the vanity and pointed at it. "A letter. To the mage."

Elle's hands trembled as she stepped once toward him, then halted again when he mentioned June. "Saying what?"

"That you've left. I will also read it. And I will make you rewrite it as many times as I fucking must if you try to write anything else. We don't need anyone looking for you. Don't need any trouble. And this way, she's not going to get herself killed. It keeps her safe if you tell her not to look for you. I *assure* you this."

Elle hesitated, but she sensed no deceit in the male's tone. He was right. Keeping June away from this would keep her safe. She had to write something that would convince June she'd left . . . and she'd have to break their bond. She was the captive of a male who could control the blood in her veins, the oldest remaining vampire lord. She needed June to stay as far away as possible.

Something in her heart shattered as she wrote the letter. Tears fell onto the page and left spots on the paper. She handed it to the male who watched her every move, and his eyes ran over each line.

"This will do." He nodded. "I appreciate your participation, princess, makes this much simpler." He folded the paper. "Dae has requested you ready for dinner in an hour."

"Ready for—?"

He pointed at a wardrobe. "There's a dress in there for you. Get dressed. In that. I'd advise you do as he requests, and look your *best*, and he might go easier on you." He looked her up and down once. "He's quite eager." He turned and exited before she could speak again, the door closing hard behind him.

She took a breath before she removed the dress from the wardrobe. She stared down at it, then she held it up in front of herself in the vanity mirror.

The room was so quiet it was deafening. She'd never felt an emptiness like this.

Elle sat in the stool before the vanity and braided her hair carefully around her head in a crown. In a drawer, she found pins for her hair, each with a ruby on the end. She pinned up any loose strands. In another drawer, she found makeup, and she painted her lips the same red as the pins, then lined her eyes with black to emphasize the bright green.

She wondered if Dae had someone watching June. If he would harm her if she rebelled against him. They knew she was important to Elle. They knew to write a letter to slow down her search for her. She'd heard rumors of Dae before . . . read about him in books as a child. He could use her pain, could use what she loved to control her. Whatever he wanted from her was his to take.

He owned her. She'd felt owned before, by men, by the money she needed to survive, by the eyes of the patrons while she danced, but nothing like this . . . nothing ever like this. This was magic, ancient magic that penetrated her very bones. She felt it in every inch of her body, every flake of her skin and strand of her hair. None of it was her own. She belonged to someone else, and that monster had dark intentions.

She stripped to get into the dress and caught sight of the curse mark in the mirror, a dark brand etched into her chest, black against her porcelain skin. The mark of his cursed bond.

Elle dressed herself in the pale cream-colored dress he'd left for her. It fit closely over her chest and back, cutouts in the fabric revealed her hips, and golden chains connected the front fabric to the back, hanging in draping swoops over her thighs. The neckline dove deep below her breasts, nearly to her stomach. A golden chain that matched those on her thighs hung just at her collarbone. The seal on her chest on grand display. Rubies lined the shoulders and neckline. She'd never seen so many gems in one place, even when she'd danced in great halls . . . She'd never seen gems like this; another reminder of the age and the power of the vampires in this castle, wealth like she had never seen accumulated here.

Dae had left a necklace as well. The same rubies pulled tightly against her neck in a design that looked like he'd slit her throat, and she bled the deep red gems down the side of her neck. Earrings that matched hung from her ears and felt heavy as they pulled her closer to hell.

She looked in the mirror once more. She was dressed as his prize. A new possession to show off. A demonstration of his power and a shiny new toy.

*****

The door opened after an hour, and she turned. Her breath left her chest as her eyes landed on him. The room immediately grew darker in his presence, the shadows came in closer, and she felt like the air in the room had been sucked away.

He strode toward her, a smiling curling on his lips as he came nearer. "Come."

As the *thought* to stand still, to disobey even a moment, began to form in her mind, pain shot through her. His power clenched the muscles in her neck and shoulders, and she held in a small scream. She stepped toward him instinctively to make the pain stop.

As she stepped into his reach, he grabbed her arm and ripped her to his side, his nails digging into her flesh. "I've gathered my court to meet you, darling. Behave," he whispered harshly into her ear, the cool and collected monster she'd met once still replaced by the cruel devil who had torn her neck to pieces.

She could only nod and follow.

*****

The main dining room, like the other rooms in the castle, was adorned with hundreds of years of vampire art and history. It would take years to understand it all, to truly dig into every detail in each room. A dining table surely once used for great vampire feasts ran down the center. An intricately embroidered runner lined the entire length of it, and before each of the few vampires seated at this table were golden place settings. Elle had never seen wealth like this on such display.

Here sat the last of Dae's court. Some of the last of the great high vampires. Their numbers had dwindled dramatically over the years, their families ravaged by humans, by each other . . . by Dae. Elle knew so little of these vampires, but she could see by how they held themselves, their body language, their posture, they were of old blood. There was an ancient air about them. They had lived many times over the lives of men. There were only five now seated at that table. Only a whisper of what had been.

Closest to Elle was a female, her hair white as fresh snow and cut short just below her ears. Her features were sharp, and her gaze was piercing. The sleeves of her deep blue dress rested off her shoulders. The bodice was fitted tightly against her slender frame. Golden lace traced the dress's neckline and wrapped around the waist, only further accentuating the hourglass shape of her body. A golden necklace hung just above her breasts with earrings to match that hung to her jawline.

Beside her sat two more, another female and a male, both with features like hers and the same pure white hair.

The second female looked younger than the first, though it was hard to tell around vampires. Her white hair hung far down her back, and her eyes were brighter than the first's, hungrier. Her dress was simple, black, less gaudy than the elder's but equally stunning. Like the blue, her shoulders were exposed, and the lace at the neckline and shoulders was white. A black lace choker rested tightly around her throat, a cross hanging from its center.

The male's hair was nearly as long as the younger female's, gracefully hanging down past his shoulders. His hair brushed his exposed chest, the neckline of his white shirt plunged nearly as low as Elle's. She knew him. He was the male who had taken her. The one who had stalked her through the streets and brought her here. The very same who'd had her write June's letter . . .

How had he made it to Torzen and back so swiftly?

He leaned back in his chair, his arms crossed, his eyes—until Dae and Elle entered—rested on the younger female, who seemed to babble on about something he appeared to be entirely disinterested in.

In her head, Dae spoke harshly, his voice in her mind as clear as if he were speaking out loud. *Saturn and her horrendous children, Silas and Venus.*

Next was another female. She was so young. She could only be eighteen. She did not carry herself like the old bloods who had had hundreds of years to grow bitter. She was nervous, inexperienced in life. She shared many of Dae's features. Her nose and her eyes mirrored his, her face shape was a more feminine version of his. Her dress was simple, out of place in the grandeur of the dining room, and her hair was tightly braided. Dirt lined the hem of her skirt and collected beneath her fingernails. She did not fit in this hall. She seemed much more fitted to wherever it was she'd been before, wherever she *clearly* wished to return to. Her eyes darted to the door often. Her hands fidgeted with her skirt. Everything about her said she longed to leave. Desperately.

Beside the nervous female was another male. He sat straight in his chair, his posture the only indication he was even slightly engaged in the room. His eyes were darker than the rest, like beneath them a light had long since died. His face was a perfect copy of Dae's. His shoulders and chest, however, were much broader. Had he been standing, he likely would have towered over the male Elle could only assume was his father. His clothes were simple, leather pants and a white shirt. He clearly had little concern for his father's affairs.

Dae's voice echoed in her head again. *Two of my bastard children. Clementine and Suho. Suho's my eldest.*

Dae flippantly motioned around the room as he walked to his seat at the head of the table. "I loathe a dinner with you all as much as you all loathe one with me, but introductions were due." His hand drifted to Elle. "She who will bear the next era of vampires is finally home."

Elle's throat closed up. So that was what he'd meant. Pureblood heirs. Her heirs. She looked at the other vampires a moment, her eyes locking with the bastard girl, Clementine, desperate for answers no one at this table could give . . . would give. Who was she? Who was she to him? Why did her heirs hold enough value for Dae to take her?

She stood beside the chair at the head of the table, her hands trembling. He sat and motioned for her to sit on the armrest. His hand was frozen against her back.

"You're not eating just yet, princess," he whispered. "Just watch and be a good little pet." He addressed the table of vampires before him. "Tonight, we're celebrating the return of my darling princess." His hand wrapped around her waist, his nails tearing into her side and blood running over his fingers.

The woman, Saturn, glared. Her two children seemed to care very little about the announcement. About Elle's presence at all. Suho's gaze was empty. The only vampire at that table who seemed concerned for Elle was the young one. Clementine. Her eyes held so much fear.

"Dinner," Dae announced and snapped the fingers not embedded in Elle's flesh.

Human and lesser-vampire servants brought women into the room. Each woman was naked, some were shaking, some were weeping, some silently looked into the eyes of their own death.

Dae removed his hand from Elle's side and licked his fingers slowly. Lines of her blood ran over his mouth and chin. He looked back over the table of his people. "Enjoy your dinner. I've selected only the best for my *family*." The word was said with such hatred for everyone in the room. His eyes ran up and down Elle, taking in the flesh she was entirely sure he intended to destroy. "I . . . have other things to attend to."

A chill ran down Elle's spine. They weren't staying for dinner.

"My darling and I shall eat *alone*." He stood and grabbed her arm.

The tremors worsened. The fear in her stomach was now entirely consuming her.

Dae's eyes moved to her throat, his gaze following the trail of blood-red rubies, then he walked toward the hall at the end of the room. "Come." His grip did not lighten as he pulled her along.

She hesitated. She hesitated because whatever was about to happen . . . Her feet faltered. She couldn't do it. She couldn't follow him. He was going to—

In front of the court, he grabbed her throat and pulled her toward him. "Do not linger when I've said *come*, princess." Blood dripped down her neck, his nails cutting into her flesh and the rubies beneath his hand tearing into her skin. He released her and continued walking out, not glancing back at the group, knowing she was following.

She glanced over her shoulder. Her eyes met Clementine's once more.

*****

He closed the door.

His room was enormous, completely and utterly enormous. A grand bed was centered on the wall opposite the door, deep red curtains around it tied at the supports of the frame with thick golden rope. Paintings on the walls, reaching nearly from the floor to the ceiling, depicted graphic scenes of violence: Vampires tearing humans apart. Women ripped to shreds with blood rolling down their naked bodies. Demons surrounded by billowing clouds of darkness, blood dripping from their claws and fangs. Ancient weapons with dried copper stains accompanied the horrific artwork on the walls.

A carved wooden desk, a bottle of wine and a glass atop it, was on one side of the room, a dresser beside a large mirror on the other. A doorway led to an attached room.

A rug of a beast's fur rested on the floor before the bed, but she couldn't identify what manner of monster it had belonged to. It was larger than she'd even known monsters to be . . .

His grip on her arm released, and he shoved her toward the bed.

She stumbled, desperately trying to regain her footing. "Please . . . please don't do this . . . *please.*" Her eyes rose to his. Her voice cracked as she begged, growing louder as the panic set in. She grew cold, sweat beading her neck and in her palms. He was going to rape her, and she couldn't run from him. She wasn't going to escape it. She couldn't

His hand rose only slightly, and she crumpled to the floor.

Screaming, she curled inward as her blood twisted in her veins, an instinct to shield herself from whatever was attacking, though her attacker was inside her own skin. She vomited as the pain overwhelmed her, and her mind went blank in agony.

He released her.

She lay on the ground, panting and sobbing as the fire and tension stopped. The pain dulled only slightly when his grip released.

"Get up." His voice was stone.

Elle stood slowly. Her knees shook and her stomach turned as the fact that she couldn't stop this barreled through her mind. It wasn't going to stop. Anxiety, fear, anger all boiled up in her throat. She felt dizzy. Her whole body was shaking. She looked at him once. He stood, silent and still, watching her. Her eyes darted back to the floor; she couldn't hold his gaze for long.

With a flicker in his red eyes, he became something else entirely. The ancient and composed creature who had been watching her was gone, replaced by one more like an animal. Feral and cruel.

He grabbed her hair tightly in one hand, wrenching her head to the side as he bit deeply into her neck.

She screamed.

He dragged his teeth through her skin, tearing her throat open as his fangs ripped down. Blood dumped from the wound, the cream color of her dress quickly as red as his eyes.

He licked at the wound, sucked at it. There was no savoring of the blood, only desperate hunger. He tore at the dress next, his claws ripping at the fabric and tearing it from her, his nails catching her pale flesh beneath and cutting her as he stripped her entirely naked. She reached up to fight against him, but that familiar pain began to surge. He would drop her again. He would twist her blood again if she resisted.

He stepped back when the last of the dress fell into the blood on the floor. Her neck had started to heal, but the blood had already run down her collar and over her chest.

Dae stared at her a moment. Her entire body was bared to him. She shook uncontrollably. Tremors ran down her spine as his eyes moved over her. Every instinct told her to run, to fight him, to scream for help, but she couldn't. Her fear held her completely still. He was going to kill her. He was going to rape her, and he was going to kill her.

On the bed. His voice in her mind was loud enough that she winced and covered her ears.

She couldn't make her feet move. She couldn't.

I said on the fucking *bed, whore.*

She stumbled toward it.

As he approached, she heard his jacket hit the floor when he dropped it from his shoulders.

On your back, he commanded.

Her arms rattled as she climbed onto his bed. *Fuck. Fuck fuck fuck fuck fuck fuck fuck. No, please. Gods. Someone help me. Please someone help me. Please please please. Kirk. Kirk, help me. Please. Kirk. June. Anyone. I'm so sorry. I'm so sorry. Help me. Help me, please. Please. Please. For the love of the moon, someone help me.*

I said, on your fucking back. He was on his knees on the bed, and he grabbed her shoulder. His nails dug in, and he threw her back onto the bed.

Her knees were pressed tightly together, her hands wrapped around her stomach. She stared up at him. He was fucking *feral.* She'd never felt dread like she did at that moment. "Dae. Please. Please, let me—" The next scream that ripped from her lungs echoed through the halls of the castle.

Dae drove his nails into her chest, directly through the seal between her breasts. He leaned closer, drawing his fingers together. His nails tore deep gashes through her skin. *Did you know this seal can't be destroyed?* As the wound started to heal on the edges, the seal seared itself into her skin again. *I can rip it off over and over, and it will keep coming back, burning exactly as it did when I put it there.*

Her eyes burned with tears. Her breaths were short and shallow. She felt like he was crushing her lungs under the weight of his hand. *Please stop.*

He dragged his nails down, stopping just below her breasts. *Listen to me, little princess. This.* His hand hovered over her stomach. *This I cannot harm. I cannot risk damaging that precious little womb. But the rest of you?* He leaned closer to her face. Her blood dripped from his chin onto her hair. *The rest of you, I can destroy.*

Dae cut her. Over and over he cut her. Her arms, her legs, her chest, her face, everywhere. Over and over and over he cut her. He drank the blood that poured from her. A small dagger in his hand cut deep gashes through her, a twisted smile on his face as he watched the blood bubble from the damage he inflicted. He dug his fingers into the wounds, tearing her apart from the inside. His claws shredded her skin, her muscle, sinew, every piece of her, torn apart.

She screamed for a while, but her screams faded as she lost her voice. She couldn't scream any longer. Her body tried to heal . . . but it slowed as she lost more and more blood. Her voice became hoarse from screeching, from begging him to stop. Consciousness began to leave her. Blackness started to creep in from the corners of her vision. She began to pray for it. Beg for the darkness to consume her. Release her, even if only for a moment. She couldn't bear the torment any longer.

He forced her legs apart.

She did not have strength to resist. But it wouldn't have mattered if she had.

She hadn't noticed when he'd unlaced his pants, when he'd slipped them down and released his erection.

Her screams brought him pleasure. Her body contorted in pain only amplified that pleasure.

Hands and knees. Now.

Someone save me. She tried to turn herself, but her limbs could no longer move. She was weak enough, she did not know how she would ever stand again. Every wound trying to heal took more energy than she had to give.

He grabbed her hips and dug his nails into her skin. He flipped her over and shoved her, jolting her hips up and back. His hands moved to her sides near her stomach, his nails dug deeply into her flesh again, and he forced her back against himself.

She dug her elbows into the bed and tried to stifle a sob, but it escaped her throat. She pressed her forehead into the bed. Once they released, the sobs could not be stopped. "Stop this. Please." Her voice was only a whisper.

Blood dripped over his fingers and into small pools beneath her hips.

Please. Please. Stop. Please. Someone. Help me. Please.

~ 29 ~

CHAPTER 29

THE HOUSE OF BLOOD

As they ate, the vampires left in the dining room discussed the new guest in the castle. Plotting and processing the return of the Lady of the House of Bone. A lost princess they'd all assumed dead. Her parents, their entire house, had been murdered by Dae. That was what they'd all known with certainty, Dae included, until Silas had seen her and brought her there.

The house had threatened Dae. Their power was greater than his own, and Elle and her brother Theo . . . they were Dae's greatest threat. When Dae had learned of Elle's birth, he'd proposed an alliance between the houses through marriage, had requested Elle as his wife. However, her parents had refused.

Dae had hired hunters and mercenaries to attack the family. Elle's parents, the infant Elle, and her young brother had fled, only escaping for a few weeks before they were found and killed.

Or so they'd assumed.

Dae had sought to eliminate the threat of Bone when they had refused the alliance. He'd needed to snuff out their house before they came after his.

But she had not died. The Princess of Bone. The female heir who could bring forth powerful vampires. She had lived, and here she was again, within Dae's grasp, and within his walls.

First, Saturn turned to her children, Silas and Venus, who were both preoccupied with the blood pouring into their mouths.

Saturn watched as Silas sighed heavily. His hand was wrapped tightly around the waist of one of the women, and as the wound he'd torn into her neck bled down her chest, he sucked and nipped at her breast. She knew eating was such a sensual experience for Silas, combining his food and his pleasure. But she also knew her glare was ruining his enjoyment.

"What?" He spoke harshly, releasing the woman to crumple onto the floor beside him, her knees on the ground and her arms and head falling into his lap.

"You're going to have to fuck the princess," she snapped.

Silas rolled his head, now petting the barely conscious woman in his lap. "I have no interest in fucking Dae's whore, Mother."

"I do not care about your interest in her. You, my son, must father a child with that whore and further our bloodline." Her whispers were harsh, using the screams and sobs from the other room to hide her voice from Dae's children on the far end of the table. She had already begun her plotting, how to get her son close to the princess, how she would elevate her family with the blood of the House of Bone. Maybe . . . maybe gain enough power to free herself from Dae. Her house had been shattered so long ago. If Silas could impregnate the little bitch for their family . . .

Venus seemed entirely disinterested in her mother's plotting, her own attention on the woman in her brother's lap, her eyes running over the pale body. Hungry.

"My experiments . . ." Silas groaned.

"They can continue," she whispered, her tone cruel. "I only ask this simple task of you. Do not fail your mother."

*****

Clementine stood after several moments sitting in the heavy air of the room. She'd lingered as long as she could stand it, waiting long enough she knew her father was far from view—and far from earshot. Brushing her dress down, she lifted from her chair and turned to leave the hall.

Suho gently grabbed ahold of her arm. "Have you eaten, my sister?"

She looked back and him, then shook her head. "I'll eat later."

He motioned toward the women. "Eat. Your dog can wait."

Clementine pulled free of his grasp, initial annoyance shifting to defeat. "I said I'll eat later, Suho. It's fine."

"Fine. Give my best to the mutt."

~ 30 ~

CHAPTER 30

ELLE

Dae threw her off the bed. *To your room*, he hissed in her head. *One of the servants will take you.*

She lay on the floor for a moment, unable to force herself to her feet. Her dress was in pieces, all of those beautiful rubies scattered on the floor around her, and drowning in pools of her blood. She shuddered against the cold air in the room, shuddered against the harsh collision with the floor. At least his hands were no longer on her . . . At least right now there was some space between them. She tried to get to her feet again, but she nearly failed as her strength wavered and her fear nearly buckled her knees. She screamed as his power coursed through her blood, as she felt like he was crushing her from the inside out.

Get out! He screamed.

She stumbled to her feet when his power released her and hurried toward the door as quickly as her shaking knees would allow.

Dae said nothing as she left the room.

*****

A human servant stood outside Dae's door.

Elle appeared in the hall as she pushed the door open, naked and shaking. Her body was covered in blood, some fresher, some dried to her skin. Red and purple marks indicated wounds that had already begun to heal. Her arms were crossed over her breasts, and her chest caved inward.

When she realized Elle was entirely bare, the servant looked around for something to cover her with. She spotted a cloth draped over one of the tables in the hall and hurriedly grabbed it. As she wrapped it around Elle's shoulders gently, her hands grazed her skin and she felt the girl trembling. She pulled the cloth tightly around her, trying to catch a glimpse of the girl's eyes.

They were dull, a shattered heart behind them, only a dimly flickering light left.

"Come now, little one. We need to get you to your room." She ushered Elle down the hall.

Elle said nothing as she followed.

*****

Elle was left alone in that room the rest of the night.

The same servant brought her fresh clothes to change into, a pair of pale pink silk shorts with a matching top.

Elle managed to dress herself before she collapsed onto the floor. She wept that day. She wept so very much that day. She lay on a rug made of a beast's skin and fur, and she wept. The seal Dae had left on her chest burned. Every wound he'd caused, everywhere his hands had touched, it all felt like his fangs continuing to devour her whole. She lay on that floor, debating if death would be simpler. Debating if this torture could be survived . . . if maybe she could escape. But darkness tapped at her mind, a foreign voice whispering torment to her.

Would Kirk forgive her if she wasn't strong enough? Would he forgive her if her strength failed and she died there? *He will move on.* He would leave Torzen and keep living, safe and happy as he should be. That was all that mattered to her. Maybe he would find another woman, a beautiful *human* woman, who would hold him close and love him as he deserved to be loved. She prayed if she did not survive, it would not hurt him. That he would not feel it in their bond if she passed, and he would be able to live on. She didn't know what the effects of the bond would be, especially since he was human. She didn't know what he would feel should she succumb to the darkness. But she prayed he could forget her. She . . . would never be able to forget him.

If she escaped—if she managed to get free—would he even want whatever pieces of her would be left?

He won't, that foreign voice whispered in her head. It sounded like her own, but it . . . wasn't. It could take years to find him. He may simply hate her. Kirk may kill her. She had lied to him, and she had run from him. She had revealed her lies, revealed every deceit, then she'd fled. If she were to see him again, she would only be a husk of what he'd known. This body was not hers anymore. It was stained. It was broken.

What if she did bear Dae's children? Would she be able to abandon her own children to *him*? No. No, of course not. Absolutely not. If she was forced to bear a vampire child that carried his blood, she could never leave them with him. She could never leave them in his grasp, to whatever torture he would have them endure. But escape with a child? If she were pregnant when she managed to find a way out . . .

He would never allow this to end with her running off into the distance with his blood in her arms, with his heir in her womb. And if she somehow managed to return to Kirk, with Dae's child pressed against her breast, how could she ask him to accept her? How could she ask Kirk to take her, and another man's child, in? She could not return to June with a child. She could not return to June with Dae on her heels. She could not endanger them. All of this—all of this only assuming she could find an escape in the first place. She could only hope. She could only pray and beg the moon that she did not bring forth Dae's children . . .

Vampire pregnancies were longer than a human. They lasted twelve months, but while the gestational period was longer, the child would mature quickly, grow quickly. She felt her body grow colder. He wasn't going to waste time. She begged the moon, begged the human gods, anyone to save her from her fate.

How was she supposed to stave off despair? The fear? How was she supposed to fight it and survive?

She needed to get out. If she wanted to survive, she needed to get out.

*****

Early in the morning, a knock on the door echoed in the room. She still lay on that same rug, unable to lift herself from the floor, her limbs weak and numb. She did not move when the knock sounded. She did not turn as the door opened.

A female entered and sighed softly. Light footsteps padded against the stone of the floor. "You need to eat." The voice was unfamiliar.

She did not turn to face them.

"Here." There was a small clatter of a glass against the table by the door. "Eat." The female turned to leave. the door creaked as she opened it. "You remind me . . . of my mother." And with that, she closed the door behind her.

*****

Only when he'd raped her had his torment seemed less calculated and more animalistic. He'd torn her apart. He was cruel. He was vicious. He'd savored every moment. He relished her screams, her pain. It'd only brought him further pleasure.

Elle knew, she knew with certainty, that if he did not wish to possess the children she'd bear, he would have already killed her. He would have killed her, and he would have *luxuriated* in it. His voices in her head did not cease, they would not end. His power was immense. He could bend blood, twist it, burn it, and he could do greater damage in a mind.

She was starting to believe that somehow the legends of the Lord of Blood were *less* than the male himself. She began to feel that the stories did not make him seem grander than he was, as most legends often did, but that they paled in comparison to the true nature of his cruelty. The legends romanticized the devil that now held her captive.

Elle stood. She didn't know exactly how long she'd lain there. She walked to the table by the door and took the glass the girl had left behind. She wondered what kind of magic kept the blood in the glass warm . . . She quietly thanked the moon for it and sipped slowly. If she was going to survive this, whatever survival looked like, she would need all the strength she could summon. If she ever hoped to return to Kirk, June, even just to see them once more, she had to survive this. Tears ran down her cheeks, and she stared into the cup in her hands.

~ 31 ~

CHAPTER 31

ELLE

The next day, Elle was lying in the bed when she heard a knock on the door. What else was she to do than sit, lie down, let her thoughts spin out of control. Yet another way Dae seemed determined to break her.

Elle sat up as the door opened.

The girl, Clementine, stood in the doorway, another glass in her hand. She stared at her for a moment. Her eyes locked on Elle were haunted, as if seeing into her own past. "May I . . . come in?" Her voice shook. Her features were so much like her father's.

Elle only nodded in reply. She did not know this girl. She could be as bad as her father. She could be cruel like him . . . She was his daughter. A child of the monster who kept them all captive here. A future vision of what Elle would bring forth, broken children who carried his face. Elle wondered why she reminded Clementine of her mother. She dreaded finding out.

Clementine set the glass on the table beside Elle's bed. "Forgive me . . . You just should eat. It'll help keep your strength up."

The young vampire seemed unable to break away from Elle's gaze.

"Why . . . me?" Elle finally spoke, her voice weaker than she thought it would be.

The girl swallowed and shifted on her feet. "You really don't know who you are? You looked lost yesterday. I just assumed it was, because he'd taken you." She motioned to the edge of the bed, and when Elle nodded in approval, she perched there. "You're the heir of a vampire house Dae destroyed."

Destroyed. Elle's head tilted. "What house?"

"You belonged to the House of Bone. A house that was growing far more powerful than my father's . . . and he had your parents assassinated after they . . . denied him your hand."

"My hand?" *This male has known of me, tried to claim me, before . . .*

"When you were a babe. I only heard about it from Suho when he was explaining our father's history, so I don't know . . . much. But Suho told me that Father asked to marry you when you were only a small baby, and your parents denied him. He retaliated by having them killed. He assumed you had been killed as well . . ."

Someone saved me. Someone brought me to Ben and Lio. I wonder how much they knew. How much of who I am they had knowledge of.

Clementine observed Elle's face a moment. "You look like your parents from the books. I've seen drawings of them in some of the historical writings . . . You look like your mother."

"My mother?" Elle had known she had parents somewhere. She'd known she'd come from *somewhere*, but this . . . this was not what she had ever dreamed of. It was all so overwhelming. It was all too much. She felt her mind and her heart growing heavy. Her vision blurred. It was too much. It was too much.

Clementine's back tensed. "My lady, you're a powerful vampire. More powerful than Dae. He wishes to breed that into his children. Control you. Please. Please be strong. I'll keep bringing you food. I'll come back. I promise." She stood and hurried toward the door. "He's coming my lady. Be strong. Please," she whispered as she ducked out of the door.

Elle stared at the warmed glass on her bedside table. An ancient house. Powerful bloodlines. Dae had desired her for so long . . .

This was why she'd been disguised as a human. Why her teeth had been filed. Her eyes permanently changed. It was all to keep her safe from him. To keep her safe from Dae. She had once be-lieved it was some attempt to keep her safe from humans, that her parents, when they had left her with these spells, had sought to protect her from men. But it had never been men. It was *him.*

And it was all for nothing.

*****

A few moments later, Dae opened the door.

The sight of him froze her in place. Already his power over her was entirely immobilizing.

He raised a hand as he stepped into the room and motioned her to stand. The sight of his hand brought back every memory of what those hands had done. What would those hands do next? They were her destruction, slow and painful. Those nails . . . those nails and everything they had torn apart. She shuddered from the memory of her body being shredded between those claws.

She stood, shaking but not moving toward him. She would not move toward him until he commanded it. It was only a slight re-bellion, the smallest stand against him, that she would only do ex-actly as he commanded. She would not move toward him without the call. She had to resist. She had to so she didn't give him any more power than he already held over her. She had to. She had to do anything she could to retain any feeling of autonomy.

He stepped forward, eyes falling to the glass of blood on the table then returning to her. "We really must do something about these . . ." Suddenly, he was close enough she felt his breath on her face. She blinked, confused since she hadn't seen him move. He was just . . . before her. He grabbed her chin and pulled her face up to his. "These eyes are such an awful green. A disgrace to your house. And those teeth." He tilted her head and ran his thumb un-der her lip and over her teeth, exposing her filed fangs. "I can't have you looking like this. You're disgusting."

She couldn't pull her face from his grasp. She only stood, silently cursing him in her mind over and over.

"Have you already forgotten?" he hissed as he leaned closer, brushing his teeth over her cheek. "I can hear every one of your thoughts when I touch you, and those really are such awful things to think about me. Especially when I'm about to make you beautiful again." His nails dug into her cheeks, and he bit her neck, tearing at her skin then running his tongue over the wounds. As he pulled away, blood dripping down his chin, he spoke again. "You taste so much sweeter when you're afraid." He wiped the side of his mouth with the back of his hand, smearing her blood across his cheek. "Now, about these eyes."

With no further warning, she felt his mind enter hers. Like shadows that quickly overtook her entirely. The curse burned into her chest rendered her useless against him. She couldn't resist as he swept into her consciousness and covered it in darkness.

She heard him whispering. Her vision was gone. It had become black. She only felt him, only heard him. His grip on her face did not waver.

"Just have to find whatever spells your parents used . . ."

Elle screamed as he dug deeper. Her knees buckled.

He held her upright by her face, his nails digging farther into her cheeks. "There."

She felt his mind grab ahold of something within her own. A wall she'd never known was there. The mask. The spells her parents had placed over her to protect her. To hide her from Dae. They were so old, nearly eighty years, that they'd been grown over in her mind. The walls had become part of her. Breaking them could break her being, could break parts of her mind.

And that was what it felt like when he crushed those walls. Like he destroyed a part of her and simultaneously freed a monster that had been trapped for years.

Elle collapsed against his grip. Her eyes rolled back into her head, and she screamed again. More.

He dropped her.

She grabbed her head as she continued to scream. Her knees collided with the floor, and she doubled over, pressing her forehead into the ground beneath her. The stone was cold against her face, but nothing could draw her from the spiral in her head. Blood dripped from her nose and her eyes as the walls that had changed her physically shattered in her mind. Her body was shifting back. Her eyes burned. Her teeth ached.

Finally the anguish ended, but she remained on the ground, panting, with her hands still tangled in her hair and her forehead against the floor.

He squatted beside her, grabbed ahold of her hair, and yanked her head back. "Show me."

Her eyes met his.

A cruel smile spread on his lips. "Oh, that's so much better."

Fangs that had not been there for so many years brushed against the tip of her tongue as she panted before him.

"Such a lovely red those eyes are. Much more fitting of our vampire princess, don't you think, darling?" He let out a small groan, and he ripped her head up toward his, pressing his lips violently against hers.

Then was the second time he raped her.

~ 32 ~

CHAPTER 32

ELLE

Dae did not return on the next day.

On the third day, she grew sick. Elle could not move from her bed. On the fourth day when he returned to her, he tried to force her to move, twisting her blood to compel her to arise, but she could not. She immediately collapsed, fell before him, screaming. Her vision went dark as her eyes rolled into her head and she crumpled. She vomited on the ground as he tried to force her up, then she passed out. He ordered a healer brought immediately, sounding frustrated with how quickly his toy had broken.

He cursed into her mind. Breaking down the walls that had disguised her for so long had broken her body, and a fever had taken hold strong enough even her ancient blood could not keep it at bay.

Weak. Fucking pathetic. You need to get stronger if you're to carry my sons.

*****

One of the servants brought the healer woman to Elle when she arrived at the castle. Dae had retreated to his study.

Elle heard a shuffle in the hall, the door opened and she saw an unfamiliar woman pushing past Clementine who had been near the doorway. For only a moment she wondered how long Clementine had been out there, she looked stiff, her arms were crossed over her chest. Her lips moved in what Elle assumed was some type of protest as the other woman disregarded her and moved toward the bed. The woman appeared to be in her fifties by human standards, though she was likely past five hundred. Her white hair was braided around her head. Beads, gems, and metal trinkets hung from the braids. Her clothes were simple compared to the elaborate clothing of the vampires in the castle. A belt wrapped around her waist held leather bags and glass bottles with a variety of liquids inside

Elle lay under the deep red blankets. Sweat beaded her forehead, and her breaths were shallow. She could barely hold her eyes open as the healer approached. She tried to open her mouth to speak but could not get words to leave her throat.

The healer shook her head. "Shh. Remain quiet, young one." She set a bag on the table beside the bed and began to rummage through it. "I'm Elainiah." She pulled out a few small glass jars, each filled with something entirely unfamiliar to Elle. Even after her years with June, what Elainiah carried was foreign . . . Her methods were ancient.

Her hand glowed ever so gently as she laid it on Elle's forehead first. Her brow furrowed, and she moved her hand, now laying it softly on Elle's chest, resting it just between her breasts.

Elle's flesh was slick with sweat.

"Oh, young one . . ." Elainiah grabbed one of the jars and, with two fingers, removed some of the paste inside. She mumbled as she worked. Elle could not make out the words. She drew runes on Elle's chest and her stomach, each with a deliberate whisper. Lingering over Elle's stomach, she placed dots of the paste in two lines, each curved inward toward her center. She returned the jar to the table and, from a different jar, removed a honey-like substance. She placed a few drops on Elle's forehead, then muttered quietly as she rubbed them in. The gentle glow of her hand was warm against Elle's face. "The fever has set in deep. He wounded your mind . . ." She breathed in before she continued, "But if you rest, you will recover by the end of tomorrow."

Elle moaned softly. She'd begun to drift in and out of consciousness as another wave of exhaustion took hold.

Elainiah stared at her for a moment, then placed the jars back into her bag. After throwing the bag over her shoulder, she leaned toward Elle, laying a hand against her cheek. "Hold fast, little one. Do not let the devil break you."

Elle only just heard this command as she fell back into darkness.

*****

CLEMENTINE

Clementine remained in the hallway. When the door opened, she asked the healer, "She will recover?"

Elainiah nodded, but her expression was deeply saddened. Her ancient eyes met Clementine's, and she spoke softly. "He will destroy her."

*****

ELLE

Elle lay in the bed, sweating profusely. Her shallow breaths were the only sound, the small noises lost in the vast space of the room. She slipped in and out of darkness. She tried to fight it off, tried desperately to stay awake, because of what awaited in that darkness . . . When she slipped back into *that* space. He would be waiting for her. He would meet her in that place, a place between dreams and nightmares. And there, he would torment her. He would not let her rest. He was relentless and unyielding.

He would never let her rest.

He was there. Again, again she'd lost consciousness and slipped back. She was standing in a white space. There was nothing around her, nothing to orient herself with. Her chest tightened as panic yet again set in. She couldn't understand her surroundings, and it was overwhelming. She grabbed at her chest and sank to her knees, trying to catch her breath, trying to right herself in the space.

"Calm yourself," his voice commanded.

She struggled to breathe. Her heart rate refused to calm. She screamed and fell forward, collapsing with her face pressed into a ground that did not exist.

"Calm yourself." His voice was louder, harsher.

She took a partial breath, trying with all she had to pull herself together. She had been here before. She had to remember. She had been here. She had been able to calm herself before. She could do it again. She had to do it again. Her breaths started to slow. Her heart rate followed suit. She slid back onto her heels, still curled over herself. Her arms wrapped around her middle. "Let me go . . . Please . . . Please let me rest . . . Please, Dae."

The shadow of him appeared before her. The shined toes of his shoes came into view. He sighed heavily as he squatted beside her.

She braced herself.

He grabbed her hair, pulling her head back and to the side, straining her neck. "If you'd not fallen ill, we wouldn't have to be in this place, since you seem to hate it so much," he hissed at her. "This is your doing, little darling."

She winced and yelped as he tore her hair. "Please—"

His grip tightened and he growled as he said, "Stop resisting me." He jerked her head toward him. "Stop resisting your fate."

She pushed the tears welling in her eyes back as best she could. This couldn't be her fate. She had to escape. Return to Kirk. She'd be in his arms again. She had to believe that. She wouldn't survive it if she didn't believe that.

"Still you think of him." He stood, dragging her up with him. "Disgusting."

*****

As the healer had said, by the end of the next day her fever had broken and she was regaining her strength. Still nausea and fatigue seemed to plague her, and the anxiety, the torment, it made her sick. Every footstep, every knock, it all meant he could be returning to her. She lived in constant fear, which only ended when sleep finally took her. Unless he sought her out in the *white space*, though with her fever passed, he'd let her be when she slept.

She awoke and sat up slowly, running her hands through her hair and pulling it back. She reached to the table beside her and grabbed a tie for her hair. The portrait of Dae on the wall stared at her. She hated it. She hated those eyes watching her *constantly*. That face that watched her even when she tried, and often failed, to rest.

Her eyes landed on a glass by the door. Clementine had left more blood for her. She stood. Her legs were still shaky, her limbs still weak, but she could nearly stand again. As she moved toward the door, she caught a glimpse of herself in the mirror. Today was her sixth day . . . seventh? But in her reflection—in her reflection, it looked as if she'd already been his captive for years. She turned away from the mirror and grabbed the glass. She cupped it in both hands and held it under her nose, taking in a deep breath of its scent, feeling its warmth in her hands. It smelled sweet.

She chose not to let herself think about where it may have come from. What poor soul had been torn apart by Dae's court for her meal. She quietly uttered a thanks to that soul, wishing her safe passage onto her next life, then she sipped slowly. It was warm against her lips, comforting as it heated her chest and her stomach. She focused on how it felt. How it soothed her. How it truly satisfied her hunger. If she focused on that, for just a moment, the darkness was kept at bay. The clouds that loomed over her were held back for a small second of relief. As she took another sip, her mind shifted to Kirk and her eyes drifted closed. She clung to thoughts of him. She thought of his voice, of his face. She thought of his hands, of his chest. She thought of how it felt to be near to him. How it felt to be with him. The sound of his laugh. She took a heavy breath and her eyes opened.

She would see him again.

She was jolted from her thoughts as a knock rattled on the door.

The door opened, and there he was. Once again. He stepped into the room. "You're up. Good. We've already lost enough time." He paced the room, looking around with a bored expression. He looked as he always did. Perfectly put together, perfectly fitted and trimmed. "I assume since you had no idea of your bloodline, you know little of our history . . . of our kind."

She nodded.

He looked over at her, his eyes running up and down her body, lingering ever so slightly too long on her neck. "Then you are unaware of how rare a vampire child is." He smiled cruelly. "I know, I know. With my count of bastards, it's hard to believe. I had five more that lived here once."

Where . . . are they?

He continued, his smile spreading when he saw the fear in her eyes. "But, my darling, it's vampire women who seem intent on ending our bloodlines. A pure-blooded vampire, born of a vampire's womb, is *truly* precious with how rarely our women conceive. Half-bloods, you see, are like rats, running around everywhere. They're cursed little creatures that we cannot seem to stop creating, myself included." He kept pacing, stopping to look at his own portrait on the wall. "Even then, females . . . You fucking females so rarely bear children." He waved a hand. "I believe it's some bitter curse you've placed on yourselves as a punishment to males. Since clearly you do not wish to do your duty and bear sons." He grumbled, "And the moon seems to protect her daughters for no good reason." He crossed his arms behind his back. "This is why you and I? We cannot waste our time. I cannot lose precious days with you if we are to bring forth the next era of pure-blooded vampires."

She felt her knees start to shake. She was afraid she was going to collapse. *Again. He's going to take me . . . again.*

He did not turn to her yet. "This could be simpler, Elle. You could submit willingly. Become my queen. I would not have to keep taking this from you. We could be something truly great."

She stepped back. She looked for a weapon in the room. Maybe if she ran something through his heart, the torture would end. But he sensed her movements. Perhaps sensed her intentions, that she searched the room for something to drive deep into his chest. He turned, a cruel smile on his lips, and his power surged within her again.

Her blood twisted in her body. It burned in her veins and she collapsed screaming.

He stepped over to her, entirely unhurried. "Have it your way, then."

The third time. The third time he raped her he took her on the bed in her room. He cut her apart with his claws. He tore into her, and she bled viscous pools that soaked into her bedding. He muffled her screams with his hand. He bit deep into her neck. He savored every taste of her blood, and he relished her agony.

Then, yet again, she found herself alone. In silence. Deafening silence. She was left to process and to suffer in her own mind. Her body started to heal, slowly, barely, but she could not stay in that bed. That bed was soaked in her blood and soaked in her screams. That bed was haunted by what he had done to her. Her body was going to heal, but her mind— Her mind wouldn't stop bleeding.

She lay on the rug again, as she had the first night, and she wept softly. With her arms tight against herself and her knees drawn up to her chest, she tried to summon any thoughts of Kirk, any thoughts of the end of this, of escaping . . . But the darkness crept closer and closer, like a tremendous hand made of shadow slowly closing around her.

*****

"What is it that you want more than anything else, Elle?" His voice was gentle. He lay behind her, his arms wrapped around her pulling her tightly against his chest.

She was quiet for a moment, taking in everything about the feeling of him. His skin pressed against hers. His heartbeat molding into her own. The scars that riddled his chest against the smooth skin of her back. Her ass pressed into his stomach. His breath hot against her neck. "What I want more than anything else?"

He pulled her closer somehow, pressing his nose between her neck and her shoulder and kissing her softly. "Mm-hmm."

Elle thought for a moment. What did she want? She loved her life with June, Bliss, she loved this, but she'd been stuck surviving for so long, she'd forgotten what she wanted . . . How could she tell him she wanted to be free, to be safe? Those are the dreams of a hunted monster. But what if . . . what if she wasn't a monster? What if she had been born a human? What would she have wanted? What would have been the desire in her soul? "A farm." Her voice was quiet. "And children. A dog." She laughed softly, but a knot formed in her throat. "A man who loves me scooping me into his arms . . . and I'm—I'm in love, and I'm safe." She felt it forming on her lips, the word you, but she couldn't. She couldn't force it out of her mouth. She wanted to. She wanted to roll over, grab his face and tell him what she wanted most in the world was him. But she couldn't . . . and she didn't.

There was something about his tone, something that led her to believe he was about to hold something back just as she had. "That sounds beautiful, Elle." He kissed her neck again.

CHAPTER 33

CLEMENTINE

Clementine moved briskly through the halls. They echoed with her mother's screams. She fucking hated those halls.

But the dungeon.

The basement.

That was where Mutt was. Where her pet was. She loved it down there. She loved being there because he was there.

She ducked around a corner to the top of the stairs leading into the darkness, and she quickly set down them.

Her dog. She loved her dog. She was always so excited to sneak away to see him. She had been so happy when Dae had finished training Mutt—when he'd let her take him. She'd been sneaking down to check on him before then anyway, and Dae had known that. Maybe it was some pathetic fatherly— Of course it wasn't. He'd grown bored and let her keep his old pet.

Mutt's eyes would always widen with excitement when she appeared. His whimpering would cease, and he'd excitedly press against the bars of his cell in anticipation of her affections.

She wished Dae would let him join her in the main corridors, but Dae would grumble about how he would not have some barely housebroken dog walking his ancient halls.

She rounded the corner and saw the cell. "Mutt!" She smiled as she approached. "How is my good boy?"

He looked up at her, his deep red eyes sparkling. The vampire boy, no older than her, tilted his head and his eyes squinted in a smile.

*****

No one knew where Mutt came from. Dae found him when he was just a child. He was returning from a human town, likely having fathered another cursed child, when he smelled blood. Dae's senses for blood were strong. Any amount of blood he could smell, though rarely did he follow the trail. Often they were simply left by animals, however, this was a lot of blood. He followed the scent, and it led him a ways off his path, toward the gentle cracking of branches, the sound of someone panting. He reached a clearing, and for a moment, even he paused to take in the sight before him. The ground was an unbroken pool of blood. Strewn about in the blood were chunks of human flesh. Arms, legs, heads, entrails . . . thrown around the clearing, in the trees. It would've been hard to decipher exactly how many men it had once been, their bodies reduced to loose piles of flesh, but counting the heads, he saw at least six. Their faces torn apart were still in states of shock, fear, agony. It must have been a human hunting party to have been this far into the woods.

But what really interested Dae was what stood at the center. In the middle of the clearing was a boy. Maybe eight. He had claws like a beast and was drenched in their blood, all of his own skin stained entirely red. He was panting, his claws still flexing as though he were ready to pounce. His fangs were bared, blood dripping from them. The boy turned to Dae, and he lunged.

Dae held up a hand, and the boy dropped to the ground. He writhed and screamed as Dae twisted his blood. A seal appeared over the boy's mouth, and his screams ceased, not because his torment ended, but because Dae muzzled him. Weary of the screeching, and wary of just what the child would be willing to bite.

*****

MUTT

Mutt's muzzle was bloody. The leather straps constantly dug into his face. If it were to ever be removed long enough for him to heal, it may even leave scars . . . He felt his heart race at the sight of Clementine. He squinted, and though it was hard to tell to anyone else, he was smiling beneath the leather that covered his mouth. It cut into his cheeks when he smiled, but he couldn't help it when he saw her. He was seated beside the front bars of his cell, and he leaned his head against them as she neared, a clear request for affection.

She smiled and squatted beside him, sliding her hand through the bars and ruffling his fluffy black hair.

He leaned into her touch, his neck arching as he pressed into her fingers. He began to purr.

She slowly pulled her hand back and sank onto the floor beside the bars.

A new scent caught his attention. He sniffed the air around her, tilting his head as he tried to identify who it was.

"Dae has a new whore."

Mutt kept sniffing. The smell was different, familiar and foreign. It was sweet . . . ancient.

"She's an old blood. From the House of Bone." Her perfect red eyes met his. "She's powerful, and Father wants to breed her."

Mutt sat back a little from the front of the cage, his questions around the scent answered. House of Bone meant nothing to the dog, however, he remembered Clementine talking about it. Breeding and power he understood . . . His eyes remained locked on Clementine. He loved when she visited. She was the only thing on earth he didn't have an insatiable drive to kill. He waited anxiously for her visits. When she appeared at the bottom of those stairs, the everlight mounted to the walls made her look like an angel.

Clementine reached to scratch his hair again. "She reminds me of Mother, Mutt." She sniffed, and he could see liquid pooling in the corners of her eyes. "He's doing the same things to her . . ."

He pulled his head away from the scratches, asking the question with his eyes and the angle of his head.

"I don't know what to do, Mutt. I don't want to let her get tortured like Mom. I don't want her to die like Mom. Or leave a child behind . . . I just . . . What can I do against my father? And if I help her escape, she'll only be hunted . . ."

He tilted his head in the other direction, reaching a hand through the bars and tapping at Clementine's heart.

She shook her head. "Soon enough she'll wish she was dead like the rest of us."

He cocked his head to the opposite side again and growled.

"I don't wish I was dead when I'm with you, stupid." She smiled softly.

~ 34 ~

CHAPTER 34

CLEMENTINE

After a few days, Clementine returned to Elle's room once again. She opened the door and winced. It smelled so strongly of blood and sex. Elle curled up on the rug, still entirely naked. Clementine averted her gaze, trying to give her any ounce of her pride back, any sense of autonomy over the body Dae was determined to break. Searching for something for Elle to wear, Clementine walked to the vanity, only to find nothing. At the bed, she paused, her hand drifting over her mouth at the sheets entirely soaked in blood.

She found a blanket with minimal blood splatter shoved to the end of the bed, and she gently draped it over Elle.

She hadn't moved since Clementine had entered, the darkness holding her tightly, her eyes glassy and dull. As Clementine laid the blanket over her, Elle pulled it close and slowly began to sit up. "Forgive me."

"No. No, there is nothing to forgive, Elle." Clementine knelt beside her, then glanced over her shoulder, listening for any sign of her father. "I'll bring you some clothes, okay? Just hold on a while longer . . ."

"I'll . . . survive." Elle's voice faltered as she spoke those words, as if she were only trying to convince herself.

When Clementine's hands began to shake, she balled them into fists and a sigh escaped. "He's nearly killed you already." She

227

looked her over, and her desire to help the poor girl, her need to save, her only grew. But she knew, she knew if she told Elle she wished to get her out, Dae would know. Anything Elle knew Dae knew.

"Clementine . . . You've been his prisoner for many years . . . It can be survived."

Clementine's heart shattered in her chest, she'd never considered herself a prisoner. And here a true prisoner looked at her with empathy, with care, and for *hope*. "Do not let him break you . . . please. Please just continue to hang on, Elle. I'll be back. With clothes."

*****

ELLE

Later that afternoon, Elle awoke still on the rug. Her eyes rose to a stack of fresh blankets by the door, atop the blankets three new sets of shorts and tops. She stood, slowly dressing herself and hiding the other two sets in case Dae wished to destroy them too. The blankets she laid in a nest on the rug. They were lavish blankets, soft and warm and thick with down. She curled up in them, thanking Clementine for this gift. The blankets brought comfort. The blood warmed her tummy. The clothes covered the body that had been exposed and abused.

As she returned to sleep, her dreams were not nightmares. Her dreams were of Kirk. His warmth wrapped around her like the blankets. For the first time since she'd been taken to this castle, she truly slept.

"Elle . . ." Kirk's knuckle rested under her chin, tipping her head back so her eyes met his.

She smiled softly, her eyes only half-open. "Yes?"

He did not speak for a moment. He simply looked at her. She could have sworn she saw the stars dancing in the blue of his eyes. He wanted to say

*something, she could feel it. Something lingered there behind those eyes .
. .*

Her eyes opened fully. Her arms were wrapped around his waist. "What is it, Kirk?"

"Kiss me." He leaned down and pressed his lips against hers.

At first, the kiss was gentle. He tasted of spices and sweat. But the kiss shifted and became desperate, passionate, as though he needed in that moment to completely consume her.

Her hands moved up his back, her fingers digging into the skin beneath them, the tense muscles resisting her grasp.

He dropped lower and swung his arm behind her knees, scooping her into his hold and pressing her against his chest. All the while, his deep kisses continued. She was so small in his arms, she felt like she might simply vanish within him.

Her hands tangled up in his hair as she kept kissing him. His arms felt warm.

His arms felt safe.

*****

DAE

The moon gifted each vampire with great power. Each vampire's power was unique to them. Sometimes there were similarities within bloodlines, but each soul carried something different from the rest. These powers were stronger the older the blood. Dae was believed to be the most powerful vampire to exist; his control of blood and mind was unmatched. He could drop men without touching them, without so much as a finger lifted, men could die by his power. But Dae knew. Only Dae knew that the House of Bone held heirs that not only rivaled his power, they could decimate it. Why else would he seek to destroy the family before the heirs could come to their full power and what would surely be his end.

This was why he held on so tightly now that the lost Princess of Bone was in his castle. He'd found her. He'd taken her. She was in his grasp. And she did not even understand the power she held. He just needed to know how they'd sealed it away. How her parents had managed to lock her power so even she was unable to access it. Even prodding deep into her mind to break the chains on her eyes, her teeth, he could not find that lock. He needed Silas.

With her under his control, he did not fear her power. He sought to use it. Breed it into his own children. Have her bear as many children as she could before she broke. He'd figure out what to do with her after that soon enough. She'd be nothing by then. He intended to do enough damage to her mind that she may not remember her own name by then, let alone remember she held power enough to be his end.

She was shattering so easily. It was pathetic. He had hoped for more. He had hungered for more. Something to be of actual entertainment. But she was weak, crumbling beneath him. At least the taste of her screams brought him some joy. He did enjoy those screams, the taste of her ancient blood filled with the fear he inspired in her. He so relished that look in her eyes, like she stared at the devil himself. Gods, it was simply divine watching her suffer. He held her beneath his power. He controlled her. He owned her. It drove him insane, holding so much power in his hand. He was going to destroy her, and it was going to taste so damn good.

He sensed that she'd found rest that night, and he chose to leave her in that peace. He couldn't afford to fully break her yet. He needed her mind in sound enough condition to sort through. The next day, they were going to shatter her. She was going to need strength if she was going to survive with anything left intact.

*****

ELLE

She was startled awake by the doorknob turning. She hadn't realized how deeply she'd fallen asleep, how badly she'd needed that sleep. She did not think about why Dae had let her rest untouched, without a trip into that dreaded space between realities. It didn't matter. Whatever he wanted, whatever his plan was, she was powerless against it. She only needed to be thankful for the rest she'd been given. Immediately, fear and instinct pushed her away from the sudden intrusion. She shoved away from the door as it opened.

Instinct was right.

Dae stood in the doorway. He glanced down at her on the floor, bundled in a nest of blankets. "Surely you'd rather sleep in your bed." His eyes darted to the bed still drenched in her blood.

"I'm fine." Her voice was barely over a whisper.

"Get up."

She stumbled to her feet.

"Come." Dae held out his hand. "Behave or Clementine doesn't get to bring you any more presents."

She tensed up. She didn't want Clementine in any danger.

"I am fully aware of *everything* that happens in my castle, little princess. You only get from her what I allow her to bring." He nodded toward his extended hand.

She swallowed hard and nodded, then grabbed the hand held out to her. It was cold. Even for a vampire.

"Now come."

She didn't dare ask where.

He led her down the hallways. She couldn't raise her eyes to see what lined them, but she could feel the eyes of the portraits burning into her as they passed.

Dae brought her to stairs that descended below the castle. "Princess, we're paying Silas a visit today."

A shock ran down her spine. Some part of her knew that visiting Silas was very bad. Very. Very. Bad. "Why?"

The sigh that left Dae's lips was laced with rage. "I do hate it when you pry, princess."

"Forgive me . . ." She felt that familiar surge. He was on the edge of sending another wave of pain through her. She bit her tongue to keep him at bay.

He turned away and continued down the stairs, motioning for her to follow.

She walked behind him through the dungeons. Rows of barred cells on either side held humans. She averted her gaze. She'd heard them scream at night, but she could not bear to see them, to know the faces of the humans that were the victims of these *monsters*. She wondered what the humans who'd fed *her* looked like. The blood Clementine had brought . . . that blood had been in these cells, afraid, wondering when death would come for them.

Some cells held the willing, the humans who came to this castle to appease gods. Some likely hoped to become vampires themselves, though vampire transformation was ugly, painful, and unlikely.

But all of them were simply prey. Caged animals. Like domestic pigs waiting for slaughter.

A heavily pregnant woman was alone in a cell. She shrunk back when she saw Dae approaching, her hand over her belly as though she could protect it from him. She refused to let Elle pass without their gazes meeting, and terror ran down Elle's spine. She had been beautiful once. Dark brown hair, like Elle's, was tied back, but her eyes were encircled with darkness. Fresh scars lined her face, her neck, any exposed skin. Unlike a vampire, she did not heal from Dae's torture swiftly.

Elle's eyes darted from the woman.

But the woman started sobbing. "Please. PLEASE. Please help me!" she screamed as they passed her.

Dae sighed as Elle shook in his grasp. "Don't mind her." He spoke harshly, shooting a glare at the woman. "Once the bastard is born, she will be free from the torture."

Because she'll be dead.

****

Silas's workspace was something from nightmares. The stone walls dripped with moisture, mold grew in the cracks, copper stains were etched into rock, and matching stains were splattered across wooden tables. Metal tools hung from the walls. An angled table in one corner sported restraints. In the opposite corner sat a pile of human bones. A few skulls perched on a shelf on the wall, holes drilled in each. Claw marks marked the stone beside heavy chains bolted into the wall where something horrible, something large had once been held . . .

This was a place of torture, horrible experiments, and cruel treatment of whoever was sent down here for Silas to play with. Shelves held a variety of books, spells, jars, and bottles filled with mysterious, ominous liquids. Humans had been tortured in this space. The screams she'd just barely heard at night, mixing in with her own, had come from this room. The scent of blood was quickly overwhelmed by the stench of rotting death that seeped out of every pore. The smell was so truly horrible, Elle wondered how anyone with vampire senses could stomach being down here.

She vomited almost as soon as they entered, pulling from Dae and crumpling near a wall.

Dae huffed. "You get accustomed to it."

"Your whore is making a mess, Dae," Silas said.

"I'll send someone to clean it." He snapped his fingers. "Get up."

She felt her body stiffen and she stood.

"Silas." Dae motioned to Elle. "She's yours until you can get it unlocked. You will contact me the moment you're through. She cannot die. Do not fail." He glanced back at Elle. "I will know if you fight him."

Her hands began to shake. She couldn't control it. She tried so hard to fight it, but she couldn't. "Y-yes." She looked to Silas, who already appeared bored, her eyes pleading for answers but finding none in the deep red that looked back at her.

Silas turned from her and reached for one of the books on the shelf and a few of the tools on the walls. He grabbed a jar and set it on the table. "Of course, my lord."

Elle turned back to Dae, but he was already headed up the stairs, leaving her alone with Silas.

Silas pointed at the angled table. The one that smelled so strongly of human blood. "You'll need to be restrained."

"What are you . . . going to do?"

He rubbed his head and sighed, setting a few more things on the table. "Unlock the rest of your vampire nature. Your parents went to great lengths to hide you from him, and I have been asked to rifle through that pretty little head of yours to find whatever else your parents locked up."

She stepped back.

"I wouldn't, if I were you." He pointed again at the angled table. "You don't want to anger him."

*****

She had been strapped to the table. Every piece of her body screamed to refuse, screamed to stop them, screamed to run, anything other than let him into her mind. She should have run. She should have run.

"Drink this or what is about to happen will kill you." He held a bottle to her lips.

She turned her head away from him.

He sighed. "Do you sense deceit in me? Drink it or this will kill you."

"What if I chose death?"

He smiled, only slightly. "Trust me, girl, while you may wish for death, and it may be better than your current station, this death is far more painful than you wish to endure. I swear that much to you."

She tried to swallow the knot in her throat, then she nodded. Her face twisting as he poured a vile liquid into her mouth, she forced herself to swallow it. "What is it?"

He turned away from her, reaching for the book on the table. "Partially a sedative."

This was no lie, she already felt her limbs begin to grow heavy, her eyelids with them. "And . . .?"

He looked over his shoulder at her as her eyes started to drift closed. "You'll find out."

~ 35 ~

CHAPTER 35

CLEMENTINE

She stared out the window on the far end of the room. She hated the library. She preferred being outside in the garden, outside in the city, *outside . . .*

Dae's prisoner. Elle considered *her* her father's prisoner. Elle had looked at *her* with care, her eyes so heartbroken for *her.*Clementine had to free her. Release her before she hung from the ceiling. If Dae didn't kill her, she'd do just as Mother had and end her own suffering. She'd abandon her baby because the torment Dae inflicted was unbearable.

But could Clementine herself truly be considered Dae's prisoner? She'd lived a comfortable life. Beside the death of her mother, she'd had anything and everything she needed. Could she consider herself a prisoner?

Every day, part of her soul eroded as she watched Elle suffer as Mother had. She was running out of time. She only had so long before Elle succumbed to the torture, before the blackness consumed her. She could sense Elle was slipping away quickly. She needed to figure out how to get her out. She ran through every scenario in her mind, any way to at least get her out of the castle and slow Dae's hunt for her enough that she could find a way to break the curse. Even Silas did not know how to break bonds and curses outside of death. That was why she found herself in the library, searching through ancient texts about bonds, looking for any way to free Elle. She had waited until Dae was fully involved in his work so she could read undisturbed. She pored over another text, seated in an armchair with her legs tucked beneath herself.

"You really must stop bringing her so many things."

Clementine's gaze shot up from the book. "Suho."

Suho stood in the doorway. "You're going to get yourself in trouble with Father, little sister." Long-dead eyes looked at her.

"He knows what I'm doing, and he knows that if I don't she'll die long before she can bear him a child."

"And I'm telling you, you're pushing it, little one. He's going to take it out on you, or *her*, if you continue to meddle with his whore."

Clementine closed the book. Her fingers turned white against the cover as she clenched them. "Brother, you cannot simply consider her a whore. Do you not see our mothers in her eyes?"

Suho sighed. "Do not be immature and naive sister. She is another of his whores. One with powerful blood, sure. But you and I both know that once she's borne a babe or two, she'll be cast aside as both our mothers were."

Clementine sniffed back tears. "Suho—"

"Dae is our blood, and the babe she'll bear for him will be ours as well. Do not waste your breath on her. Save your energy for guarding the child, if you must care."

Clementine opened her mouth, about to say something stupid, about to get into a fight with Suho and get herself in trouble, but she was interrupted.

From the basement, they heard screaming. The kind of screaming that could turn even an ancient vampire's blood cold. Elle's screaming.

"What is he doing, brother?"

Suho shrugged. "He left her with Silas for the day. Even I do not know his reasons."

"With . . . Silas?"

"There may not be much left to save by the end of the day."

*****

SILAS

He leaned against the table, his hands braced on the surface behind him as he stared at her. She'd passed out, but he'd found it. He'd rifled through that mind for hours, dug through every corner of her consciousness until he found it. He rubbed his forehead with his sleeve. He was sweating. Even he got tired after searching for that long, that deep in another's being. Her mind was disgustingly good. Such kindness made him nauseous. Nevertheless, he'd found what Dae sought: the lock her parents had placed on her vampiric power. They'd tucked it so far, so deep, he was unsure how much damage he'd done to destroy it. He'd sent for Dae as soon as he was out of her mind and the power was released, but who knew how long it would be before she awoke. . . And who knew what would remain of her when she did.

The door swung open, and Dae shoved through. "You've done it?"

Silas shoved himself away from the table. "It's released."

Dae looked at the small body still strapped to the table. "And she's alive?"

Silas nodded. "Alive is all I can assure."

"I will send someone to take her to her room and see to it that she's watched. You've done well, Silas."

"Thank you, my lord. Glad I could be of service." He rubbed his forehead. "My lord, if I may. The power I just unleashed, it's unlike anything I've ever felt before. If she were to harness it, if she were to understand it fully, I fear she may—"

"That's enough, Silas," Dae growled. "I am aware of what she possesses." He ran a hand through his hair and turned to head back up the stairs. "Do what you can to bring her back to her senses."

"Yes, my lord."

*****

Silas tied back his hair as he walked to his room. Tension gripped his shoulders; he was entirely exhausted and he needed relief. He motioned one of the human servants over as he passed her in a hall. "Send them to my room."

"The same as always, my lord?"

"Yes. But more wine." He waved her away as she scurried off to gather his meal and continued toward his room, rubbing his temples. Sorting through that princess's head had taken a toll on him.

He opened the door and stepped into the enormous space. The bed at the center was large enough to sleep at least six comfortably, though when not asleep, he'd seen plenty more on the mattress. There were three couches around the room, and the rug was as strikingly large as everything else. He was not a fan of the red *everywhere* in the castle and had created a space for himself in the tones he enjoyed the most, mostly dark green with gold lining the edges. He unbuttoned his shirt as he waited for dinner to arrive.

A knock on the door turned him, his hands falling from the last button on his shirt. "Come in."

The servant opened the door. "My lord," she said and ushered a group of three humans into the room, a man and two women. "I'll be by later . . ." To clean.

Silas nodded and motioned the three of them in. The man and one of the women stepped in confidently, willing participants in what was about to take place. The third, however, seemed afraid. She was tucked back, her arms wrapped around herself, and she was visibly shaking.

He hated when they brought him the scared ones. He was already so exhausted, he really didn't want to have to do this. He walked toward her.

She looked up at him.

He sighed heavily as he took in the fear in her expression. "Shh." He touched her face, his hand resting on her cheek. *Relax,* he said into her mind, easing the fear, covering it with his own command. He wanted her calm.

As his command took over, her shoulders dropped, and her eyes drooped a little.

"There you go." His hand shifted from her cheek to her chin, tilting it up toward himself. "Such simple minds humans have." He leaned forward and kissed her. "Easy to manipulate." He kissed her again.

The other woman stepped behind him, her palms sliding over either side of his waist under his shirt, her touch warm against his frozen skin. Her hands moved beneath the waist of his pants. He continued to kiss the woman before him, his hands moving to her head, his fingers in her hair. The woman behind him found his cock, and his head tilted back. "Gods," he purred. Then he leaned forward again, biting down on the neck of the woman he'd kissed. His fangs tore into her throat, and blood ran down her collar. He'd bit hard. He had been hungrier than he thought. *Shit . . . she's going to die a little sooner than I'd have liked.* He lapped at the blood, his face sticky with it quickly.

The woman did not scream, but her body grew cold as the blood poured from the punctures in her neck. She began to sink toward the floor, and he let her fall. Turning to the woman behind him, he found the man draped on the bed, naked.

He wiped the blood from the side of his mouth and stepped forward, gesturing for the woman to join the man before him as he unbuckled his pants. They let their hands explore each other as the vampire undressed, the woman on the floor behind him quietly bleeding to death. As his pants hit the ground, he joined them on the bed.

*****

Silas moaned softly. The man's grip on his hips was strong, lighter now after he'd drained a decent amount of blood from him, but enough. The woman lay on the pillows, exhausted, blood dripping from the punctures in her neck.

The door opened.

The man turned.

Silas sighed and fell forward onto the bed. "Venus, must you always interrupt my dinner?"

Venus flitted about the room, cocking her head to the side as she looked over the dead woman. "I hate it when I'm not invited."

Silas's eyes found the woman on the pillows. "Tend to my sister."

The woman nodded, standing slowly then making her way toward Venus.

He heard Venus giggle. "Oh, you're SO pretty!" She grabbed the woman and pulled her close, her hands running down her bare back, her fingers tracing the warm flesh. "Wonderful, lovely, and so soft. You're so very soft." She kissed her neck, then she bit it.

*****

CLEMENTINE

Clementine snuck into Elle's room when she heard she'd been returned from the basement. "Elle." She spoke to a room that did not reply. Elle's body was curled on the giant bed. One of the servants luckily had changed the sheets, and she lay beneath a new comforter.

Her brow was furrowed, her entire body beaded with sweat. Clearly, the tiny form was in deep distress. Her breathing was labored, and her eyes moved chaotically beneath closed lids.

"Oh gods . . . Elle." Clementine came up to her bedside and stared down, grasping Elle's delicate hand in her own. It was drenched in sweat, clammy, and shaking violently. "Fuck." She sat on the bed and pressed her hand to Elle's forehead, hunched over beside the girl. "I'll get you out of here. I swear it. Please just hang on."

No response from the girl on the bed.

Clementine shuddered when she felt a presence approach, when she heard her father open the door. She released Elle's hand and dropped it back onto the bed as Dae entered behind her. "Father."

Dae's red eyes were on fire. His chin rose as he looked over his daughter. "You're pushing your luck, Clementine."

Clementine stood quickly and stepped away from Elle's beside. "Forgive me, Father. I only wished to check on her . . ."

"Leave."

"Father—"

"LEAVE."

*****

That night, Clementine couldn't force herself to sleep. She sat on her bed with her knees pulled up to her chest, her forehead resting atop them as she desperately tried to figure out how to get Elle out. She couldn't rest until Elle was free. Even if Dae hunted Elle forever. Even if she ran for the next hundred years, she couldn't stay here. She couldn't. They had nearly killed her already, and Clementine didn't care if she died in the process of freeing her. All that mattered was getting her out of here. That was all that mattered. The girl that lay on that bed would not survive. Her mind was already shattered beyond repair.

Clementine might already be too late.

She shoved herself from her bed and left her room, her hair falling over her shoulders and into her face, out of its usual braids. Her footsteps echoed in the hallway as she hurried toward the basement. She needed Mutt right now.

She fell before Mutt's cage and wept.

He hurried to the bars and reached through them to touch her hair, his head cocked to the side. He whimpered softly in confusion.

She shook her head violently, her arms wrapping tightly around herself. "I don't know what to do, Mutt. I don't know what to do. They're going to kill her like they killed Mother. Elle's going to die like she did, and I don't know what to do to help her."

He gently ran his hand through her hair, his whimpers softening further. His hand was gentle, bringing the warmth and comfort she found in him,

*****

ELAINIAH

The healer was called back when Elle still could not rise even days later. She hurried through the castle halls toward the girl's room.

Suho stood beside the doorway, leaning against the wall. He shoved off it as she approached and extended his hand. "Dae has commanded that no one see her without him present."

"He was the one who sent for me. Move out of my way, bastard prince," she said and shoved at his chest.

"It's his request. I'll go get him." He was evidently unfazed by her age or station.

Dae's voice nearly rattled the paintings off the walls. "Send her in." He strode down the hall toward them.

She pushed past Suho and into Elle's room. As she stepped through the door, she stopped for only a moment. Even with everything she'd seen, Dae's cruelty shocked her. The aura in the room, the smell, the sight, it frightened even one as ancient as she.

Dae walked casually past her directly toward the girl on the bed. "I fear her mind is shattered. I do not need her the same as she was, but I need her alive enough to bear children. Fix it, witch."

Elainiah rushed past Dae, shoving him slightly as she knelt beside the bed. "What have you *done* to her?" She glared over her shoulder before returning her gaze to Elle. She gently rested her hand on her cheek.

"I have freed her."

"You've nearly killed her. You *might have* killed her." She reached into her bag and rifled through the jars. Her voice was sharp as anger laced her tone. "She will be of no use to you, *my lord*, in this state. She's nearly died by your hand. She cannot bear you children like this." She gently rubbed a paste into Elle's forehead, muttering words ancient enough even Dae could not understand them.

His expression did not change. His heart clearly held no compassion for her. In his mind, she was just a whore to breed, a vessel for his children. If she did not survive this, all he would mourn would be the loss of the power of the babe she had not brought forth before he tossed her corpse into the woods to be fed on by beasts.

Elainiah's hands moved over the body of the girl. She applied salves, whispered hushed spells. She laid her forehead against Elle's. Her compassion shifted to pity. She wondered if she could simply put the girl to rest. If she should help usher her back to the moon's embrace. But as she worked to heal the girl, she just barely sensed it. The smallest presence. The smallest form *within* her. It was not her choice to make. It was Elle's . . . because of what she carried.

She stood, glaring at Dae as she wiped her hands on her dress. "Lord Dae, let her rest. I implore you to let her rest. I've done all I can."

~ 36 ~

CHAPTER 36

Elle

She was unconscious for days. Her last memories were her own screams. She remembered seeing herself crying out, strapped to that table, as if from outside of her own body, watching her own torment. Then she remembered nothing. For days . . . weeks.

When she awoke, she sat up suddenly. She was in her bed. She was in *that* bed. Phantom blood pooled within the sheets underneath her, and she screamed. Desperately, she scrambled out of the bed to collide with the floor. She had to push herself away from the mattress before she managed to calm herself, before she managed to pull herself into whatever reality she was in. The one where the bed was not coated in blood. Those sheets were clean. Those were not where he'd taken her . . . She fought to calm her own breaths; she fought to force herself to breathe. Then she winced, the pounding in her head rushing in as the panic subsided.

Her head throbbed, and her limbs were weak as she struggled to stand. She tried to remember anything, anything about what Silas had done, but it was entirely dark in her mind. And the more she tried to think about it, the worse her head ached, the worse her head pounded. She looked at the mirror to her left, and her eyes widened. The girl looking back at her was so different from the girl who had stepped in here two weeks ago. Her eyes were entirely sunken back, dark circles underneath them. She'd lost weight. She was sure her ribs were visible. Her stomach was bloated from hunger. How had two weeks taken such a toll? Had it been only two?

Suddenly, she became aware of how *hungry* she was. Gods, she was starving. She needed food. She needed blood. The desire, the hunger was like when she'd attacked June years ago, that desperate need. She looked at the door, hoping to see a glass from Clementine, but there was nothing there. Shit.

She leaned forward, wrapping her arms around her stomach. Her breathing quickened as a type of panic she'd never known began to overwhelm her. The darkness snuck back into her vision, slowly creeping in the corners of her eyes. She was disoriented and confused. The world was collapsing in on her. It felt like drowning. It felt like she was dying. Her head pounded harder. She didn't understand. Her breathing quickened even further. She was hungry, scared, and everything hurt. She screamed as she crumpled, her forehead pressing into the ground. *Fuck. Fuck. Fuck. Fuck.*

She heard a voice, and she screamed once more. Someone was behind her.

Then darkness consumed her again.

*****

Time became . . . blurry. Her memories were foggy. She slid in and out of consciousness, and when she returned, she would be somewhere else, with someone else. Dae would be there, Suho, Clementine. She would be in Silas's lab, in rooms of the castle she didn't recognize. She'd catch sight of herself in a mirror and wouldn't recognize the eyes that stared back at her. The woman whose gaze met her own. There was no life left behind those eyes.

*****

SATURN

Dae glanced up from his desk. Maps spread out over the wood, their edges torn and discolored as the years had deeply weathered them. "Ahh. Saturn." He motioned to the chair in the corner of the room. "Sit."

His tone was so cold even Saturn shook at his command. She was only reaching her three hundredth year, but he'd become so powerful so quickly, it was hard to believe he was only in his four hundredth. She felt as though he had been stalking this earth since the dawn of time.

"Why would you summon me?" She remained standing, some false courage—or stupidity—urging her to stay on her feet.

"To form an alliance with your house."

She huffed. "What house? You killed all but myself and my children."

"And why would I have saved you?"

She stepped back. The look he shot her startled her. The power behind his eyes pushed her backward. "I don't . . . know." A phantom hand around her throat slid over her neck, the invisible fingers barely tightening against her skin.

He looked back down at the map. "You, the women of your house, are blessed. You've birthed two children in three hundred years when many women cannot conceive at all in their first two hundred."

She remained quiet as he spoke, unease creeping over her, but her face remained unchanged.

"You're a tired old hag by now, but when Elle bears me a son, I wish to have him married to your daughter."

Her eyes widened. "My lord—"

"*Yes, my lord.*" His eyes moved up, looking at her through his eyebrows for only a moment before drifting back to his work. "And in exchange, you keep your son away from my princess."

How the fuck did he know?

"I know *everything* that happens between my walls, Saturn. You made it clear with your glances the moment I brought her before the court. You wanted her to bear your son's bastard for your line."

He grabbed at the desk as his tone rose only slightly, his nails digging into the wood as his fingers clenched. "Be thankful that I do not tear your throat out. Be thankful I offer you a *marriage* proposal to bind our families instead of burning your children in front of your eyes before I tear them from your skull."

The hand around her throat tightened as his nails clawed at the desk. "Forgive me, my lord." Her voice cracked as the hand tightened further and air no longer made it into her lungs. "For—give—me."

*****

ELAINIAH

Elainiah returned often in the months that followed Elle's capture. Elle's health shifted from bad to worse and back again, so she would return frequently to do what she could for her. Help the girl as best she could though her mind had been shattered and her body torn apart. As long as she could, she kept the secret from Dae, but only so long could she hide it from him. He would learn of it, and he would learn of it soon. Dae's torment of Elle had been skillful. Precision work to break her mind, her body, and her soul.

This time she visited, the girl was awake, the most conscious Elainiah had seen her in such a long time. The most aware she'd seen the girl since they'd broken the barrier in her mind.

Elle was sitting up in her bed. She turned to Elainiah. Her voice was so delicate as she spoke, barely above a whisper. "Am I . . . pregnant?"

Elainiah stopped short of Elle's bed. Her long-frozen heart shattered in her chest. "You are."

Elle's lip quivered, and she sucked in a breath as though the air had been pulled from her lungs. She fell forward, her arms wrapped around her waist, and she began to weep. Her weeping grew louder, harder. Her shoulders shook, and her chest heaved with sobs that were shifting into screams.

The door opened.

Dae stood in the doorway. "What is this?" He stormed toward the bed. His eyes burned as he grabbed Elle's hair, ripping her head back. "What is this?"

Elainiah ran toward him and grabbed his arm. "She's pregnant, Dae." She pulled at him, trying to tear him from Elle, to put any space she could between Elle and the male. "She's pregnant."

Dae released his grip on Elle's hair, and his hand slowly lowered. "She's—" For a moment, shock crossed his face, surprise in eyes that had not held surprise in decades, but it quickly became something far more sinister. Then he *smiled*. "This is the best thing I've ever heard."

*****

DAE

Elle was flopped unnaturally over a chair in his study. She was mostly naked, stripped down to undergarments Dae had had a servant help her into. Her eyes were half-open, the dull red barely visible under drooped eyelids.

He grumbled as he carved one of his nails into a viciously sharp point, the knife slowly taking the edges of the nail away. He glanced at the husk of a female before him and stepped toward her, dropping the knife on the table he'd leaned against.

He knelt before her, and for a moment, his hands cupped her stomach, the gentle curve of her tummy, still so subtle, so small. But his child . . . the babe all of it was for was growing there. His blood. His heir. He'd done it. "Finally, an heir worthy of me." He kissed her stomach, then leaned back. He started to drag his sharpened nail over her perfect flesh. Only with enough pressure to break the skin. He carved the symbols over her womb, a seal, a curse over the unborn babe.

She squirmed under the sharp nail, but she did not scream. Her mind was far from her. Her body barely reacted.

"Consider this . . . insurance," he hissed as her blood dripped slowly from the symbols he carved into her. "This child will be bound to me. Far beyond the binding of blood." He placed both hands on the fresh wounds, the blood coating them and a black smoke drifted from him, seeping into the gashes. "He's bound to me. My son. And it cannot be undone." Smiling, he stood and licked the blood from the tips of his fingers. Arousal settled deep into him. Her blood. Gods, her blood tasted sweet, ancient and pure, and it hardened his cock.

This time. This time was not for an heir. He'd already achieved that goal. This was simply an urge, primal and cruel. She was an object now. Nothing but his doll. The blood dripping from her wounds only heightened his desire. He grinned and unbuckled his pants.

He raped her again. She could not resist. Her mind was too broken. He grabbed her throat, digging his claws into the sides of her neck, and ripped away the little fabric that still covered her. Her body could only twist in response to the pain. Small yelps left her lips every so often, but she could not fight against him. Maybe it was a mercy that she would not remember.

As he stepped away from her again, readjusting his pants, he walked toward the table where a bottle of wine rested. He poured some into a glass. "You've done so well so quickly. An heir already." He smiled to himself, knowing the female could not hear him. "Maybe after the babe arrives, and you birth a few more, I'll grant you what I've heard you beg for." He eyed her body. Her eyes had drifted closed a while before. "Maybe, little princess, I'll let you die. But for now"—he raised the glass of wine before himself, swirling the liquid and watching it move—"we plan an announcement. My true heir is coming."

*****

CLEMENTINE

Clementine threw her cloak over her shoulders. She had waited too long. She was too *fucking* late. She had to do something. Elle was pregnant. The girl was pregnant. *Fuck fuck fuck fuck.* How the *hell* was she supposed to get her out? She was hurrying through the halls toward the basement when she heard Suho and Silas speaking in a room as she passed.

She would have never stopped before. Except.

"There's been sightings in Torzen of the vampire hunter again."

"The one mated to Bone?"

"Apparently. I wonder why he's returned."

Her mate was back. The hunter who had been cursed by the moon to be fated to a vampire had returned to Torzen. There was no way he wasn't there to try to find his mate. He could help. He could help her get Elle out. She couldn't do it alone, but with a hunter . . . maybe they'd be able to get Elle far enough away. She ran down the stairs to the basement, but she passed Mutt's cage.

She was headed for Silas's lab.

She knew how he traveled to Torzen, and if she could steal one of the vials, she could get there, find the hunter, and get back quickly enough . . . No, wait. She could just tell them she was headed on a run. No one had any reason to suspect otherwise . . . Yeah. Yeah. Steal two rounds, then "leave" to go collect more humans like her and Mutt did often enough. She could get to the hunter, then if he didn't kill her on sight, she could convince him to help her get Elle out.

It could work.

It had to work.

*****

Clementine hated Silas's lab. It was so . . . unsettling. Even for her. She'd grown up in this gods-forsaken castle with Dae as a father, and Silas's lab was bad enough it made her skin crawl. But she needed his travel spells.

He'd long ago honed blood travel, something very few vampires could perform. And what Silas had done with it was condense it. It was truly a work of genius.

Blood travel required the blood of a human to move to a location known by the vampire using it, and it had required a *lot* of blood before Silas found a way to make it portable.

The work, time, *humans* it'd taken to create the two vials she was about to steal made sure that while this was a true innovation in science, it was not one used often. He was still working to hone it. To streamline it.

But none of that mattered to Clementine at this point. She needed two. One to get herself to Torzen, and one to get home. That was all she needed. In and out. Silas was likely still with Suho upstairs, but that would only entertain him for so long. If Silas was not bedding his dinner, he was in his lab. He preferred it to the goings-on of the castle.

She understood that much. She spent her days anywhere else too.

But it meant she only had moments to retrieve what she needed.

She slipped into the room and sucked in a breath as the smells overwhelmed her. In. Out. She just needed to grab two. Then get the *fuck* out.

She'd seen him get them out of the cabinet on the far wall. She hurried toward it, trying to keep her steps light. Once she opened the cabinet, she quickly found them, took two, and shoved them down the top of her dress so they rested hidden between her breasts.

Then she heard footsteps.

Heavy footsteps she'd heard down there before.

Silas.

~ 37 ~

CHAPTER 37

CLEMENTINE

She turned and was face-to-face with Silas.

He tilted his head, his long white hair falling over his shoulder as he did. "What are you doing in here, Clem?"

"I . . . was looking for a sedative."

His brow furrowed. "And why do you need a sedative? If you need something for your hunts, you only have to ask, young one." He began to tie up his hair as he walked toward her.

She shook her head. "It's for the princess."

"You're sedating the princess?" He strode past her. "That's why you're down here in secret then? Because you know Dae would be quite upset if he knew you were interfering with her. I understand now."

For a genius, Silas was easy to fool.

"I must advise you against angering your father, youngling." Silas shuffled through glass bottles on a shelf. "But I will not stop you. The woman's screams have put a damper on my activities."

"I'm sorry that her torment inconveniences you," Clementine growled.

"Do you want my help or not, child?" Silas glared over his shoulder. "That being said, this is an exchange. I'll give you what you wish, but I need your assistance."

"And what is it that you need?"

"Your power. I'd like you to use it on a pair of humans."

"For what purpose?" Clementine shuffled nervously.

"To observe what happens to their minds when combined with something I've been developing. Shouldn't take you more than a moment. And then I'll give you whatever you wish. But if I get word that Dae knows I gave you *anything*, I'll rip your throat out. Understood, bastard princess?"

She nodded, her eyes lowered. "Yes."

*****

Silas dragged a pair of humans into the room and restrained them on the tables he used for his experiments.

Two men. Both young, neither likely to be more than a few years Clementine's elder.

One looked at Silas fondly. The other had desperate fear in his eyes.

Silas injected them both with something Clementine had no knowledge of and wished not to. He kissed the one with the gentle eyes, who then said something Clementine couldn't hear.

Silas shook his head and turned to her. "This one. Show him his greatest fear."

That was her power. Clementine could take control of a mind for ten seconds. Within those seconds, she could force the mind to live, as if it were truly and wholly real, their greatest fear or their greatest joy.

The human's eyes had gone glassy like Elle's. Whatever he'd been injected with had begun its work.

She stepped toward him and extended her hand, gently touching his arm. "Show me your greatest fear."

She hated the next part.

Chaos erupted in the room, and the man was screaming. Screeching. His eyes rolled back into his head.

But the response of this human was stronger than she'd ever seen. His eyes, nose, and ears began to bleed. He writhed in his restraints, and he twisted unnaturally until the ten seconds ended.

But when her power left him, when the nightmare was over, the man went entirely still. He was dead.

She looked at Silas, her brow furrowed in confusion. "You—"

"Interesting." He looked at the man, no emotion behind the crimson eyes. He walked over and wiped some of the blood running from his eyes with two fingers. He licked the blood from them as he observed the body for a moment. Then, without looking at her directly, he pointed at the other. "And him. His greatest joy."

He looked as dull as the first had, otherwise he might have been screaming at the sight that had just unfolded before them.

She repeated her movements, repeated the gentle touch, but her command changed. "Show me your greatest joy."

The response wasn't normal. It wasn't like it had been any time she'd used her power before.

The human writhed again. Blood poured again.

But the male smiled. He was smiling as his body revolted.

It was truly horrible to watch. As his joy . . . as his greatest joy killed him.

"It's done, Silas. Give me the sedative. I want to leave." Her eyes could not leave the bodies of the men she'd just killed. The two humans who had just died by her hands . . . somewhat.

Silas rolled his eyes and grabbed a small glass bottle. "Here. Go, young one. I'm going to continue on with my work here."

*****

Her eyes met Mutt's as she hurried upstairs as quickly as she could. She rushed to tell Suho she had "a hunt" to attend to, and then she would find the hunter. The mate.

She stopped before Elle's room, the small, bottled sedative in her hand. It hadn't been her plan, but sedating the poor soul would be a gift she could grant her before she left. She knocked twice, then opened the door slowly. "Elle . . . ?"

Elle was sitting up, her head drooped to the side and her eyes half-open. Her hands rested on the tiny curve of her tummy that had started to show. She didn't turn to face Clementine when she entered. She only continued breathing slow and labored breaths.

Clementine closed the door behind her as she stepped into the room. "Elle."

"Clementine." Elle's voice was so small. She still did not turn to face her.

Stepping up to the bed, she gently touched Elle's arm as she neared. "It's time to sleep a bit, Ellie. But first . . ." A tear rolled down Clementine's cheek. "Show me your greatest joy."

At the command, Clementine saw it as though looking through a lens at Elle's mind. Experienced it with Elle as if she were living it with her. Her greatest joy.

Flowers gently bent as a breeze washed over them, tall grass almost an off-yellow against the green and blue of the flowers. In the field before her, three figures stood. One she knew immediately. Kirk. He smiled softly at her, a few loose strands of his hair blowing across his face. The white shirt he wore was unlaced deep down his chest. His blue eyes were gentle and locked on hers. Before him stood two little boys. Children. One of his hands on the shoulder of each. They only stood to his waist. She could not see their faces, she did not yet know their faces, but she knew they were her sons. Tears rolled down her cheeks. She was warm, she was safe, and this was her home. They were her home. Kirk and those children before her were her entire world, and as she looked at them, she felt truly and fully . . . okay. She glanced down at her tummy. It was heavily swollen, the boys before her vanishing because they were not yet in this world. She placed her hand on her stomach. "I'm so excited to meet you."

As Elle slipped down toward the bed, her eyes closed softly and her breathing calmed The vision faded, and Clementine drugged her so she could rest.

*****

Suho did not question her when she said she would return soon enough after a hunt. He nodded and flipped a hand to send her off.

She pulled her cloak over her shoulders, sheathed the dagger at her belt, then grabbed one of the vials hidden in her shirt. She stood in her room, the door closed, and poured out the contents. A pool of blood, far greater than what should have been contained in such a small glass, spread on the floor before her.

She stepped into the blood.

She was standing before the walls of Torzen, tucked out of sight so as not to alert the humans that she had simply *appeared*. She pulled her cloak over her head tighter and hurried into the bustling city.

Now to find a vampire hunter.

Not get killed.

And convince him to save his mate.

Part 4

Can The Devil Die

~ 38 ~

INTERLUDE

Elle's hands shook as she held them in front of her face. "Alder!"

His eyes darkened. He grabbed a blade, and his fist tightened around it. "A vampire?! I've been fucking a VAMPIRE?"

She whimpered, tears pouring down her cheeks. "Alder, please. Please. I'm only telling you because I love you. Please!"

"You're a fucking monster." He grabbed her throat and squeezed.

Choking and gasping, she clawed at his hand wrapped around her throat. "P-please."

"Fuck you—"

She saw it in his eyes. She knew with certainty. Alder was about to kill her. He was about to tear her life from her. She should have known. He'd been controlling. He'd been abusive. He'd hit her so many times. But she'd wanted to love him. She'd wanted to trust him.

And he chose to kill her.

Instincts took control of her body. A will to live. A monster in her soul that would not let a human take her life from her this simply.

She scratched at his face and dragged her nails through one of his eyes.

It was enough to break his concentration and his grip on her.

Then she attacked. She bit into his throat with dulled teeth, tearing at his flesh.

She'd never tasted blood before.

She'd never known the taste of human blood.

It was exquisite.

She felt stronger, powerful. Alive. She hadn't realized how far from alive she'd felt until the metallic liquid crossed her lips.

She tore Alder to pieces.

She drank his blood until her belly was full for the first time in her life. She'd never known satisfaction like she did in that moment.

Then it stopped.

And she stared at the remains of the man below her.

And she panicked.

And she ran.

~ 39 ~

CHAPTER 39

K^{IRK}
A vampire girl stood before him.

"I need your help. We have to get her out of the castle," she said, desperation in her eyes.

His hand on the hilt of his sword tightened. It had moved there on instinct but now remained until he could understand fully what was happening. "She's *where*?" he growled. "Where is my mate?"

The vampire girl stepped back. "She's been taken by Dae. He's keeping her in the castle. He's torturing her, hunter."

Kirk would have sprinted out the door then. His feet moved.

The vampire held up her hand. "You can't just run in there. You'll get both of you killed—"

"You said she's being *tortured*." That fear he'd felt. That dread he'd felt. She was being tortured. *Tortured.* He grabbed her arm and tugged her closer. "You're one of his bastards."

The girl trembled in his grasp. "Hunter, sir. Yes. I-I came here looking for you, or the mage she lived with, to figure out a way to get her out. Please." She winced as his grip on her arm only tightened.

Kirk released her. "Let me get dressed. Then we need to talk."

~ 40 ~

CHAPTER 40

CLEMENTINE

Clementine soon found herself standing in Morel, nervously checking over her shoulder. Her hood was pulled over her head, and she held it closed tightly. The three other figures watched her.

The mage.

The hunter.

Her half brother the half-breed.

What exactly had she been thinking? Asking this mismatched trio to help her steal away the future vampire queen. Dae's future queen.

Dae's *heir*. They were going to try to steal away the fucking heir of the last great vampiric lord. These three and herself.

Maybe Mutt.

They were truly and fully *fucked*. But they needed to get her out. Clementine couldn't see another woman go through what her mother had. Or see another baby live through what she had.

She still hadn't told them about the baby. She knew the three of them were desperate for the return of their princess, but she did not know if the mate or the mage would reject her if they knew she carried the spawn of the devil. She wondered if her brother would be like her, desperate to protect another of Dae's children. Another of their siblings cursed by his blood.

None of them seemed like the type to turn her away.

But Dae had false faces too.

She would keep the secret for now. They'd know soon enough. If they managed to save her . . .

If they all didn't die in the process.

The hunter spoke first, his voice deep and ragged. He'd been falling apart for a while, clearly. "So you can get her out?"

Focused on the task, as she had expected a hunter to be.

She could see a thousand questions about the happenings within the castle walls bubbling beneath his surface, but his task was clear, and like a well-trained dog, he had steps to take.

She nodded. "Only out. And they'll know quickly. I don't know what he'll send after her, but I wouldn't be surprised if he sends everything, even chases her himself. And sir, hunter, even with your experience, Dae is far beyond any vampire you've encountered."

"So I transport us and we run," the mage said, her voice laced with frozen rage.

Her brother spoke next. "No. No. Dae *will* come after her." He was seated on the mage's worktable. She looked ready to shove the bastard onto the floor. His legs were crossed beneath him, his hands held to his shins, and he shook his head. "If she is actually that important, he's going to hunt her down if we simply *take* her."

Clementine bobbed her head in agreement. "He won't let her get away again. Either we need a way to hide her from him forever, or he needs—" She noted bags packed by the doors, they were leaving. They had been leaving to find Elle.

"We kill him," the hunter said, his attempts at keeping his rage hidden in a stone demeanor slipped quickly. He wanted Dae's head on a stick.

So did Clementine.

Bliss looked uneasy. Killing his father was a task far beyond the skills of this group, even fueled by their devotion to Elle, and he clearly knew it.

Clementine knew it too.

Even with the whispers she'd heard from Silas that Elle contained immense power, the girl likely was nowhere near a state where she could help them in a fight. Her mind had all but left her completely. The girl's eyes had become glassy, doll-like. Nothing remained behind them. Clementine could only hope that being reunited with her mate, her family, might bring her back to life.

Again. That was if they all didn't die in the process.

"And how do you plan on killing a vampire like Dae?" Bliss leaned forward a bit. "He can bend your fucking blood in your veins. How are *we* going to kill something like that?"

June ran her hand through her hair. "We figure it out, Bliss. I'd rather die trying to save Elle than leave her one more fucking minute in that castle."

Clementine could nearly *see* the weight of the mage's guilt on her spine. She'd brushed by her earlier, seen the glimpse of her greatest fear. Of course it was about Elle and Bliss. Her greatest joy too. Both about them being at her side. Or *not*. "There's a dinner tomorrow," Clementine finally said, "to announce . . . a celebration. I can get Dae drunk, distracted with food and women, and sneak her away. No one bats an eye anymore if she needs rest . . ."

The hunter's eyes shot to Clementine's and his resolve, his focus, broke. "Why?"

Clementine's heart constricted at the desperation in his voice. "Dae has been cruel to her, hunter. She will be only a whisper of who you knew."

"A . . . whisper . . ." He faltered. For a fraction of a moment, that rage burning in his eyes just evaporated, replaced with solely grief. It returned quickly, boiling over the sorrow and returning the anger. "But even then, if Bliss is right and Dae hunts her, we need to be ready for whatever comes after us."

"Dae." Bliss swallowed. "Dae comes after us and kills us all. Takes Ellie back, and it's for nothing. This isn't a plan, Kirk."

"It's what we have." He looked between Clementine, June, and Bliss. "The mage is more powerful than she's let on. I'm *trained* for this, and I can smell power on this vampire." He gestured to Clementine. "It's all we have so it *has* to be enough."

"There's one more I might be able to sway . . . I would have to find a way to release him." Clementine hoped she would be able to break Mutt of Dae's influence. She *hoped*.

"That's going to have to be enough," Kirk repeated. "She's spoken it before, but if you do not wish to come along, then *don't*." His voice rumbled as he addressed her brother. This was a man dead set on protecting his mate. This was a different type of instinct.

Bliss closed his eyes and breathed. "I only want us to ensure Ellie's safe. And has a family to come home to . . . That's all."

"I will ensure it." The hunter spoke confidently. Far more confidently than he should, given their situation. But she understood that if they didn't believe in it, they were doomed from the start. "Tomorrow, we're getting Elle *out*."

~ 41 ~

CHAPTER 41

KIRK
They were about to start a war with Dae, but nothing in him hesitated. Nothing in him faltered as he walked toward where Clementine had told him to be. He was going to wait there to retrieve Elle.

June was off deeper in the woods preparing a spell to transport the girl farther away, to give them more time, to put more space between her and Dae.

Bliss was with her, guarding her.

It was all they had.

And it had to be enough to save Elle.

He'd spent the entire night thinking about what had happened to Elle. Clementine had returned to the castle, so he had no answers. No knowledge outside of the few things she'd mentioned. A husk. Elle was a tortured husk of who he'd known. And it was his fucking fault. He hadn't protected her. He'd let her go.

But now, as he trekked through the woods, all he could think of was her smell. Her taste. What it would feel like to hold her again . . .

He'd already decided. He was going to accept their bond. Accept their fate as mated souls and become one with her. Become entirely and wholly hers. Without hesitation. Without question. He was going to accept what the moon had *gifted* them. And then he would protect her with everything he was and everything he had.

But first, he waited.

~ 42 ~

CHAPTER 42

C LEMENTINE
    Dae sat at the head of the table, which was set with the most extravagant of his tableware. Candles ran down the center, hundreds and hundreds of candles. The wax dripped onto the blood-red runner beneath them. He was dressed in his best suit. It fit against his body flawlessly, black with red and gold embellishments that sparkled when the light of the candles hit them.

Elle sat on one of his thighs, her body leaned against his chest and her head on his shoulder. Her eyes were closed. She'd drifted out of consciousness again . . . They'd dressed her in a gown of black fabric that sparkled with thousands of gems and draped gently over her body. The neckline plunged low, and the sleeves hung off her shoulders. Slits up the skirt revealed bare thighs past her hips. His hand was wrapped around her waist, his nails dug through the dress into the flesh of her side.

The dress was meant to conceal the small curve of her tummy.

They all knew.

But he still wished to announce it.

The court's anxiety was thick in the room, their gazes flitting between each other and their lord at the head of the table. This was gaudy even for Dae. The air hung heavy with tension.

Clementine's foot tapped nervously under the table. It was the night she was going to set her free. The night she was going to get her out.

Dae spoke. "I've gathered you all to share great news."

They all already knew.

They knew.

"My darling princess is pregnant." The smile on Dae's lips, one of cruelest pride, burned into every one of their souls. "The first son of a great bloodline is on the way."

Clementine tried to control her emotions. Her face. Elle wouldn't suffer as Mother had. Elle wouldn't die like Mother did. This was her last night in this wretched prison.

*****

ELLE

Her mind came back from the darkness. She was . . . in the dining room? When had she gotten there? She was seated . . . she was seated on Dae's lap. His hand was wrapped around her waist, and his nails dug deep into her side. It hurt. Maybe that was what had drawn her back? There was blood dripping from where he pierced her flesh, warm as it rolled down her hip. She winced and blinked, scanning the room to try to understand her surroundings. Her eyes landed on Clementine, who was looking so intently at her. She looked so sad. There were other voices. Other people. She was sitting on Dae. Dae was touching her. He was so close. She fidgeted, her body screaming at her to get away from him. His nails only dug deeper, and she whimpered. Pain washed over her, and her fear rendered her immobile.

I see you've returned, little princess. For now, at least. You keep disappearing on me. His voice rattled in her mind. *In and out, over and over . . . I'll have Silas sedate you again. You've become so difficult when you're lucid.*

She grabbed at her head when his voice entered. It was overwhelming.

Hands down. Get ahold of yourself. His nails dug deeper as he dragged his fingers tighter, threatening to rip a piece of her side from her body.

But she couldn't. His voice was too much. It was all too much. She crumpled, and he caught her around her waist as she fell.

"Fucking hell," he hissed.

Clementine's chair squealed against the ground as she shoved it back and stood. "Father, let me take her to her room. She's clearly unwell and should rest. For the baby."

Elle's hands were still on either side of her head. It was so loud. It was so loud.

Clementine was quickly beside them, trying to help Elle up before Dae's answer was fully formed on his lips. "I'll take her to her room, Father."

Dae hissed through his teeth. "Fine." He glared at both of them as Clementine pulled her onto her feet. "I'll call for the healer. Silas, after dinner I want her sedated again. I will not risk damage to my child."

And Dae waved them away.

*****

Clementine held Elle tightly as she pulled her into the hall. "Are you still with me, Elle?"

Dae's voice had quieted. The room was spinning, but she could see again. She could hear her own thoughts again. "Yeah . . . yeah."

"Good." Clementine propped her against her shoulder. "Listen to me. Look at me."

She turned to face her.

Clementine's eyes were so stern. The look in them was so intense. "I'm going to keep Dae busy. Get him drunk and occupied . . ." She took in a deep breath. Her voice grew quieter as she said, "You're going to run."

Her eyes widened, and she stumbled backward. "He'll kill me . . . I can't. I can't." Her voice rattled.

"Kirk's waiting for you."

Kirk? Kirk. Kirk Kirk Kirk Kirk Kirk Kirk. Kirk's waiting for me. Kirk's here. Kirk. My mate. My mate is here. "He's—"

"He's waiting. You have to run to him, okay? Run as fast as you fucking can to him." A tear rolled down Clementine's cheek. "Run, Ellie. He's just on the east side of the castle. In the woods. He's waiting. Run, for the love of the moon." Clementine brought her to a door that led to the garden. "Hurry. He's going to grow suspicious." She grasped tightly to her arms. "Go. Protect that baby. Go."

And Elle ran.

*****

It was still afternoon. When she opened the door and the sun hit her face, she could barely keep her eyes open. It was too hot. It was too bright. It was so much. It burned. But she had to run. Clementine told her to run. To keep running. She couldn't stop. She had to run. Clementine would keep Dae at bay as long as she could . . . But they were bonded. He would find her. He would chase her. Soon. She had to get as far as she could. She had to run as far as she could. Dae was on her heels.

But Kirk was waiting. Kirk was here. Kirk had come back for her. Kirk had come back to her. She had to get to him. She had to get to him no matter what. No matter what.

She didn't have shoes. Her feet were bleeding as the ground of the garden, then the forest around it, tore into her soles. She was leaving a blood trail. Not that Dae would need it. The curse would be like a beacon. Leading him straight to her until she found some way to break it. Her dress tore and snagged on branches and bushes as she passed them. She didn't care. She had to run. Why had she run? He was going to come after her. He was going to hunt her, and he was going to kill her. She couldn't escape him. She couldn't escape him no matter how far she ran. Even with Kirk waiting for her, he would find her. He would kill her.

The seal on her chest began to burn. Why run? She had behaved so Dae would have no reason to hurt those she loved. If she was good, he wouldn't hurt her or them. Why was she running? He was going to hurt her. Them. She should stop. No. No, if she stopped, she would die. He would kill her in that castle. She would die on that stone, and her blood would join the lake underneath it.

But if she died . . . Choosing her own life was selfish. If she died, it still kept them all safe. But if she died in the castle, she couldn't protect the baby. She couldn't keep them safe from Dae if she died in those walls. But he would chase them. He wouldn't stop. Running only prolonged her suffering. Their suffering. But she had to. She couldn't bear it any longer. Shit. Shit. Shit. Shit. Her heart rate quickened. She couldn't calm it. She couldn't calm her breathing. Darkness was closing in. Her vision was getting spotty. Shit. It was collapsing. She was drowning again.

WHERE HAVE YOU GONE, LITTLE PRINCESS?

Her knees buckled as his voice echoed in her head, and she collapsed, falling hard against the earth. She screamed, but she tried to stand again, she tried to pull herself back up. She tried.

DARLING LITTLE PRINCESS, YOU'VE RUN OFF. WHAT A STUPID LITTLE BITCH YOU ARE. THE DOG IS COMING FOR YOU.

The dog. Mutt. He'd released Mutt.

~ 43 ~

CHAPTER 43

MUTT

Dae stood beside Mutt, his hand wrapped tightly around the leather leash around his neck. "Bring her back to me," he commanded.

Mutt rolled his head and anxiously shifted from foot to foot, waiting to be released. Waiting to hunt.

Dae dropped the leash. "Go."

Mutt must have been good. They hadn't let him out in so long. And so rarely without his leash. His vision went entirely red. He followed her trail, his senses locked onto the escaped princess. He was so excited to tear into her. He was so excited to feel flesh under his claws. If only they'd taken off the muzzle. If only he'd been able to bite. He missed it. Biting. He wanted to feel flesh in his teeth so badly. He wanted to tear into someone and feel the warmth of their blood on his face. But at least he got to hunt. He got to hunt down prey that smelled so strongly of fear it was nearly overpowering. She would taste so good. All that fear, all that blood, she would taste so good if only he could . . .

He wanted to kill her. Dae didn't want him to, but he *really* wanted to . . . He would smell her blood as it poured from her body, see it on his hands, feel it on his face. He was so very excited to hunt again. His senses overpowered what control he had. When he saw her, he was going to tear her apart, and he was going to *love* it.

*****

She hadn't even sensed Mutt coming. He was a predator, and she was simply prey, a deer that could not sense a wolf about to rip her to shreds. She hadn't stood a chance when they released his leash. Mutt was built for this. Mutt was trained for this. She never could have escaped him. She had started to turn around, only hearing him behind her when it was far too late. He dug his claws into her flesh and tore at her skin, removing chunks of the muscle beneath. Gaping wounds in her back began to bleed profusely, heavy rivers of wine pounded into the dirt beneath her.

The edges of Mutt's vision darkened and focused when the smell of that blood collided with him. He needed it. He needed *all of it.* He *needed* to see her insides, her intestines, her heart, her lungs, in his hands, in his mouth. He wanted to tear her apart and feel that warmth. Feel the life in her body fade away. Those glorious sounds, that incredible taste, the feeling, the liquids pouring from her body, her chest cavity sucking air in, death rattles, gurgles; he *craved* it all. He shook with excitement.

She had made Clementine cry. She had made his angel sad. She was why the angel was sad and why the master was mad. She should die. She should die because she made his angel cry. She needed to die. He needed her to die.

*****

ELLE

She screamed and fell forward, crashing into the ground. That was it. They'd caught her. She'd failed and it was over. He was going to drag her back into that castle, and whatever awaited her when she returned . . . Dae would surely make her regret running. *Fuck. Fuck. Fuck.* She had been so close to town. Maybe she would have seen June again. Maybe she would have seen Kirk again. Just for a moment. She screamed as he tore at her, her head rearing up as the pain caused her body to twist.

He slammed her face into the ground and pressed her head down with one hand. She could hear him panting. His drool dripped onto the wounds in her shoulders. He had her pinned. He had caught her. But he didn't stop.

If he was supposed to bring her back to the castle he was surely supposed to stop.

Her mind had been muddy for days . . . weeks . . . blurry and chaotic, but in one moment, Elle knew with absolute clarity she was about to die. Mutt was going to kill her. Right there. Mutt was going to kill her.

She heard herself screaming. Begging him to stop. She hadn't made it out. Clementine was going to suffer for this. Kirk and June might if Dae was angry enough and he caught them. This wasn't how it was supposed to end. She was supposed to see them all again. She wanted to see *him* again. He was waiting for her. She'd nearly made it to him. She'd nearly seen him again . . . But now she was going to *die.* Her baby was going to die. His claws made contact again. Pain crashed into her as he tore a hole through her back. His hand wrapped around one of her lungs . . .

His hand ripped through her chest. His claws grasped at her lungs and tore at her heart. He hadn't stopped. Something had driven him further. Something must have broken in him. She could nearly feel it as his ferocity only increased.

She screamed one more time. A flash of bright light burst from her. Mutt screamed as it consumed him. He fell off her, her lung still in his grip. She barely heard crashing as he stumbled away from her. He fell into the bushes around them and kept pushing seemingly to get as far from Elle as he could before his limbs gave out and he crumpled onto the ground. He kept screaming.

Elle lay on her stomach, the pool of blood beneath her spreading quickly. Her cheek was pressed into the ground and her face was pointed toward where the dog scrambled away, screaming and grasping at his face. The light faded. Then it all went numb. It overwhelmed her until she felt nothing. White-hot pain shifted into unfeeling darkness.

Elle felt warm. For a moment. Like someone was holding her, and she could have sworn she'd heard his voice. Kirk's voice. Then she felt nothing at all, and the darkness consumed her entirely.

Elle was dead.

~ 44 ~

CHAPTER 44

K IRK
He waited patiently, searching for any sign she was near. This was close to when Clementine had said she'd get Elle out. Get her to him . . . But the forest was quiet and still, uneasily silent. Until he suddenly *felt* her. He felt her *strongly.* The small pull exploded in his chest. She was near, and she was getting closer. He broke into a sprint toward her. As he got closer, he heard her steps in the distance, crashing steps through the brush. She was close. She was close.

Then the bond was overwhelmed with pain.

He screamed. Something in his soul screamed. Something was wrong. He had been getting closer and closer to her, but now something ripped at his chest. It felt like something was being driven into his heart. Something happened. Something happened to her. He picked up the pace after he regained his footing, and he ran toward where he'd been drawn, toward where he desperately hoped she would be. He'd felt her so close, he still did, but now something was wrong. Something was so wrong.

Then he saw her. Her body on the forest floor. *No.* Her tiny body lay in pools of blood and viscera. She was not breathing. She was not moving. She was dead. Elle was dead. He was too late. They were too late. He'd found her too late, and she was *dead.*

He slid onto his knees beside her. He could barely take in the sight of her, the sight of the broken woman before him. She made a sound. She wasn't dead yet. A spark of hope shot through his bones. She wasn't dead yet. But she was going to be. Soon. "Elle! *Elle.* Hey . . ." He scooped her up into his arms.

She was gasping and choking. The sounds coming from the wound in her chest made it clear that even a vampire could not survive it. Gurgling sounds bubbled from her throat, the wound went all the way through her chest and back. She was choking on blood. It ran from her mouth and sprayed every time her chest heaved as she tried to suck in any air. Blood poured from her like a steady river, creating a puddle beneath them and coating Kirk entirely. It gushed and spurted from the holes in her flesh, from the wounds that were deep enough to damage her organs. Her attempts at breaths faltered.

She was going to die in his arms. He had to do something. He had to do anything. He had to save her.

She needed blood.

Kirk nearly dropped her as he reached for his knife, desperate. He had to try anything, anything. He was screaming her name. Frantically, he cut open his arm, the wound messy and jagged. His blood was black. His blood was cursed. But it was all he had. Maybe. Maybe his blood would be enough. "Elle, *please.*" He pressed his arm to her open mouth. "Please. Please. Fuck. Fuck, Elle. Drink this, Elle, please. *Elle.*"

The black blood mixed with the red running over her chin. She sputtered once more, the black and red spraying Kirk's face as he screamed. Then she went entirely still in his arms. Her chest ceased its desperate heaving, and her eyes stared past him.

Elle died. Kirk screamed. Half of his soul. His soul-bound mate. Dead in his arms. The other half of himself without breath. He doubled over her, pulling her broken body to his chest. He pressed his forehead against hers. "Elle. Elle. Please. Please. Don't do this. Don't leave me. Gods damn it, I love you, Elle. I am *bound* to you. You are my salvation. Please. Please. You can't leave me. I will give anything. Anything and everything. My entire soul. My life. Anything." He held her tighter, pulled her closer. "I beg any god, every god, the sun, the moon, don't leave me. I've only just found you. I cannot lose you. I cannot breathe when you're not with me. The world crashes. The world ends. Elle. Elle, I'm yours. I'm yours entirely. Don't leave me."

*****

The moon looked down at her child, the broken girl in the arms of her lover. She listened as the human boy screamed. As the human boy begged and pleaded for the life of a vampire. A human boy who had spent his life killing her children now begging to spare one he had come to *love*. She felt the girl's soul drifting toward her, coming home to her mother's embrace . . . But the moon heard the man's screams. She felt the soul of the girl long for him. She listened as he promised to bond his soul to hers. She heard his words, she heard the soul of her child begging to return to him. She smiled softly. *Protect my daughter, human. You've given your blood to save her, and you've bonded your soul to hers. I will grant you this*, the moon whispered and returned Elle's soul, ushering her back to her body and giving her a second life.

A pair of tiny souls, unsure of their identities, followed behind Elle, first drifting with her toward the moon, and then returning to Elle's body with the moon's blessing.

*****

Dae
There was an enormous sound, like an explosion. Deafening. It left his ears ringing. Dae was overwhelmed as the chains between him and Elle shattered.

He felt every string attached to every nerve in his body tear. Ripping her away from him. His heart stopped for a moment. His head felt like it would burst. Every inch of him burned with pain all at once. It buckled his knees. Loss. Everything was stripped away so fast it felt like the air left his lungs.

He collapsed, gasping, grabbing at his heart. The glass in his hand fell and shattered on the ground beside him.

Dae screamed, not in pain, but rage.

*****

ELLE

She gasped first. She had been gone. The darkness had taken her. Then she felt everything break all at once. Her body was torn away from her, then dropped back to earth. Dae was gone. She could breathe. A flash of excruciating pain in every nerve, then it was all gone. She felt so much lighter she nearly felt nothing, then she sank back into her body. The body she'd left. She'd died. Elle had died. She'd heard Kirk calling to her. Kirk begging and screaming. She'd heard his voice, the deep rolling of it, pulling her back.

Her wound, now healing, reminded her of its presence. She was in Kirk's arms . . . She was wounded. She had died. She dropped back into reality . . . but reality looked different, like the fog, like the screen over her soul was gone. The scars remained, but his control was gone. She was free of Dae. She'd died, she'd felt the moon's embrace, but now, now she was back in her body and her bond to Dae was gone.

*****

KIRK

Searing pain scorched Kirk's chest, his heart . . . No, above it. Like a brand applied to his skin, it burned for a moment then vanished. Something washed over him, something went through him. He was not the same.

"Elle . . . Elle?!" He pulled his face back from hers. She'd started breathing. There was breath in her lungs, her breath on his face. Then she screamed; she was in pain. "Shh. Shh. You're okay. You're just—" He glanced down at her and watched as her wounds slowly started to heal, glowing gently as they began to close. "You're healing." He spoke the words so quietly, as if to himself, a whisper to assure himself. "Elle, you're healing . . ."

Her breaths were still short, hitching as her lungs tried to close the wounds Mutt had put through them. She let out a small yelp as Kirk moved her slightly. Tears welled up in the corners of her eyes. "Kirk . . . ?"

He kissed her. Desperately and passionately, he kissed her.

Then he heard something in the bushes.

~ 45 ~

CHAPTER 45

CLEMENTINE

She ran after Mutt. It was falling apart. She wasn't sure who she'd thought Dae would send but not Mutt. Had he known she'd released his princess? Had he sent the only joy in her world deliberately to torment her? She ran as fast as she could after her dog. Praying she wasn't too late.

She burst through the bushes and found Kirk kneeling with Elle in his arms. The girl was bloody, but she was breathing. Alive.

"Mutt. Where's my dog?"

She heard his soft whimpering in the bushes and ran to him.

He was crying even through his muzzle. His hands clasped tightly over his eyes, he just kept crying. Blood coated his face, so much blood, And he smelled like burning flesh. She pulled at the muzzle which easily fell away, the straps had barely been hanging on. The volume of his screams grew as soon as his mouth was free.

She clasped the sides of his face. "Mutt, Mutt, what's wrong? Move your hands. You've got to move your hands and let me see, Mutt. Please."

His hands shook profusely as he pulled them stiffly from his face. His screams shifted to whimpers and panting.

She stifled a gasp when she saw his face . . . what was *left*. "Oh my gods. Oh my gods, Mutt. Mutt . . ."

His eyes were gone. Burned away. The top of his face, from his nose up, was badly and severely burned. Blood poured from where his eyes had been. It ran down from the sides of his open mouth. Dae's seal was burned into his tongue, the mark of the bond Dae had placed on him.

"Oh my gods. Oh my gods."

He was gasping as he lay in her arms. She looked at that mouth, a mouth she'd only seen glimpses of. His jawline was handsome. He would have had such a lovely face. She leaned close to him and kissed just beside his lips. She felt his body tense for a moment, then he relaxed, even leaned into the gentle touch.

*****

MUTT

He'd never been kissed. He'd never known a touch as gentle. It felt warm. It felt safe. She felt warm and safe.

She kissed him again, this time her lips against his. "Please . . . just hang on. I'll get you away from here, somewhere safe," she whispered, holding his face close to hers, their foreheads together.

He shook his head. He wouldn't be able to run from Dae. Not from the consequences. He wouldn't be able to run. Mutt was going to die.

He'd killed Dae's whore. He'd killed Dae's heir.

Mutt felt her tears hitting his face. He couldn't see her. He wished he could see her face. He just wanted to see her face. She always looked like an angel. His eyes weren't healing. The magic. The princess's magic was strong enough she'd taken his eyes. He almost felt it was fair. He'd taken her life . . .

He must look so ugly to Clem. But she kissed him again. It was so soft. So good. He'd been a bad dog. He'd disobeyed, and he'd broken his commands, yet she rewarded him so sweetly. He did not deserve such delicate touches. Every time she kissed him, he forgot the pain. He forgot the fear. He just felt *her*. He did not wish to die. He wished to feel this forever . . . her kisses. Over and over. But if he did, he could die knowing a peace that resonated through his bestial soul. The animal he was felt *loved*. He'd been kissed by an angel.

"Mutt, we have to run. We have to run."

Mutt shook his head, leaning his face into her. He couldn't see, but he could smell her, he could feel her.

"Please, Mutt." Her voice cracked with panic. "Please. Please. Father will kill you."

The pain had grown numb. He was already dying. He could not run . . . And the seal burned into his tongue meant Dae would find him. Dae would have a beacon that led him directly to him, to her, and since he'd killed Dae's whore, he would be hunted. He shook his head *no* again, whimpering.

She took his hand and squeezed it. "I'm your handler, good boy . . ." She slowly helped him stand, leaning his body against hers. His knees shook. "I'm going back with you then."

He shook his head again, far more violently this time. He pressed his hand blindly against her chest, pushing against her.

A man, one who smelled of the princess, called out, "Vampire! We need to move!" His tone was cold. He had lifted Elle to her feet.

His heart sank. Clementine needed to run. She needed to run. He wanted to beg her to run, to be safe.

Dae was already on his way. He had to be.

~ 46 ~

CHAPTER 46

K IRK
"Vampire, we have to go!" he called to her. If she wished to run beside them, they would take her. They would welcome her. The male she held . . . was near death.

He held Elle closely against his chest. Her wounds began to heal quickly, emitting the soft white glow of the moon. This . . . this was not the Elle he'd known. This was not the Elle he'd left. But this was still Elle. Still his mate. Still his Elle.

They had to go. They had to get as far as they could.

But they were already too late.

He heard him approaching.

Dae was already here.

Elle crumpled against him, her body contorting unnaturally, and she was screaming.

The curse was broken. Kirk knew it well. He and Elle were bonded. He felt as she felt. But that did not take away Dae's ability to bend and twist her blood within her. He tried to keep her upright, hold her against himself to keep her from collapsing, but he needed to grab his sword. He needed to be ready to kill the bastard who had hurt her.

Dae stepped slowly through the bushes toward them. His eyes burned with a rage unlike any Kirk had seen in a vampire before. "You try to steal my queen, hunter?"

293

Kirk held her tightly, unable to reach for his sword. "You stole my mate."

Dae stepped toward them again, and Elle got louder. "You've accepted the bond. I can smell it. I felt it as you ripped my female from me." He growled softly. "I'm surprised you'd accept a bond with a female in such a state."

"What?"

Dae paused for a moment, tilting his head toward the sounds of Clementine and Mutt in the bushes just out of view. "Oh yes, dear hunter, you really must congratulate me. My darling princess is with child. *My child.*"

Kirk's stomach dropped, like the world had vanished beneath his very feet. She . . . she was . . .

But this meant something important.

Dae wouldn't kill her.

He tried something he had read about mates doing. He didn't know how, or if it worked, but he had to do something. He tried to speak to Elle in her mind.

Elle. Elle, if you can hear me. I'm going to let you go. I'm going to rush him. Take his attention from you. June's in the woods. Run to her, Elle. Run to her, please. The moment he releases, you run.

When he opened his mind to hers, he only heard screaming. Hers.

Then he let her go.

He reached for his sword, but another vampire, Clementine, rushed at Dae from behind.

He turned and caught her by her neck. "Darling daughter, you're far too much like your mother. Weak. Emotional." He squeezed. "Truly disgusting."

She glared at him as she sputtered in his ever-tightening grasp. "Father, show me your greatest fear."

Dae *stumbled.*

Clementine dropped onto the ground as he released her.

Elle fell backward as his hold on her blood ceased.

Kirk raised his sword. No sooner were his arms raised, was his sword above his head to strike the vampire, than he felt a grip tighten around his blood.

This was what Dae's power felt like.

He froze.

Dae's eyes met his, strands of his dark hair falling into his face. He panted. A drop of sweat ran down from his temple. "Fuck you. Fuck all of you." One hand extended toward Kirk, who he held in place. The other lifted, and he pointed at Clementine. "Enough of you." He snapped his fingers and she screeched. Her eyes rolled back into her head, and she fell into a pile on the ground.

Her breath stopped.

Kirk stood, shaking, sweat running down his face in streams, unable to break free of the grasp around him. "You—bastard—"

Dae glared at him. "I'd kill you if I could. But you've bound yourself to my darling. I could risk her life if I take yours, you fucking human. You'll spend the rest of your life in my dungeon listening to her scream. Listening to me fuck her. Listening to her birth my children only for me to put another in its fucking place." He tightened his hold on Kirk. "And you'll feel everything. I won't let your bond dull. I won't let it grow numb. You'll feel *everything* I do to her."

~ 47 ~

CHAPTER 47

E^{LLE}

She was getting to her feet, one hand protectively over her belly. She glared at Dae. "Just release him. Just release him."

"And let him hang himself and free you in death?" Dae growled. "Darling, you're a fucking fool if you think I'll let him free."

Her hands began to glow. Light danced at her fingertips. Something deep in her soul had been unlocked. Had been unleashed. Something vampiric. Something powerful.

The Princess of Bone was free of her bondage

Dae's grip shifted to her, and he held her tightly before him. His eyes darted to her fingers growing ever brighter. "Don't make this harder, *Bone.*"

Then.

She heard more voices. Familiar voices.

June.

Bliss.

Her family.

They were here.

June ran toward them.

Dae released Elle to try to grasp at June, but she vanished from this plane before he could take hold of her blood. She appeared behind him, driving a blade gleaming with light into his back.

He turned toward her, and his eyes widened when instead he found himself face-to-face with one of his bastards. Where a mo-

297

ment ago Bliss had stood a few yards away, he was now before Dae, his nails digging into his father's throat.

"Good to see you, Daddy." He grasped tightly, his father's blood running over his fingers.

"Bliss. Duck," Elle said. Dae's grip on her was released. Her hands were then fully consumed in light.

Bliss dropped out of her way.

Before Dae could speak, her hands covered his face. "Close your eyes!" she yelled before light erupted from her and began to burn away Dae's flesh.

His eyes melted in their sockets and ran down the sizzling skin of his cheeks. He screeched, and he moved to try to tear her hands away. He fell back, away from her, screaming and cursing.

The light around them was bright enough that Bliss and June stumbled.

Kirk rushed past her. She only caught a glimpse of his solid black eyes and the flames dancing on his sword.

Then she watched a flash of fire as his sword came down surely on Dae's neck.

The head of the devil rolled toward her feet, still stuck in a burned, contorted scream.

Light danced around them in small flecks, the remnants of her power twinkling like stars fallen to earth.

Dae was dead.

Part 5

Home

~ 48 ~

INTERLUDE

*S*how me your greatest fear.

Dae had known little fear in his lifetime. Little true fear. But when his daughter had grasped his arm and commanded it, he saw two figures.

That was all.

One he knew immediately. Elle.

She stood before him dressed in the old style of Bone. A white dress. Her family's crest embroidered on her chest. Her father's sword in her hand.

The second.

The second, he did not know. At first.

The second was a male. He stood taller than Dae. Broader shoulders. But his face . . .

His face was Dae's own.

That . . . that was his son.

The son who rested in Elle's womb.

The male he feared more than any other.

*****

Mutt crawled toward Clementine's body. He could barely smell her, but he followed what he could to reach her.

His angel.

He dragged himself to lie beside her. He rested his head on her chest and lifted his hand to her hair. He petted it gently as his breathing slowed.

With his final breath he tried, for the first time, to speak.

His final word was his first.

"Clementine."

~ 49 ~

CHAPTER 49

K IRK

It was over.

He was dead.

Dae was dead.

But they had no home to return to. Torzen could not be home to Elle, and Kirk would never let her out of his sight again.

June either, for that matter.

They also couldn't travel forever.

Elle was pregnant.

Kirk lingered on the thought. She was pregnant. He'd never considered a life as a father. Not that the baby was his by blood, but his mate carried offspring. If she would have it, he would love them and care for them as his own flesh and blood.

He needed her to be somewhere she could rest. Heal. Grow the baby she carried. He needed to find her somewhere quiet. Quickly.

She'd already suffered long enough. She needed peace.

He needed peace.

He would find them peace.

*****

The aftermath of their ordeal hung heavy on the air. It smelled strongly of blood and death. They did not dare linger or dispose of bodies as they wished they could. They needed to get far from Torzen quickly. Elle was too well known. Recognized. And with

303

how rumors and word spread through the city, anyone who had known her was well aware of her . . . nature . . . by then.

June was far too exhausted to move anyone, so they would have to begin their travels toward Spiritmire by foot with only one horse between them. Elle stood beside Love, and Kirk took one of his furs from his pack and draped it around her shoulders, wrapping the vampire in warmth.

Her eyes met his and shakily she pressed her hand against his chest, right above where he was now marked. Their mated bond sealed above his heart.

She was still covered in blood. She was still so . . . pale.

He took the hand that she'd placed over his heart and brought it to his lips, kissing her knuckles then holding them to his forehead for a moment.

Her voice was so small. "We . . . have a lot to discuss."

He nodded. "We do." He kissed her hand again. "At camp." He gently grabbed her waist. "For now, just rest as best you can while you ride, okay?" He lifted her onto Love. She weighed next to nothing. One hand lingered on the dip of her lower back, the other rested on her leg. "You're safe now, Elle."

She swallowed hard. Her eyes searched him. She was looking for . . . something. Now wasn't the time to tell her everything. To beg her to forgive him. To tell her just how desperately he needed to be beside her. Soon. Soon they could talk. About all of it.

He couldn't help it as his eyes fell to her middle for only a moment.

Soon they could talk about *everything*.

*****

June rode on Love behind Elle. Her powers had drained her energy enough she would have been unable to travel otherwise.

Bliss walked beside Kirk. Their steps paced by Love who walked slowly, carefully as she carried Elle and June on her back. Bliss kept a hand on June's leg most of the walk, a gentle and simple touch to remind her of his presence at her side and keep watch over his weary lover.

June and Elle didn't speak as they rode. They leaned against each other, simply resting in the other's presence.

The looks they shared told Kirk that they could all sense it. How far Elle was from them.

Were we too late?

They had to find some sort of shelter for their camp. Winter had settled deeply over the countryside, and while Kirk may have been practiced in some harsh conditions, June and Bliss, Elle, weren't ready for the elements that awaited them.

Kirk knew what to search for in the terrain, and by the grace of the moon, he found what had to be enough. A large stone overhang. The mound of rock stood tall enough, and the small cover it would provide combined with him keeping a fire would be enough to shelter his little party through the night.

He prayed silently to the moon to keep snow from falling. There were no clouds, but he'd seen the sky change in moments before. He lifted Elle, bundled still in the fur, from Love's back and set her on the ground before him.

Her knees wobbled after ridding for most of the day. "Thank you."

He would never grow weary of hearing that voice. He thanked the moon for it again. Getting to hear that voice *again*.

He leaned to kiss her forehead.

She ducked away from him. She panicked when she realized she had. He could see her eyes widen after the initial fear of his touch passed. "No. No, Kirk. I'm sorry. I—"

He shook his head. "It's okay." He tried to mask how badly it hurt.

But they *felt* each other now. She felt his hurt as deeply as he'd just felt her fear.

Fuck, this is going to be complicated.

$$\sim 50 \sim$$

CHAPTER 50

E^{LLE} After she'd torn away from him, Kirk had gotten to work setting up camp. She knew he wanted to do something useful with his hands to help distract him from how hard this all was.

They'd all just been through so, so much.

No one had come close to reconciling with any of it.

They were all on autopilot. Just surviving for now.

She felt awake for the first time in so long. She had *so much* to process.

June took her elbow gently in her hand. "Let's get you beside that fire, yeah?" she said so softly.

Everyone looked at her differently.

Of course they did.

She nodded as June walked beside her beneath the stone cover. Kirk had started a fire first, and June sat beside it with Elle at her side.

Elle wrapped the fur around her shoulders tighter, pulling it as close as she possibly could. "I missed you," she said quietly.

June sniffled and nodded. "I missed you, Elle." She held up a hand, a silent request for permission before she touched her.

Elle leaned in slowly. Hesitating for a moment at first.

June cupped Elle's cheek and looked into her eyes. "I'm so sorry, Ellie."

Elle leaned into her hand, shaking her head gently. "It's *none* of your fault."

There was a quiet moment.

"Can you check on them, June?" Elle whispered, pulling her face back from June's touch. "Make sure they're . . . okay?"

June tilted her head as her brow furrowed. "The baby?"

Elle nodded.

June sucked in a breath. Her expression shifted. So much pain crossed her face at the mention of it. But Elle needed to know they were okay. She . . . she needed to keep them safe. She'd *died.* What if something had happened to the baby?

June moved slowly, holding her hands out and visible as she moved toward Elle's middle. Every motion was careful as she shifted the fur to the side and laid a hand so delicately on Elle's tummy. Her hand glowed just barely, and the anxiety in her eyes melted away into a warm smile, her eyes drooping a bit as she felt it.

That warm smile shifted into shock. "Ellie."

Elle didn't know what it meant. Panic set in in seconds when June's eyes met hers. Had something happened? Did she lose them? "What's wrong?" Her voice cracked.

"There's two."

Kirk dropped the firewood in his hands.

Elle smiled.

So tenderly, so hesitantly, she smiled. "I saw them. When Clementine showed me my greatest joy, I saw them. Two little boys." She looked into June's eyes. "They're okay?"

June nodded. "They're strong. Like their momma." She removed her hand slowly. "Elle—"

"You should rest," Elle interrupted whatever she was about to say. She wasn't ready to hear it.

*****

The fire flickered and crackled before her. Three of them had eaten some of what they'd packed before June and Bliss had taken the first turn to sleep. June had lain down near Elle, pulling her pack beneath her head, and Bliss had slid over beside her and pulled her close, nuzzling into the back of her neck.

They were out in minutes.

Elle hadn't wanted to eat. She'd eaten recently enough it wasn't a danger to the babies if she didn't. She couldn't stomach the thought of Kirk or June's blood then. Not yet. She sat across from Kirk at the fire, holding that same fur as close as she could. She watched the flames dance, focusing on the flitting movements, the shifting of the shape, and the changing of its colors.

She could feel Kirk's eyes on her. A loving and broken gaze, unable to be torn from her. She could feel his heart aching.

He could feel hers too.

She spoke, keeping her voice down so as not to wake the others. "You were there too."

"Where, Elle?"

"The vision of my joy. You were there with the boys." She lifted her eyes to his. His lips parted as he prepared to reply, but she spoke over him. "Kirk, you accepted our bond. I don't know if there's a way to break it, but I cannot ask you to stay and raise another male's sons."

He shuffled a bit, shifting his feet before him. "Do you *want* me to stay?"

She felt his soul twist with nerves. *He* wanted to stay. Of course, she wanted him to stay. But the words tripped on her tongue. Wanting him at her side, fear twisted her stomach into knots.

But he spoke again. "Ellie, I want to stay beside you. I accepted our bond because I *want* you. And that includes those babies. If *you* want me at your side, I will never part from you again. I won't make that mistake a second time." His voice trailed off a bit. Regret overwhelmed them both. His regret.

Then, Elle broke. "Don't leave, Kirk. Please. Please. Stay with me." She crumpled inward. Her feelings, her desperation, the true desires of her heart pouring out of her mouth without restraint. "Please—"

He hurried to her side, then paused, unsure if he should touch her.

"Hold me," she whimpered through the tears.

He wrapped his arms around her and held her against his chest, kneeling beside her on the ground. He pulled her so deeply into himself he nearly consumed her. He pressed his nose into the hair on the top of her head and breathed deeply.

Elle leaned into his embrace. Her eyes began to drift closed. She inhaled him, soaked in his scent. She felt his heartbeat against her face.

Her mate.

Her mate.

Her mate.

*****

She awoke against her lover's chest, one of his massive arms wrapped tightly around her. His own head was bowed, and soft snores left his lips. She reached her hand up to his cheek, gently touching it. The stubble above his beard was rough against her fingertips. Her thumb brushed over his cheekbone.

He stirred and his eyes half opened, his expression softening as he saw her gazing at him. He whispered, "Can I kiss you?"

She smiled a bit and nodded.

He brushed his lips to hers.

They both felt a twinge of fear in her, but she leaned into his touch. She kissed him tentatively.

As they pulled only slightly away from each other, he whispered beside her ear, "You're hungry."

She was. She'd woken up *incredibly* hungry. The smell of June was frustratingly sweet. Kirk, nearly irresistible. She already wrestled with her hatred of taking from them, but knowing she needed *something* for her sons . . . *her sons* . . .

"It's okay, Ellie." He shifted and brushed his hair off his neck. He leaned his head to the side, exposing the column of his throat to her.

By the moon, it looked delicious. She stared at the tanned flesh of his neck for a moment. "Kirk . . ."

"Eat. Please."

She nodded, hesitantly. Then she leaned into his neck, taking in the scent of him. She breathed deeply. Her lips parted, and she brushed the tips of her fangs against his skin, a sudden desperate hunger pang nearly drove her to bite down immediately, hard. But she moved slowly. Carefully. Her teeth punctured his neck, and Kirk sucked in a breath as she broke his skin. As her tongue delicately ran over the wounds and his black blood dripping from them, he relaxed into the sensations. The intimacy of it. She could sense a peace in him knowing he was sustaining his mate and the babies she carried. That very peace slipped into her own heart as it warmed through her. Then feelings new to them both began to tangle amongst them. He was aroused. He stiffened as she fed, as he felt the prick of pain and the warmth of her mouth on his skin.

She fed on him, her eyes closed and her nose nestled just below his ear.

When she finished, she sat back, her tummy a bit bloated from her first real meal in days and the pair of baby boys. She sighed. "I'm sorry about this all. All of it. Please—"

Kirk pulled back from her. "We will take this slowly. We will figure it out together."

She nodded, letting his voice soothe her. "Together."

~ 51 ~

CHAPTER 51

K IRK
Traveling was difficult. They needed to keep Elle hidden. She was often exhausted and required frequent feedings, which left Kirk weak himself.

They were headed toward the city Elle had grown up in. It was on the way to Spiritmire, and Elle had assured them they would be able to rest there. Bathe. That the men who raised her would give them somewhere to breathe, if for only a moment.

She directed them from Love's back as they continued their journey.

It was a farm on the outside of a city, far enough that it would be safe for Elle. And if she was correct, if they were willing to give them somewhere to pause, it would be a welcome rest.

They approached the house. A large building made mostly of stone with wooden doors and slatted windows. Vines grew up the sides of the home, though they were currently covered in snow. That same snow covered what would be a generous garden in the spring, surrounded by a short stone wall. Elle's steps quickened as they grew near, and her face lightened some. Kirk felt a sense of familiarity and nostalgia rush through their bond. It wasn't the same feeling as when he returned to the keep. It was warmer. Safe. If this was what *home* felt like, he would do anything to give her such a feeling forever. She kept her hood pulled over her head, the cloak obscuring her face just in case. Kirk stayed within inches of her, June and Bliss close behind. his hand gently grazed her lower back as she stopped before the door, and he felt her take a breath before knocking.

Male voices could be heard from inside. They grew closer until heavy footsteps stopped when they reached the door.

A human man opened the door. He stood a few inches shorter than Kirk. Black hair fell around his face and highlighted bright blue eyes. He was dressed simply, sleeves of a green tunic pushed up just below his elbows. His round features were kind and gentle. "Hello— Ellie?" His eyebrows rose in shock. "Ellie, is that you?!"

Elle pulled the hood from her head. "Ben." She smiled softly.

Ben wrapped his arms around her and squeezed her tightly into his chest. "GODS, Ellie!" He kissed her cheek. "I'm so glad to see you. Gods, Elle. Come in, come in." He pulled her into the house, gesturing to the others to follow. "Lio, love, Ellie's here!"

Another male entered the room where they stood. A lean man, of a similar height to Ben. Long blond hair was pulled into a ponytail, a few strands framing his face. His features were sharp and his eyes a deep maroon. His fangs flashed as he smiled when he saw her. "Elle." He took her from Ben's embrace into his own.

Ben looked at the other three. "Where are my manners? I assume if Ellie has brought you here, she's mentioned who we are, but I'm Ben and this is my husband, Lio."

The blond man nodded at them after releasing Elle from a strong hug.

"Ben, Lio." Elle's voice was louder than it had been since her escape. "June and Bliss, my family from my last home." She gestured, looking fondly at them, then her hand directed them to Kirk. "And Kirk. My *mate*."

Ben's shock returned. "Elle. Elle, your mate?!" He smiled broadly. "Gods, you've been busy since we've seen you!"

With a soft smile she said, "One last surprise." She pulled her dress tight over her growing tummy, her hands wrapping on either side of the bump.

Kirk could feel something in her heart shift.

His hand covered his mouth. "Ellie, you're—"

She nodded, releasing her stomach. "I've missed you both so much." She sniffed, tears beginning to well up in the corners of her eyes. "I've missed you so fucking much."

Ben wrapped her up again. "C'mon, I'll make tea. We have a lot to talk about." He kissed the top of her head gently. "A mate. A fucking mate. And a baby! Good gods, Ellie." He ushered her out of the main room toward the kitchen, leaving the others, his attention solely on Elle.

Lio smiled softly at Ben, but when his gaze moved to Kirk, it darkened. "You're her mate?" He spoke with a protective growl, his arms crossed. "And you're her, companions?" He looked June and Bliss over.

June nodded, stepping toward Lio and extending her hand. Her expression was as cold as his. "She's my roommate. My best friend. This is my—" She looked at Bliss, her eyes running over him for a moment.

Bliss looked at her with a smile. "I'm her lover."

She sighed heavily. "Yes. He is."

Lio huffed. "I truly don't care." He glanced back at Kirk. "Tell me why you're in my home, hunter."

Ben yelled from the kitchen, "Over tea, my love! We discuss over tea!"

Lio's expression softened a moment, then he motioned toward the hall. "Over tea."

~ 52 ~

CHAPTER 52

E^{LLE} Ben sat across from Elle. He'd made tea and made sure everyone was appropriately cozy before they dove into just why she had come home. Kirk stood behind her chair, his hand resting on her shoulder and his thumb gently moving over the collar of her dress. She leaned her face into his arm. Finding comfort in a touch was rare these days, and she pressed further when she did. She needed to reclaim this. *Herself.*

Bliss sat on the floor beside June who was seated in a kitchen chair, leaning back at an angle that almost looked uncomfortable with her arms crossed.

Lio mirrored Kirk, quietly behind his partner, his eyes resting on the group now in his home.

"So Ellie baby, why have you come to visit? I do hope it's only to tell us we're uncles." Ben's voice was laden with anxiety.

Ben had always been able to tell when something bothered her. Even when she was young and determined to keep her feelings to herself, he'd known. Of course he could tell this was not only a visit to share her sons with them. "We're— I'm running again . . ." She was so quiet Ben leaned closer to hear her.

"Is it Alder's family? Again? I thought you—"

She shook her head, her eyes averted from him now. "It's not Alder."

Kirk gently squeezed her arm. "We're headed north. It's no longer safe in Torzen for Elle. She wanted to see you two as we passed and hoped we might be able to rest a day or so."

Ben nodded. "Of course you can." He reached across the table and rested his hand on Elle's arm. "As long as you need."

"We can't stay long. It's not safe for you two—"

"We've hidden you here before." He squeezed her arm. "And we'll hide you again. You're our family." Ben looked at the others, his eyes moving between them. "We have a few spare rooms just for such occasions. Lio, show the companions to a room, please?"

Lio nodded. "Of course, my love. Come." He motioned they follow him and he left.

June stood quickly. Bliss stumbled to his feet.

"And you can stay in your old room, Elle." He stood, holding out his hand to her. "Drop off your things and settle in, then we can talk more, love. I . . . I'm worried."

"Of course."

*****

Ben led them to her old room before squeezing Elle's hand as he left them. "I'll be in the kitchen if you need, and I'm sure Lio's in the library. I'll start dinner. We've got to celebrate our Elle coming home to see us."

She thanked him again, then stepped into a familiar space. They hadn't changed the room much in the time she'd been away. Her old chest was still in the corner. She wondered how much of her childhood was stored in it. Later she would open it and dig through some memories. The bookshelves still held books she lovingly remembered, books Lio had so heavily urged her to read, but she'd usually chosen to spend her days in the garden with Ben. She looked over her shoulder at Kirk, who watched her with such kind eyes. "I spent a lot of time in this room."

"Fond memories?" He wrapped a hand around her waist and pulled her close, kissing her forehead.

"Very." She leaned into his touch.

His kiss.

Him.

*****

Their packs were moved into the house, Love into Ben and Lio's pasture. Elle pulled a dress she'd once known from the chest. It flowed loosely, and she was grateful to change into something clean, something that did not smell of their journey. She walked by the mirror in her old room and stopped, staring at herself for a moment. Kirk sat on the bed behind her. Months ago, she had been a different woman. Months ago, the eyes that looked back at her were not the eyes that met hers now. She was different, she was changed, broken . . . but she was going to be a mother now. She'd met her mate now. She spoke it so often in her head it had become like breath. *I'm going to be okay.* Her eyes met Kirk's in the mirror and she stood, walking back to him.

"I'll be back soon." Elle squeezed his arm. "Try to rest . . . I'm going to go catch up with them."

Kirk leaned forward and kissed her cheek. "I'll try, but hurry back to me."

She smiled softly. "You're so needy."

*****

Ben turned as she approached. He wiped his hands on his pants and left white flour handprints on them. "There you are." He wrapped her up in his arms yet again. "Gods, Elle." He took a deep breath and stepped back, his hand moved to her cheek and his brow furrowed. "Your eyes . . . The world hurt my precious sister."

She leaned against his hand. "A lot . . . happened." The tears began to roll down her face. "So much happened." Her voice quivered.

"Tell me what happened, little one." He motioned to the kitchen chairs. "You've met your mate, and you two have started a family." He spoke as he pulled a chair for her then sat at one adjacent, but her gaze was cast down and her shoulders trembled as he spoke. "What is it, Ellie?"

She wrapped her arms around herself, the fear sinking back in. Even Ben's comfort could not keep it fully at bay. "They're not Kirk's."

"Then my Ellie *has* been—"

"Ben, I was taken."

Immediately, his body froze, his expression went blank for a moment. "Who took you?"

"Dae." She saw him begin to shake as she uttered the devil's name. "The Lord of Blood took me, and he raped me, and he—he hurt me." Her voice hitched on the words, and she curled further inward. Visions of all she'd endured slammed against the back of her mind. They screamed at her to let them in, to let them tear her apart.

She'd been lost in her mind a moment and had not realized as Ben had shoved his chair back and rushed to wrap his arms around her and press her into his chest.

She sobbed against him.

He petted her hair gently. "My sweet Elle. My sister. My friend. I'm so sorry." He hung his head as he spoke. "I cannot begin—"

She shook as sobs racked through her. "Kirk killed him for it. The bastard is dead, but he still haunts me. He still torments me."

"Elle—"

"And Kirk. Kirk barely knows me, and he's been thrown into being mated to a vampire. A pregnant vampire. And he's amazing, and he's wonderful, and he's at my side even now, but how can I ask him to be?" Her voice rose as anxiety took hold of her heart. "How can I ask him to love this? How can I ask him to be any part of my fucked-up existence? How do I raise the devil's children, Ben?"

Ben rested his cheek on the top of her head, and his hand moved to gently rub her back. "You'll do amazing, little one."

She felt a tear drop into her hair.

"I know without a doubt you'll be an incredible mother. I know without a doubt that Lio and I love you. I don't know how Kirk couldn't fall head over heels for you. He'd be a fool not to." His voice wobbled in a way Elle had heard so rarely from him. Ben was a gentle soul, but she knew when those he cared for were threatened, it provoked an anger that rooted deeply into his heart. It was the pain in his voice that gave him away, though he seemed to be desperately attempting to mask it. He'd always sought to be her comfort. "And that evil fuck won't hurt you again. Not ever again."

She wept in his arms for some time.

~ 53 ~

CHAPTER 53

K^{IRK}

Kirk grew restless in the room. He'd tried to rest as she'd asked, but he had not rested well in such a long time. He wasn't sure he ever would. Not until he knew she was safe. And then shortly there would be newborns, and sleep would evade him again. He did not mind. He found himself excited for it. Life with *her*. Life beside her. Building them a home, raising the children there, with her.

All these things he'd never considered he'd be able to have now within his reach. If only he could take her torment from her.

He removed his outer layers, only leaving on a simple button-down and leather pants. He tied his hair half up after running his fingers through the tangles as best he could. He laid his sword at the side of the bed, leaning it against the frame, then he stepped into the hall.

He glanced to either side, unsure which direction she'd gone. He moved back toward the kitchen, his footsteps falling heavy in quiet passages. He hoped June and Bliss had found some rest. Gods knew they needed it as badly as he did.

He heard June's voice from a room as he walked by. The vampire, Lio's, as well.

"Kirk. Hey. Come in here."

He stopped and turned. June had leaned her head out of the door and was beckoning him in. He stepped into the room, a li-

323

brary. Books lined every wall, some older, some newer, between them were collected pieces of a life of vampiric length lived. Skulls, jars, stone statues, metal figures. There were two chairs in the room, deep and lined with thick pillows, where Kirk assumed Lio and Ben spent time reading beside each other. Between the chairs was a small table, on it a cup of tea, steam lazily drifting from it.

Standing in the room were June and Lio, both with their arms crossed.

"Kirk," June said, "Bliss and I are going to leave tomorrow to head to"—she paused—"the city." She dared not speak its name, dared not curse Lio with the knowledge of their location should someone come after them. "And Lio has offered to let you and Elle stay here until we've found somewhere to settle."

Kirk looked at Lio, whose stone expression did not shift. "It is a danger to harbor us. You do not need—"

Lio shook his head, his hands falling from crossed over his chest. He pointed at Kirk as he spoke. "I do not offer this for you, hunter." He lowered his hand and calmed his tone. "I do this for Elle. Ben and I spoke of it earlier. If we can offer her a safe haven until you have somewhere for her to go, we will gladly provide it. You, being her mate, may stay with her. I've read plenty of soul-bound mates. Leaving her would only do both of you harm. Would only do *Elle* harm."

Kirk bowed slightly. "Thank you. Please tell me what I can do to be of service while we're here. To repay you."

Lio waved a hand and sighed again. "I'm sure Ben will have you do chores." He looked between them. "Has she told you of how she came to us?"

Kirk shook his head.

"A pair of hunters come to my door. Hunters." He huffed as he spoke to another hunter in his home. "And they're carrying the Princess of Bone in their arms. They'd killed her parents, her brother dead by Dae's hand before then, but then after murdering two vampires, they had some change of heart." Frustration built in his voice. "They had heard of Ben and me—of me—and brought her here. I wasn't thrilled about hiding such a high-profile vampire in my house, knowing that Dae himself was searching for her. But Ben, Ben loved her immediately, and she stayed with us until she was in her forties. Then she left to dance. She wanted to repay us, she sent money back, but Ben would only store it for her. Then after everything that happened with Alder, we stopped hearing from her. She disappeared, and we knew she was hiding. It broke Ben completely . . ." Lio walked to one of the bookshelves and grabbed a small wooden box off it. "This is every coin she sent to us." He handed it to June. "Buy her a safe home with this. Please."

June took the box from him. "Absolutely."

~ 54 ~

CHAPTER 54

B^{EN}

Ben smiled at her beside him, carefully laying a thin sheet of pastry over the pie. He remembered when a young Elle had stood in that same place, when she'd helped him make meat pies before. Her bright green eyes had looked up at him, and she'd smiled so broadly. Now a pair of deep red eyes turned to meet his, and the smile that greeted him was fragile. There was pain behind it now. "Do you want boys? Girls? Both?" He spoke softly, his own smile gentle.

She looked back at the pie before her. "They're boys . . . I've seen it in a vision." She watched her own hands folding the edges of the dough. "I'm glad. I think Kirk will raise boys well."

"And you." He bumped her hip with his own. "You'll raise them well."

She looked down at her tummy. Flour stuck to her dress where she'd bumped into the counter. "I'm excited to meet them."

"I am too. You promise you'll bring them back someday, okay?"

She nodded. "If it's safe."

"Fuck safe. I want to meet my nephews. They're going to be incredible, Elle."

*****

KIRK

The fireplace was lit, and flames roared softly. Ben had opened the best wine he had to celebrate the occasion. He smiled and lifted the bottle. June lifted her glass and nodded. Kirk sipped his wine, seated in one of the chairs beside the fire. Elle sat on his thigh, her legs hanging between his. His arm was wrapped around her waist, and he smiled at her. Lio strummed softly on a guitar, and Bliss sat beside him on the floor, both of them singing a song Kirk had not heard before. Elle however seemed to know it intimately. She leaned toward Lio, her eyes closed. Kirk could feel how the familiar voice, the familiar song soothed her soul.

Elle stood and held out a hand toward June. "Dance with me."

June took the hand. She set her own wineglass down and pulled Elle toward herself, grabbing her other hand. They began to swing around the room, smiling, *dancing*.

His heart skipped. She was dancing. It felt like the world had lifted off his shoulders. She was dancing. *Thank the gods.* She smiled. She smiled as the music swept them around the room. As she spun June. Then he heard it and his lungs nearly sealed shut.

She laughed. *Fuck.* She was laughing. It was all he wanted in the world in that moment, her laugh. He took another sip of wine, pushing back the emotions welling up in his chest with the harsh burn of alcohol.

June caught his gaze and smiled. She broke off from Elle and pulled him to his feet, then lifted the wine from his hand to shove him toward Elle.

Elle stopped her twirling and faced him, her cheeks red from the movement, her ears tipped the same crimson. She held out her hand to him, but before he could take it, she grabbed his, pulling him close.

It was as though the music had released chains on her soul. Lio's singing, being home, this safety and this comfort had given her a moment of breath. It was as though the dance had broken some of the binds that had kept her in darkness. Even if this was only for a moment, she felt brighter. Their bond felt lighter. Her heart lifted. He smiled at her and held her hands as she spun with him around the room. "Elle . . ."

She tugged him to the side, leaning her weight away from him, their hands tightly interlocked. Then she pulled him close, their chests colliding. "Kirk." She released his hands and reached around his back. Rising to her toes, she whispered into his neck, "Kirk, I want you to fuck me." Her voice was quiet enough the room did not hear her, only him.

Heat washed over his face. Thank gods for the wine to hide the redness that now surely rested on his ears. "Are you sure? If you're not—"

"I want you to fuck me." She kissed his neck.

Somehow Kirk forgot everyone else in the room. Everything else vanished, and all he felt, heard, saw, was her. Her body pressed against his. Her lips on his neck. Just *her*. His cock was already rebelling against the confines of his pants, pressing against the fabric that kept him from her body. Gods, he wanted her. "Are you *certain*, Elle?"

She kissed his neck again then laid her head against his chest. Still, she swayed to the music, holding onto him tightly. "Certain."

*****

ELLE

They'd excused themselves. Bliss and June laughed when she said she was tired and pulled Kirk from the room. Ben had smiled and laughed himself. Lio had sighed, but even he smiled softly. She cursed such an ungraceful and obvious exit, but she would have time to regret that later. In that moment, all she wanted was him.

Now she stood in her room, and her eyes took in the man before her. The human man that had stolen her heart and soul. "Kiss me, Kirk."

He smiled and wrapped an arm around her waist, drawing her in. His kisses started so delicately. He bent to kiss her lips, her jaw, her neck. Each kiss more tender than the last, lingering on her skin.

Her hand slid down his back, and she leaned into every touch of his lips, closing her eyes and focusing on each one. Making sure she felt every touch, embraced every kiss, let the comfort, the safety, the pleasure sink into her. Her hands gingerly moved toward his belt, her fingers wrapping around the cold metal and sliding the leather through the buckle. She felt his cock strain against the confines of his leather pants.

Kirk pulled back, his hands still. "If it's *ever* too much, Elle, stop me. Please."

She nodded. Her hands were hooked in the waist of his pants, then moved to undo the buttons.

A soft noise broke free from his mouth as her hand gently wrapped around his cock.

The depth of how much he'd missed her seeped into their bond, a relief mixed into the closeness of the moment.

She hooked her hands on either side of his pants, then she slid them down, dropping onto her knees with them.

His hand rested on her head, his fingers digging into the braids. His own head tilted back and he smiled. "Gods, Elle." Fuck. Fuck, it was overwhelming them both how deeply they needed each other.

She closed her eyes, feeling his hands in her hair, his thighs beneath her hands. He rocked his hips toward her, and she met his movements until she brought him over the edge and he came.

She smiled and leaned back, her eyes rising to meet his.

He raked his hand through his hair. "My gods, my love. You're simply wicked."

Elle stood and placed her hands on his chest. "Fuck me, Kirk."

He cupped her chin, raising her eyes to meet his. He leaned down and kissed her. "As you wish, my love."

Eagerly he swept her into his arms. He kissed her forehead and then laid her back. He knelt before her on the bed, lifted her to sitting, and slowly slid her dress up and off.

Her eyes locked on his. The room was cold. The air bit against her exposed body. But she was sure. She was so certain as she motioned to his shirt. "Take it off."

He laughed and began to undo the buttons. "Yes, my love."

He pulled his shirt from his shoulders, and she absorbed every piece of him. Every curve, every line. He leaned forward and kissed her, one hand moving to support her back, the other gripping her breast, his thumb running over her nipple. Those passionate kisses she'd missed so much returned, and she sank deeper and deeper into the taste of him.

They lay back against the bed, his chest pressed against hers.

He paused his kisses. Just once. "Elle, are you—"

"Fuck me, Kirk." She grasped his hair and pulled his face back down to hers. A small gasp loosed itself from between their interlocked tongues as he guided himself in. She was not overtaken with fear. She was overtaken with pleasure, warmth, safety. She felt as though the world only revolved around them, intertwined in mind, body, and soul. All that mattered in the universe in that moment was *them*.

*****

She awoke in his arms. He snored softly behind her. It was still dark outside. One arm was tucked under his head, the other draped over her, his massive hand gently holding her belly. She'd found rest that night. Free from nightmares. Free from the torment. She'd simply slept, resting in the arms of her lover.

She hoped he'd rested too. Maybe this was what their life could be like. If they ran far enough. Hid well enough. They could sleep, and rest, together. They could find peace together. Maybe. They could raise the children and live a quiet life. Maybe moments like this could be common.

The fear began to sink in again. She feared they would never rest. Dae's followers would be unrelenting. Even in death, he would take the children. Take her . . .

Kirk stirred, and he nuzzled into her neck, his lips brushing just behind her ear. His arm tightened around her, and his hand cradled the curve of her tummy.

"Kirk, my love," she whispered.

"Hmm?" He pressed his nose farther into her.

"I'm going to go get some air."

His grip released, and his arm slowly pulled back from her.

"I'll be back soon." She wrapped a blanket around her shoulders and walked through familiar halls. Even if she hadn't been able to see in the dark, she knew this place well enough, it wouldn't have mattered. She tried to keep her steps quiet so as not to wake anyone else in the house. At the back door that led to the garden, she slid into a pair of Ben's boots. He wouldn't mind.

She stepped outside, and the winter air hit her square in the face. It was cold. Very, very cold. She wrapped the blanket tighter around her shoulders and stepped out farther into the night. The sky was gray, heavy with clouds threatening another winter snow. She could not see the moon or the stars, though she knew they watched. The frozen ground crunched beneath the boots as she stumbled in them. They were far too large, but they kept her feet warm as she breathed as deeply as she could of the frozen air.

The cold broke through the blur that was her mind. It woke her from what felt like a daze she'd drifted back into. She'd gotten up before her mind had been allowed to spiral. If she'd lain in that bed, awake, it would have taken her again. The darkness. Even Kirk couldn't keep it at bay. He could ward it off for a time, but not forever. She heard the door open behind her, and she jumped, spinning around. "Wh—"

*****

LIO

Lio stood in the doorway looking out into the snowy garden, his jacket pulled tightly around his shoulders. "For the moon's sake, Ellie, it's cold as hell. Come inside."

She just stared at him a moment.

That. That wasn't the Elle he'd known. The little girl he'd known had been taken by the world . . . by the cruelty of men and vampires both. If the bastards weren't already dead, he would have killed them himself. Not that that would fix what they'd done, not that killing them could save her . . . *Ben's turned you soft.* He walked toward her and extended a hand. "Elle, come. It's far too cold out here."

She took his hand, and he led her back into the house. He didn't let go as she kicked off Ben's boots, and then he ushered her toward the library. The room had changed little since she had last seen it, their chairs still in the center, the same books lining the walls, all of Lio's trinkets and treasures tucked among them.

"I'll start a fire."

"You don't have to—"

"I'll start a fire." He walked past her and began arranging wood in the fireplace. "I'll make your *mate* get more firewood later." He smiled just a little. He didn't turn to look at her as he spoke, but he heard her sit in Ben's chair. "Is he a good man?"

"Yes."

Lio finished arranging the wood. He squatted beside the fireplace and rested his arms on his thighs a moment. "Good. I'd hate to have to kill him." He wasn't good at making jokes, but Elle always laughed at them.

She giggled just a little. "I don't deserve—"

"Stop that right there." He looked back at her. "You deserve the best. Only the best. And you *will not* settle for less. So if that asshole hunter steps out of line, you tell me and he's dead, you understand?"

"Of course." She smiled softly, but it faded after a quiet moment between them. "Do you ever hate being a vampire, Lio?"

Lio shook his head as he knelt beside the fire again to light it. "Not once."

"You've never wished to be human?"

"Never." The flames warmed his face as they began to consume the wood. He dusted his hands off as he stood back up and looked at her once again. "Elle, I have lived a long time, and men call us monsters, but you and I both know, we've both seen, monsters live in both men and vampires." She looked shattered; it killed him inside. "Do not hate your blood because they've called you a beast. You know their nature as well as I do."

She wrapped up tighter into the blanket, shifting so she sank farther into Ben's chair. "I pray my sons do not hate their blood."

The chill that shot through his spine nearly brought him to his knees. *Of course, they'll hate their blood. Their father was a monster. In its truest sense, a monster.* "You will show them true kindness and true nature. They will know the nature of a monster has nothing to do with *what* they are. Their blood will not define them. Just as ours does not define who we are, yeah?"

She nodded, holding the blanket against her face as she stifled a tiny sob. "Thank you."

"Rest." The flames danced behind him, and he walked toward his chair, which sat beside Ben's. He grabbed a book from a shelf before he sat down, opening it and crossing one leg over the other. "I'll be right here." He reached toward her over the table between the chairs. She delicately placed her hand in his, and his fingers closed around it. "I'll be *right here*, Elle."

It wasn't long before she was asleep in the chair, her hand still wrapped up in his.

She must be so fucking tired. He sat beside her, if only to guard her from the demons within herself, for a moment at least.

~ 55 ~

CHAPTER 55

L IO

Heavy footsteps came down the hall toward the room, and Lio closed his book softly. He'd figured the hunter would show up soon, unable to go too long without making sure she was okay. Especially as she was now. He understood the hunter's concern, his wariness to leave her be for any length of time.

The hunter poked his head through the doorway.

"She's asleep," he said quietly.

Kirk entered, nodding and moving toward Ben's chair where she slept. "Thank you."

Lio sighed, rubbing his forehead and laying the book in his lap. "She is precious, hunter."

"I know."

"No, I don't think you fully understand. I will hunt you to the ends of the earth should you harm her, and I will see your head removed from your shoulders as you've done to my kind for years." His voice was harsh. "Elle brought life into our world, and I have already failed her enough." The harshness turned into something pained, something mournful.

Kirk's eyes rested on her little sleeping form. "She's brought life into mine." He spoke softly. "Do not for a second doubt that I will protect her and her joy with my very life." He leaned down and slid an arm under her knees and the other under her shoulders, then he gently lifted her and cradled her against his chest. "Her and *our* sons."

Lio smiled just barely, though he could not trust the hunter entirely just yet. "Good."

Before he left the room, Kirk whispered, "Why did you never tell her who she was?"

Lio glared, worried Elle might have heard, but as he looked at her asleep in Kirk's arms, he quickly softened. "We thought it was safer. If she didn't know. And then when she ran, we couldn't reach her. Warn her. Hunter, I carry some of this blame. If she'd known who she was . . ." His fists balled and his teeth clenched. "I've failed her."

"We all have." Kirk spoke it gently as he turned to leave, and his footsteps retreated back toward Elle's room and her bed.

*****

The following morning, they gathered outside as June and Bliss loaded their gear onto the horses. Kirk stood beside Elle with his arm wrapped around her waist, Ben near to her, and Lio helping prepare the horses.

June cinched the last bag, then turned back to Elle and ran to her, wrapping her arms around her and burying her face into her neck. "I'll see you soon. Rest while I'm gone." She pressed her nose into Elle's cheek, just in front of her ear. "Please please please rest for me, Elle." She kissed her cheek, then gently cupped Elle's tummy. "Grow my little nephews and fucking rest."

Elle's face was already running with streams of tears. "I will. Promise."

Lio strolled back toward the house, his hands moving to his pockets as he watched Elle and June's exchange.

Bliss stood with the horses, holding both their leads as they said goodbye. They'd see each other soon. "Don't cry, Ellie! We'll come get you once we find you the perfect farm." He smiled broadly. "Come on, June. The sooner we get going, the sooner we can come get her."

June kissed Elle's cheek once more, grasping the back of her head. "Just a few weeks."

~ 56 ~

CHAPTER 56

E^{LLE} In the days and weeks that followed, Elle and Kirk settled into the house, quickly falling into a routine with their hosts.

Elle spent her days sleeping, helping Ben around the house, reading about vampire history with Lio, and spending time with Kirk talking, fucking, resting . . . existing. Her nightmares did not stop, but they lessened. They did not haunt her every night. The first night Ben and Lio heard her screams, they'd run to the bedroom, throwing open the door and stopping as they saw her. She'd been curled up in Kirk's arms, her hands gripped tightly at her hair, and she'd screamed. She'd been coated in sweat, her body shaking. The nightmares, the darkness had a grip so tight they could only hold her and wait until it passed, whispering what they could to try to calm her.

She spoke with all three of them about what had happened in Dae's castle. She wept as she shared the details of the torment. Some Kirk had known, some she had not had the strength yet to share. But as she spoke the evils, as she confided in those she found the most safe, the power over her weakened just a bit. She spoke excitedly about her future as a mother, she and Kirk dreamed of what their life could be, what raising the children could look like.

"I want them to call you Father."

"I would be honored, Elle."

Kirk helped with as many chores as he possibly could, desperately working to repay the kindness of Ben and Lio. He gathered firewood, fixed anything he could around the house, helped make dinner, and prepared the garden for spring.

Elle was halfway through her pregnancy, and she looked close to a human at full-term with a single babe thanks to the twins. She hobbled around the house, and all three of the men fussed over her, refusing to let her do much. She argued with them, but they were persistent with their care.

They all began to worry about the birth. She was only halfway through, and already carrying them had begun to take its toll. Her body was delicate, and it seemed like birth might tear her apart. Kirk began studying vampire pregnancies as best he could, pulling from Lio's library and reading as she fell asleep beside him, her head resting on his chest. But there was little to know, and twins in the vampire world were nearly unheard of. But she knew he would do everything he could. Anything.

Then two months after Bliss and June had left, there was a knock at the door. Elle went to answer it until Ben moved past her. "Love, let me, just in case."

She stepped back, her hand moving below her belly to support it. "Of course." She stood just out of sight, quietly tucked around the corner in the hall.

She heard Ben open the door. "Oh my gods, you're back."

She didn't wait for a cue or Ben's signal that she could approach. She rushed toward the door, and the moment she saw Bliss's face, she stumbled to him and wrapped her arms around his neck. "Bliss!"

He took a step back as she collided with him, his hands falling and grazing the sides of her tummy. "Hey, Elle." He leaned down and kissed her cheek. "Told you I'd come back for you."

She smiled at him. Something in her felt lighter, something reminiscent of who she had been before. "How's June?"

"She's well." Bliss pulled a coin from his pocket and flicked it between his fingers. "Waiting at your new farm. We found it, Elle. Land's gorgeous and hidden, and it will be perfect for you and those babies."

Elle began to sniffle. "I'm just so glad to see you, and I'm excited to see June."

Ben grabbed her shoulder. "Let's get your things together then, little one."

*****

The goodbye with Ben and Lio was tearful but not without hope. Ben whispered gently to Elle, his hands resting on her swollen belly, and he wished her and his nephews the best, begging that they return so he could know them someday. Lio hugged her tightly and kissed her forehead. Reminding her, should she need anything in the world, he and Ben would be there in an instant.

She smiled at them both, breathing heavily as it had grown difficult to catch her breath. "Thank you. Both." She sniffed, but it did not stop the tears from running down her face. "I love you."

They both kissed either side of her head again, each laying a hand where their nephews rested. "We love you too, Ellie."

The spell June used to transport them to the new farm must've taken days to prepare and would take days to recover from. But they were moved, the three of them, to a farm. Spiritmire. The city was in the distance, just barely within view.

The house they appeared before was small and in desperate need of repair, but it was still *everything*. Elle couldn't believe how perfect it was. A stone home, vines growing up the gray walls, a covered porch with a wooden roof that needed fixing, slatted windows that only revealed hints of what awaited them inside. Just beyond the porch was a massive tree, ancient and stunning. Elle couldn't tear her eyes away from it. Her new home. Their new home. The babies started to move in her womb, as though they sensed it too. *Home.* Her hand moved to where little feet kicked at her stomach. "We're going to be okay, little ones."

Kirk stepped closer to her, his hand wrapping around her waist and over top of hers. "They know they're home."

She looked up at him. "We're home."

June came out of the door. She looked exhausted but so relieved when she saw Elle. "Elle! My love! Look at you!" She held her arms open.

Elle hobbled toward her as quickly as she could muster, then fell into her arms.

June hugged her a moment, then stepped back, both of her hands on Elle's arms. "Welcome home. We have our own just down the road. We won't be far. But I don't think I can move out until these two make their appearance, now can I? Gods, you look amazing."

"I'm so very, very pregnant, June." Elle laughed. "And I've got so many months left. I truly don't know how they're going to grow any more."

"Don't you worry about it." June grabbed the side of her head and pulled her close to kiss her cheek, just beside her ear. "C'mon. Let's see your home, yeah?"

Of course, Elle was going to worry about it. But for now, for right now, she was going to just enjoy this moment.

~ 57 ~

CHAPTER 57

Kirk
Five months later

Kirk slid off his horse as he neared the house. He'd been sent to town to grab a few things for June so she could help Elle. Fall was settling into the valley, and the garden he had planted was winding down for the year. The leaves were changing colors and just beginning their last trek from the trees. It was early in the first autumn months, and it reminded him of when he'd first met her, when he'd first found her. He hurried to get his horse into the pasture and grab his things from her back. His steps were quick as he made his way back to the house.

Elle's labor had begun days ago, and he hated every second away from her side. She'd been in bed for nearly two months now, but finally, the babies were nearing their arrival, though they were sooner than anticipated.

He stepped into the house, past the porch he'd fixed that past spring. Past the chair he'd built. He had never built a chair before. He'd never built anything really, but he'd done his best, taken his time, and soon she would sit in that chair rocking their children. Soon. But his mind was ripped from that daydream when he heard her screaming. That was when he ran.

He slid into their bedroom, nearly colliding with the doorframe as he rounded the corner. It was a modest room, but it was theirs. The bed in the center, another project he and Bliss had fumbled

343

their way through, was solid wood and took up a good portion of the wall it rested against. She was beside it, on her knees. Her head was lifted, her elbows pressed deep into the mattress, her hands clasped before her face. It almost looked like she was in prayer, but what left her lips were not prayers. They were screams.

Elle's hair was braided back. Her face, neck, everything was drenched in sweat. The nightgown draped over her was stuck to her body with it, and she screamed again.

June caught Kirk's eyes as he entered. He tossed her the bag of herbs he'd brought back from town as he ran to Elle's side, sliding onto his knees beside her, his hand immediately on her back. "Hey. Hey, Elle."

She looked at him, tears running down her cheeks. "I can't, Kirk. I can't. I can't I can't I can't."

He shook his head, rubbed her back, and kissed her cheek, tasting her sweat and her pain. Through their bond, he ached. He wanted to scream. There was so much fear and pain in her it was overwhelming. Yet she looked him dead in the eyes. She was incredible. "Elle, You absolutely can. You're doing amazing."

June's voice was firm as she yelled, "Get her onto the bed. On her side."

Kirk looked over his shoulder at her then back at Elle. "C'mon, my love." He held her arm as he slowly stood, pulling her up with him.

She doubled over. Another scream ripped through her body, and she nearly collapsed.

He caught her as she crumpled, and he held her until the pain passed. He tried to calm his own shaking as he watched her, as he felt her. "You can do this, Elle. C'mon, onto the bed." He helped her up and onto her side.

She whimpered softly and cried as she lay down. Kirk felt something beneath his boot. He glanced at the floor. There was a pool of blood where she'd knelt. A lot of blood. He swallowed hard, then his attention was quickly back on her.

"Kirk, she's going to need to feed. She's going to need blood." June walked swiftly to the bedside, standing at Elle's back. In a small bowl, she'd made a paste with the herbs he'd returned with. She lifted Elle's nightgown delicately. "This should help with the pain just a little, Ellie." With two fingers, she scooped some of the paste from the bowl. She muttered a spell over it, and it glowed softly. She gently traced Elle's spine with the paste, speaking ancient words Kirk did not understand. Then she looked at him. "Blood, Kirk. Now."

Elle shook her head. "I can't, June."

June continued her work to reduce the pain, even a little. "You *have* to, Elle. You have to if you and those babies are going to survive."

*****

It dragged on. For hours upon hours, it continued. The hours felt like lifetimes. Bliss gathered anything June needed. June desperately tended to Elle. Kirk sat at her side, his attention fully on Elle, his hand wrapped around hers. Black blood dripped from Elle's mouth where Kirk had tried to help her feed. She needed the strength, but it had been so hard for her to keep down. Even then, his blood slowly leaked from her mouth when she didn't have the strength to swallow. Her body desperately healed as it broke, her vampiric blood keeping her just barely alive. She cried out and begged for it to end, for the moon to have mercy.

Then it was time.

"You have to push, Elle," June coached. Her tone was direct and firm but laced deeply with love, kindness. "You have to push."

She screamed. Her grip on Kirk's hands tightened beyond a strength he knew she had.

"Good. Good. You've got this, Elle. One more. Just one more." June's hands shook. "He's almost here."

Another scream.

Then he started to cry. A baby boy with black hair. He immediately started screaming in June's hold, his little fists tightly balled as he told the entire room he'd arrived. They called him Felix. Already, even with his tiny face scrunched and dirty, he so clearly resembled Dae. Just a hint of anger made its way into the sea of emotions that washed over Kirk as he laid his eyes on his son.

Elle kept screaming.

It wasn't over.

She twisted and cried. Her body was shattering. Blood pooled deeply between her legs, soaking into their bed and even further into Kirk's soul. Forty-seven more minutes passed before June's command repeated. Forty-seven minutes her torment continued.

"One more time, Elle. One more time. Push, love."

She cried out once more, her throat dry from hours upon hours of screaming. Layers of tears dried on her cheeks only to be wet again as more began to pour. She gripped Kirk's hand desperately. Her limbs shook.

Then the second was born.

A baby boy with dark blond hair entered the world. Like his brother, he screamed. He announced his presence with all the power in those little lungs. They called him August. His face, however, did not look like his brother's. And when he opened his eyes to see the world for the first time, his eyes were solid black, like his father's.

~ 58 ~

EPILOGUE

K^{IRK}
Six months later

Kirk wiped his forehead with the back of his hand as he stood up straight. He groaned. For all his newfound youth, his back still hurt like hell. He leaned a bit against the hoe in his hand, glancing around at the garden before him. It was almost time to plant their second year's vegetables. Only a month or so. For now, he worked to prepare the space, turn the soil, build the fence around it. The dog was seated beside him, its tail wagging incessantly as Kirk had stopped his work and had not immediately given it adequate head scratches. He smiled softly and patted the dog's head a few times. "C'mon. Let's grab something to drink, eh?"

He leaned the hoe against the fence and began his walk back to the house, adjusting the rolled ends of his sleeves. The dog trotted beside him, keeping its steps matched with his. Kirk's boots left mud prints against the porch as he stepped into the house. He kicked them off as he walked through the entry and toward the bucket of water he'd gotten earlier that day. Even though the weather had not grown hot, working in the sun still drew quite a sweat from him. His calloused hands were dotted with blisters from new tools. His sword traded for farmer's equipment. His vampire-hunting blades for woodworking tools. As he scooped up some water, he heard delicate footsteps enter behind him.

"I finally got them to sleep." Her tone and her eyes carried weariness. The boys did not sleep easily. They fought them at every turn and resisted naps with all the strength they had.

He turned to her, wrapping a hand around her waist and kissing the top of her head. "Thank you, my love."

She smiled up at him. "How's the garden?" Those red eyes ran up his chest, taking in every inch of the sweat and dirt covering him. His hair was falling from its ties, and his forehead was almost certainly smudged with soil.

"Nearly ready." He squeezed her hip. "Now we just need those two to grow up so they can start helping me."

She laughed softly, then she stepped closer. "Kirk." She placed her hand on his chest, her fingers playing with the ties near the neckline. "We *do* have a moment while they're asleep . . ."

He laughed softly, masking a hint of concern. She'd been growing more and more confident with touch, but he still feared pushing it, hurting her . . . "Oh? And what do you have in mind?"

She stood on her toes and reached for a kiss while her hand slid down his chest and gently cupped his cock. "Maybe . . .?"

"I am incredibly sweaty and dirty right now, Elle." He smirked. He already knew he was toast. This woman owned his very soul, and when she reached out for him, it brought him to his knees.

"I prefer it that way." She laughed and grabbed his shirt. "C'mon."

He smiled. "As you command." He grabbed her thighs and effortlessly lifted her, wrapping her legs around his waist, drawing her close, and kissing her. He pressed deep against her and pulled her hard into himself. He held tightly to her back to keep her against him, and she threw her arms over his shoulders. Her thighs gripped his hips, and her feet crossed behind his back.

She leaned forward and whispered against his ear, "Bed."

A shiver of excitement ran down his neck and directly into his cock, and he smiled. "Yes, my love."

*****

He stirred. He hadn't realized he'd fallen asleep. She was curled up beside him, tucked beneath his arm with her head on his chest. He thanked the moon for any rest like this she could have. Between the nightmares and the babies, he protected any sleep she could get.

The boys started to cry.

Her eyes opened, and she shifted to get up nearly instantly. "The boys—"

Kirk squeezed her close and kissed her forehead. "I'll get them and bring them to you, okay?" He slid away from her and swung his legs off the side of the bed. He grabbed his pants from the floor, they had barely stayed on past the doorframe, and then he walked out of the room to the boys'.

*****

ELLE

Elle sat up slowly. The blankets slid from her shoulders, and she smiled sleepily, glancing around the room where she and Kirk had . . . enjoyed each other. She had actually fallen asleep. Gods, his arms had become somewhere she felt safe enough to sleep again. This year she'd spent with him, healing, it made it seem possible.

Happiness.

She looked up as he stepped through the door, August and Felix in either arm. She held out her hands. "They're quite hungry, I'm sure."

Kirk nodded, tilting his head toward the fussy boys. He handed Felix to her as he scooted onto the bed. He helped her situate both to nurse and supported them as best he could, his eyes drifting between his sons and her. "Ellie."

She looked up briefly. "Yes, my love?"

He smiled and leaned in to kiss her forehead. "Marry me."

She laughed, and the boys expressed their frustration with the interruption to dinner. "I think we're beyond that."

"I mean it. I bought you a ring the last time I was in town. I was going to come up with some way to . . . I want to call you my wife. I want to stand with you as humans do and declare you my wife before the gods. Marry me, Elle. Be my wife."

She smiled. "Of course. Of course, I'll marry you."

Ed wanted a self Portrait to carry with
her since I've drawn everyone else, I'll finish
it one of these days

First self
Portrait

~ 59 ~

BONUS CHAPTER 1

A vampire couple sat at a table in the cabin where they'd hidden. They'd only been there for a few months. The father had returned from gathering supplies. The mother was weary and conserving what energy she could. They had not found food in days.

The father sighed as he looked at her, his heart deeply saddened and his body fatigued. "I'll travel closer to the human town tomorrow. You cannot go much longer without blood, my love." Her eyes had grown hollow. They'd already lost a son. He could not lose his wife. He could not lose his daughter.

She nodded solemnly. "Do be careful."

"Of course." His voice drifted as his eyes moved to their daughter sleeping softly on a bed in the corner. She was only a babe, small and precious.

They were quiet for a moment, then she spoke softly. "She has a soul-bound mate."

He glanced at her. "My daughter is already bound to another being?" He cocked a half smile, teasing in his exhaustion. Father had tried so desperately to keep positive for Mother. Her heart had been shattered.

"I've seen him." Her smile was forced. Mother had been gifted with foresight. She could not see what was not gifted to her by the moon, and she only saw small pieces, but she would get visions of the future, small images of what was to come. They would come and go. Uncertain flashes of the future that she had yet to be able to change.

"Well?" The father nodded, motioning with his hand for her to continue. "Tell me of this man. The man who steals away my daughter." It helped them both. To imagine a future for her. A future where maybe she would not have to hide from Dae. Where she could be loved . . . not hunted. If Mother saw a mate, it meant their daughter would survive, right?

"He is a human," Mother said quietly.

"A human?"

Mother nodded slowly. "Yes, but he is a good man. I can . . . tell." She did not smile. Her eyes cast toward the floor.

"I am not a fan of a human man stealing her heart. If they bond, she'll only live nearly a human lifetime." He rubbed his forehead. "Have you seen us yet?" He knew this was what worried Mother so. She had not seen any image of them in so long.

"No."

Father was quiet again for a moment, taking a deep breath that shook no matter how hard he tried to hold it back. "Fate was wrong, you know."

She looked up at him, tilting her head slightly.

He forced back his own fear, his own anxieties, if only to give her a moment's peace. "You and me." He gestured between them. "The moon was wrong when we were not bound by our souls. You are truly the other half of my own."

She smiled and shook her head. "You're quite the romantic."

"Only with you."

Mother laughed just slightly. "And what if I've seen her? Your fated mate. And I've never spoken of her to keep you all to myself?"

He reached across the table and grabbed her hand. "Then I will die happily in ignorance, because you are the only mate I have ever and will ever desire."

~ 60 ~

BONUS CHAPTER 2

June ran an exhausted hand through her hair, a long sigh escaping her lips. She began to untie the braids that hung on either side of her head and then slipped out of her shirt.

Before she was able to remove anything else, the door behind her opened, and she turned to find herself face-to-face with him. Bliss.

He smiled, flashing that single fang and those dark eyes she unfortunately found herself getting lost in.

"You're back." Quickly his arm was wrapped around her waist, and he'd pulled her against his chest. "How's Ellie? The babies?"

"They're well." She half-heartedly pushed against his grasp, not *really* wanting to be free of his arms. "Let me get changed and we can make dinner."

A familiar look flashed in his eyes that met hers so intently. "There's something I'd rather eat first."

*****

Bliss was behind her, his cock buried deep in her ass. He groaned loudly in her ear, "My gods, June."

Shadows surrounded them. Three of her shadows wrapped in and around them as their bodies intertwined with each other. One in Bliss's ass, one wrapped around her needy center, and another twisted around her breasts.

They both moaned as they fucked each other while the shadows caressed everything they couldn't touch of each other themselves.

"June June June." His voice was laced with lust and pleasure behind her.

Her face was pressed into their bed, drool pooling beneath her cheek as she was nearly delirious with the sensations overwhelming her. "Bliss," she moaned his name, letting it drip from her lips like honey.

She felt him give in and thrust once more, deep, release taking him.

The orgasm she'd been building rattled through her, and stars flashed in front of her eyes. "Fucking hells." He nuzzled into her neck. "I love you." His breath was warm on her collar, his flesh warm against hers, both still slick with sweat.

She hesitated for a moment, only a moment, then she let the words slip. "I love you too."

"Thank you for your help." Felix stood, setting down his pen on the dark wooden desk and sipping his glass of wine. "My parents' story should be remembered. It should be in our history." He ran a hand through the black curls that had fallen into his face. "They deserve that much." He sighed and sipped the wine again before grabbing his pen and sliding it behind his ear. He flipped the parchment before him to a new page and stared at the blank space. "Now to write mine . . . And my brother's."

E. M. Roselynn is located in the Pacific Northwest, the perfect rainy backdrop to write dark romance.

They love rainy days curled up with a book and the fireplace roaring. They've been writing since they were young, but only later in life did they finally get it together to turn their passion into actual novels.

They live with their husband, a pile of fur babies, and their flock of chickens, ducks, and geese.

They love the darker side of life. They love finding the beauty in darkness and even in death itself. Dark romance, collecting oddities, watching horror movies, dark chocolate, and coffee.

9 798218 567453